THE HARLEQUIN

SINCLAIR MACLEOD

I0596576

MARPLES
BOOKS

Published in 2014 by Marplesi

Copyright © Sinclair Macleod 2014

ISBN Paperback: 978-0-9931307-0-0
ISBN eBook: 978-0-9931307-2-4

DEDICATION

To Morven, Isla and Emma, my wonderful nieces
with all my love.
As always, in memory of Calum,
my incredible son and constant inspiration.

ACKNOWLEDGEMENTS

Thanks are due to Emma Hamilton, Geoff Fisher and my patient editor Ardy Melvin.

As always my love and thanks also go to Kim, my wife of 25 years and my incredibly wise and gorgeous daughter, Kirsten. I could not write these books without their continued love, support and inspiration.

PART ONE

April 1st 1993

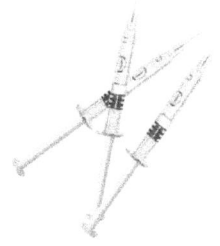

CHAPTER 1

B enjamin Blake loved comic books; it was his single true passion. He would walk to the comic store in the city centre every Thursday to buy the latest issues featuring his favourite characters, just as he had done religiously every week in the seven years that had passed since his twelfth birthday.

On that Thursday, as he walked back to his house in Hyndland clutching a bag packed with his purchases, he stopped to buy some doughnuts at a local supermarket. It was another vital part of his regular routine. Benjamin liked routine.

When he reached the flat he lived in with his mother and father, he walked into the spacious living area that comprised both the lounge and an open-plan kitchen. He took out a chilled can of cola from the fridge and then pulled some sheets of kitchen towel from a roll on the wall. It was a short walk to the dining table where he settled down with his doughnut and drink, laying the sheets of towel between the snacks and the bag with the comics. He lifted each of the delicate books from the bag, taking care not to wrinkle or fold any of the pages as he laid them on the wooden surface in front of him.

There was always a small thrill of anticipation as he placed them on the table, the excitement of knowing he was about to be transported out of his boring life into a world of good guys battling the villains in ever more fantastical ways. Each story would be read through once before he placed the comic in a clear polythene sleeve to preserve forever the cherished item. A folded page or single stain would render them soiled and worthless, so he was very careful to keep the doughnut and drink well away from the precious paper. He used the kitchen towel to wipe his hands after every bite of the cake, which helped to ensure the pristine condition of the comics.

Of all the superheroes that jumped from the pages to excite his imagination, Master Melter was the one that he related to the most. The red-suited superhero was a recent addition to the broad pantheon of comics. Like Benjamin he was an only child who had been bullied at school, making him Benjamin's ideal alter ego. When Benjamin's fictional friend was caught by a toxic explosion during a science experiment, the boy recovered to find he had the power to blind a villain with light cast from his hands, or if he was really angry, blast them away in a wave of deadly radiation. Benjamin wished he could deal in a similar way with the school bullies and all those who made his life a misery.

This week's edition of the comic featured the blue-suited Lightning Gale doing her worst to defeat the hero. Lightning Gale was alright but she wasn't Benjamin's favourite villain; he preferred the scarier, more sinister criminals such as Moon Master, Death Shade and the best of all the Night Trickster. Despite his disappointment at the choice of villain for this series, Master Melter would still be the first part of his weekly reading routine.

While Benjamin was sitting at the table, the comic opened in front of him, he began to feel a strange tingle. He was finding it difficult to concentrate on the action and his head felt a little foggy. As he stared at them, the images on the page started to move; at first there were little vibrations but soon the characters limbs and lips became animated. Strange voices began to drift up from the pages like they were echoing from the end of a long tunnel. He shook his head, trying to clear the weird sights and sensations but the images continued to writhe and twist as the indistinct words became louder. Initially he was fascinated but slowly chills began to run down his spine and goosebumps appeared on his arms. When Lightning Gale began to laugh at him, the now terrified teenager began to back away from the table, his body shaking in shock.

No, no, this isn't happening, he told himself. From somewhere deep inside him a feeling that something terrible was about to happen was beginning to overwhelm him. He felt a real palpable sense of impending danger, worse than when the bullies used to chase him home from school. He felt the need to defend himself, so he stood up and ran into the kitchen to retrieve a long, sharp knife from the block on the counter.

By the time he got back to the dining table the characters were beginning to crawl out of the pages; clambering as if they were pulling themselves up from a deep pit. Even the heroic Master Melter looked horrific as he dragged himself off the page and stood upright.

Benjamin felt he was losing control of his mind, that he was plunging rapidly into dangerous insanity but his eyes and ears were telling him that this was all too real. Then a noise from the hall startled him into a scream as the irrational panic seized him completely. He held the knife in front of him, taking up a defensive posture, determined to protect himself against whatever came through the door.

The old, heavy door that opened from the hall creaked as it swung towards him. Ominous footsteps preceded the appearance of a terrible nightmare vision; Death Shade walked into the room, his head hanging lopsidedly and luminous green eyes shining. He was followed closely by the leering, white-rimmed, rigid grin of the Night Trickster whose face was painted like a black theatrical mask. They were both laughing at Benjamin, the disparaging tone of the Trickster's cackle and Death Shade's breathy rasp piled rage on top of his fear.

This can't be happening to me, he thought.

"No stay away from me," he shouted waving the knife like a sword.

They started to edge towards him and he decided that he needed to take the initiative. Master Melter would never run away.

Death Shade was holding out his bony arms as if he was going to envelop Benjamin in a gruesome hug. The terrified young man pulled a roar from deep within him and plunged the knife into the chest of his attacker. The villain collapsed to the floor and Benjamin felt a rush of pleasure and power.

He turned his attention to the Trickster who was still leering but had begun to back away. Benjamin rushed towards the hideous creature and swung the knife in an arc that sliced through the criminal's neck. A fountain of crimson blood arced across the room as the man went down at the hero's feet.

***

Debbie Carlisle finished her lunchtime shift at the Golden Eagle pub, put on her coat and walked the short distance to her flat in Byres Road.

She was extremely tired but knew that she still had to face a few hours of studying for her second year Psychology exam. The exam was only two weeks away and she had been trying to balance the weight of the revision with pulling pints because she needed the money, but it was beginning to feel like she couldn't do both for much longer.

Her flatmate Declan was in the shower when she walked into the square hallway of the flat. She called out to let him know she was home but he couldn't hear her due to the water cascading and echoing in the high-ceilinged bathroom.

She dumped her bag and removed her Walkman from her pocket and laid it on the hall table. She placed her denim jacket on the coat rack and tutted as she lifted Declan's leather coat from the floor. *He is a messy pain in the arse at times*, she thought.

In the galley kitchen, she made a cup of instant coffee and lifted an iced bun from a pack that was sitting on the tiny worktop.

"I'm sure he won't mind," she said to herself.

She felt she needed ten minutes of relaxation before she could face the enormous pile of thick textbooks again. She slumped into the ragged settee with the coffee in one hand and the bun in the other.

She sat for a short time, feeling a release of some of the stress but suddenly she felt the room begin to chill and darken. She looked at the window but it still seemed to be bright outside; the darkness was closing in from the walls of the flat, not because of anything that was happening in the street. She jumped up, as a disconcerting feeling of alarm descended upon her like a menacing veil. The temperature continued to drop and she began to shake. She sniffed the air, the smell of ozone and brine filled her nostrils as clearly as if she was standing on the seashore.

She was about to run out of the room when a figure stepped into the doorway. He was massive, covered in tattoos and dripping wet. She backed away, unable to believe that Max Cady was standing in front of her. She and Declan had watched the video of Cape Fear two nights previously and now here was the killer standing in her living room.

"Get out!" she screamed at the cruel, savage sneering face.

Cady started to talk but she couldn't understand a word he was saying, it was like he was speaking in tongues. He moved around her with his arms out wide, as if he was showing off his tattoos; the images of death, a broken heart and lightning bolts that were inked darkly into his skin. The shadow concentrated itself around him like a ghastly, semi-transparent cloak.

He's going to kill me, he's going to kill me, was the only thought that kept screaming around her head. He continued to speak incomprehensible gibberish but she was convinced from the tone that he was threatening her.

He had moved around her so that his back was to the window. In a fit of uncontrollable panic she decided to rush the killer and try to get him off balance before he could act. She charged at him like a rugby player. Cady was too surprised to act and despite Debbie's diminutive stature she managed to propel him backwards. As he stumbled, his heel caught on the rug and the two fell into the enormous bay window. The glass splintered and shattered into hundreds of pieces; all resistance gone, the two people fell four floors to their death.

***

John Morrison was sick of university. He was sick of the work, he was sick of the staff but most of all he was sick of the students.

They were pretentious little bastards who thought they knew everything and that they were destined to rule the world. Most of them didn't even know he existed; they would pass him in the corridor without even an acknowledgement, not a word nor even a nod. However, if he didn't do his job properly then they would notice. They'd complain about untidy classrooms and filthy toilets; they'd moan about the amount of rubbish that mounted up after they had cast it aside; they'd notice that their shite smelled just as bad as everybody else.

With his mop he pushed his bucket-on-wheels into a chemistry class on the top floor of the building. He looked at the floor and thought that it didn't look too bad; it would be fine after a quick flick through with the mop. On the lecturer's table were a few cake boxes marked with the logo of the local supermarket.

"How can they no' put this stuff intae the bin?" he grumbled to himself. He began to flatten the boxes but when he got to the last one he spotted that there was a solitary éclair to tempt him.

"Bonus," he said as he lifted the chocolate covered confection to his lips. It was sweet and delicious, and immediately lifted his mood. When it was finished he placed all the cake boxes into a bin bag that he dropped outside the door of the room to be collected later that evening.

Feeling a lot happier, he began to whistle The Bluebells song 'Young At Heart' as he swished the broad mop around the desks. He didn't like much of the modern music he heard - he was more an Eagles man - but he had to admit that he thought it was a good tune.

As he was getting close to finishing the room he noticed a drop in temperature. He checked the windows, they were all firmly closed but it was definitely getting colder. His head began to pound and he thought that he might be coming down with something.

As he turned away from the window, at the edge of his vision he sensed movement. He spun all the way round to see blood seeping from the walls; little drops coalescing and running down in narrow rivulets that grew thicker as they flowed together. At the junction of the walls and the ceiling, shapes began to push through as if the wall was made of latex. Grotesque demonic faces emerged, pushing through the skin like an alien birth. Twisted and mutated bodies followed rapidly.

He dropped the mop and began to move backwards, the classroom door was his only thought as the multi-limbed visions of hell began to crawl down towards the floor. He crossed himself and began to recite the Lord's Prayer.

The mutilated monsters began to edge in his direction, their movement made awkward by the distorted forms they took. No two were alike; some looked like they were the result of some mad experiment to combine humans with animals; they had any number of combinations of hooves or paws or talons or horns. Others had small heads with sharp fangs bared in a morbidly malformed grin. Yet others had long curved claws where their hands should be.

He felt the door at his back and he turned to open it, scared that they would attack him he stepped quickly out into the hall. The sight that greeted him was even worse than the one he had escaped, as pools of blood, vomit and bile oozed across the floor making it extremely slippery. He turned towards the lift but there were many more of the terrors lurching up the corridor in his direction. His only escape was the door to the roof about twenty metres away. As he tried to gain purchase to run from the creatures, his feet slipped in the liquid and he fell into a puddle of yellow bile. He could feel it stinging his eyes as he scrambled to his feet. As he fumbled with the keys he could hear the demons edging ever closer. Their chattering and moans made it difficult for him to concentrate on choosing the correct key from the huge collection he had on his belt.

Finally, he opened the door, closed it and locked it behind him. He ran up the short stairs to the flat roof, his breathing ragged as his heart pounded. He thought that he was safe until he turned to see the monsters emerging through the door as if it wasn't there. They kept coming at him as he moved closer to the edge. They all appeared to know that he was trapped, their mangled and monstrous faces contorted in insane grins of anticipatory pleasure.

When they raised their limbs all he could see was a forest of talons, skeletal hands and vicious blades. Seeing no alternative, he ran to the edge and jumped.

CHAPTER 2

Police Constable Alan Henderson led his younger colleague P.C. Robbie McNish up three flights of stairs to the flat in Hyndland. They had received a call from a neighbour concerning a domestic disturbance at the Blake family home.

"Probably some drunk slapping his wife around," Henderson had suggested when the call had come in.

At the third-floor landing, Henderson said, "Sounds all quiet at the moment." He lifted his hand and thumped a fist against the door. "Police, open up." There was no response so he placed his ear to the door but he couldn't hear any movement in the flat.

From the house on the opposite side of the close an elderly woman appeared.

"We're looking for the Blakes," Henderson said.

"I know. I'm the one who called you," she replied with a soft Irish accent.

"And you are?'

"Mrs Patricia O'Doyle. Most people call me Pat."

"Can you tell us what happened?"

"Oh dear, it was awful. Young Benjamin was screaming and shouting like he was really scared for his life. It lasted about ten minutes and then it stopped just after I called the police."

"Who is Benjamin?"

"He's Agnes and Abraham's son."

"What age is he?"

"About nineteen I think."

"Are there any other children?"

"No, it's only Benjamin."

Henderson turned back to the Blake home and shouted but this time in a more friendly tone, "Benjamin, is everything OK? It's the police, we're here to help."

There was still no indication that there was anyone in the flat. Henderson was about to charge the door when McNish turned the door handle and it swung open. The two constables walked into the house, Henderson calling out, telling whoever might be inside that they were coming and not to be alarmed.

When they reached the living room, the scene that greeted them resembled an abattoir. There was darkening red blood everywhere; it was congealing on each of the walls, dripping from the ceiling and splashes covered every piece of furniture. The majority of it was collected in a huge puddle surrounding the three bodies that lay in a morbid triangle of death.

A middle-aged woman lay on her back with a wound in her chest that appeared to have punctured her heart. With her blue eyes wide open, she looked surprised at what had happened to her. A slightly older man lay within two feet of her, a scarlet line across his neck that resembled a narrow cravat. The majority of the blood must have come from him as his carotid artery had pumped it into the air and across the room before draining what remained on to the floor as he suffered a lingering death.

There was no surprise on his face, just a sad realisation that his life was over. The young man that Henderson presumed was Benjamin, formed the point of the triangle, equidistant from his parents. He had been eviscerated; his intestines lay in a tangled greyish-blue pile in front of where he had slumped on to his side. Close to his right hand was a large flat-bladed knife that was covered in the crimson evidence of the crime it had committed.

"Is everything... oh my Go..." Mrs O'Doyle had followed the police officers into the house and when she saw the scene of carnage she fainted, collapsing behind McNish.

"Get her out of here," the senior P.C. bawled at his partner.

The young man succeeded in getting his hands under the elderly woman's arms and dragged her unceremoniously into the hall. A shocked Henderson walked to a bedroom and perched himself on the end of the bed while he used his radio to initiate the murder investigation.

***

Detective Inspector Harry Newman turned to Detective Constable Tom Russell and said, "What do you think?"

They were sitting in the senior detective's brand new Ford Mondeo. The new car had only been on sale a matter of months but Newman had been among the first in the city to buy one.

"Aye, it's nice enough." Russell knew little and cared less about cars. As far as he was concerned they were a means to get from A to B; as long as they did that he was happy. His boss was a different proposition. He was a man who saw the car as one part of his identity, a reflection of his status in society.

He was obsessed by material things and liked to show off his latest toys at every opportunity.

"Look at this, electric windows, an airbag and ABS. Top of the line, boy."

"We should maybe get going to the crime scene, sir," Russell suggested.

"Aye, don't get your knickers in a twist." Newman started the engine. "Lovely tone isn't it? Two litre, 136 brake horsepower."

"Yes, sir," Russell replied politely but with little enthusiasm. He muttered similar positive sounds as they took the short trip to Hyndland.

***

When he walked into the Blake's living room, Tom Russell gasped. In his three years as a detective he had attended many crime scenes but this was by far the worst. The blood spatter that decorated the walls had dried to a rusty brown but the large pool in the middle of floor still shone a livid red. The three bodies lay like a dreadful sculpture created in hell.

"Holy fuckin' Christ," was Newman's reaction as he took in the devastation.

Professor Lionel Marriot, the senior pathologist for Glasgow, was bent over Benjamin's corpse, peering intently at the young man's intestines. He looked up, "I know I might be a God in your eyes, Newman, but it's OK, you can call me professor," he said, smiling broadly. Marriot thought of himself as a bit of a wit and tended to black humour, even at the grimmest of crime scenes. It was something that made the young detective uncomfortable despite the fact that it was quite common for his colleagues to join in the jokes: for many it was their way of coping but Russell always felt that it was disrespectful to the dead.

"Prof, you're more a demon than a God in my eyes. What the hell happened here?"

"My guess would be murder and suicide but I'll need to get to the guts of it to be sure, " he said indicating the inert coils on the floor.

"Don't professor, you'll make me belly laugh,' Newman cracked back as Russell squirmed.

"Nice one," Marriot said as he nodded.

"What do we know about the victims?"

"According to their neighbour, this is Abraham, Agnes and Benjamin Blake. From what I can gather from the blood patterns, the mother was killed first with a stab to the heart, followed by the father and then the killer took his own life in Japanese-style seppuku ritual suicide."

"At least it's all nicely contained. Tidy up the paperwork and we'll be done."

"Who called it in?" Russell asked.

"What does it matter? We know who did it. Case closed," Newman asserted.

"I'd like to know a little more, that's all," Russell replied defensively.

"It was Mrs O'Doyle, she heard shouting and was concerned," Marriot said.

"I'd like to speak to her, find out what she heard," Russell said.

"Don't waste too much time on it, Russell," Newman warned, keen to be back at the station to wrap things up.

"Yes, sir."

Russell walked away from the gruesome scene and across the landing to Mrs O'Doyle's flat. He knocked gently on the door, Alan Henderson opened it. Russell introduced himself and flashed his credentials to the constable.

"Come in, she's through here."

The shocked woman was sitting in a plush floral armchair holding a handkerchief in her right hand. P.C. McNish sat opposite her with a cup and saucer that he put down hurriedly when he saw the detective in the doorway.

"Mrs O'Doyle, this is D.C. Russell. He'd like to ask you a few questions," Henderson informed her.

"Oh, is it really necessary?" the distraught woman asked.

"I'm afraid it is, Mrs O'Doyle." Russell then dismissed the uniformed officers as politely as possible. "That's fine guys, I'll give you a shout if I need you."

When they had gone, Mrs O'Doyle looked nervously at the detective as if she was expecting an inquisition.

"Mrs O'Doyle, I wonder if you could tell me a little about the Blakes."

She lifted the handkerchief to her nose and blew loudly as tears began to trickle from her eyes.

"Detective Russell, I've never seen anything like that," she said.

"I know Mrs O'Doyle it's very distressing. Can you tell me about the Blakes?" he prompted once more.

"Yes, I'm sorry. They were very nice people. Abraham worked as a tailor, Agnes stayed home. Benjamin wasn't working yet and he was in the house most days."

"What kind of man was Benjamin?"

"He wasn't a man, Detective Russell; he was a child not ready for the big bad world. He was always very quiet but polite enough. Agnes worried about him because he was very shy and didn't have many friends."

"Was he a violent lad?"

"No, that's why I can't understand it. When I heard all the screaming and shouting this afternoon I thought someone was attacking him."

"What was he shouting?"

"He was bawling at the top of his voice, telling someone to get back. He sounded so scared."

"Did Benjamin ever take drugs?"

"No, well not as far as I know."

"Was there a history of mental illness maybe?"

"I don't think so son, he was always very shy but if he had mental problems, Agnes never told me."

"Is there any reason that Benjamin would have killed his parents and then taken his own life? Was he ill maybe?"

"I don't know for sure but he was a gentle lad who was always helpful to his mother around the house. He read his comics and played music. I think that was his whole life really, he didn't seem to have many friends or other interests."

"Thanks Mrs O'Doyle, we'll get a constable over to take your official statement as soon as possible. Is there anybody you would like me to call?"

"No son, it's fine. I'll phone my Padraig. He'll come over and keep me company."

Russell left the elderly woman drying her eyes with the handkerchief, as the shock from what she had seen set in once more.

***

When Russell returned to the Blake's flat, Newman was impatient to return to the station. He saw no point in lingering at the crime scene and told the pathologist he would see him at the mortuary for the three post mortems the following morning. Russell was concerned that his boss was being hasty in taking the crime scene at face value, but there was little he could do to change Newman's mind.

As they walked back to the car - which had been left parked on a double yellow line with a laminated card in the windscreen that read, 'Police. Official Business' - Russell voiced his concerns, "Sir, I think there is more to this than a simple murder suicide."

"You know what your problem is, Russell? You think too much. This is real life, no' the telly. Things are just what they seem."

"The Blake's neighbour said the son was a quiet lad who seemed to get on well with his parents."

"The quiet one's are the worst. Thank fuck he didn't have a gun or we'd be looking at a massacre."

Russell decided to silence his doubts for the time being. The detective inspector liked things to be straightforward, particularly if it meant it cut down the amount of work he had to do.

They drove back to Partick police station with Newman singing loudly to 'The Bodyguard' soundtrack CD that was playing to show Russell how great the stereo was in the new Mondeo. All it proved was the D.I. Newman was no Whitney Houston.

***

On their return, Russell and Newman found the C.I.D. room in Partick station deserted, apart from their civilian support worker, Allanah Usher.

"Where the hell is everybody, Allanah?"

"It's been quite a day. D.I. McLelland and D.C. Stephens are in Byres Road at a suspected domestic that ended in the couple crashing through a windae and dropping four floors to their death. D.S. Burgess and D.C. Magowan are at a suspected suicide up at the university.

"Bloody hell, is it a full moon or something?" Newman asked rhetorically. "You get the report typed up and when the P.M.s are done tomorrow we can put it to bed," he told Russell.

Tom Russell groaned as there was nothing he hated more than trying to use the computer. His typing was awful, he could never find where all the relevant files were and it took him forever to complete a report.

"Sir, shouldn't we investigate a bit further?"

"No, get it done or you'll be back out picking up drunks," the D.I. replied curtly.

As Russell worked diligently and slowly on the report, the first of the other detectives began to drift back into the room.

At thirty-seven, D.I. Mark McLelland was young for his rank. He had made his name when he worked undercover in a drugs gang, where he helped to secure twenty-four convictions. He was ambitious and his sharp intellect was propelling him up the promotional ladder at a rapid pace.

He walked into the C.I.D. room with D.C. Ruth Stephens at his back. Ruth had been on the same course as Tom Russell at the Police College in Tulliallan but she was struggling with life as a detective. Although things had improved over the previous ten years, there was still an element of the service in Glasgow who believed that female officers should stay in uniform; tending to the victims of crime as if they were nurses rather than out investigating and catching criminals. Her confidence had taken a bit of a battering and she had told Russell that she was thinking of quitting.

"Well that was a weird one," McLelland said.

"What was?" Newman asked.

"Two flatmates; Declan Murphy and Debbie Carlisle, good friends from what we gather and it looks like they either committed suicide together or she fell with him when she pushed him out the window. No history of depression and as far as anyone knew they weren't even lovers. I've never seen anything like it."

"Must be the day for the crazies," Newman said as he shook his head.

"Why?" D.C. Stephens asked.

Russell replied, "We got called to a double murder and suicide in Hyndland." He then told the two other officers of the details of the grisly scene and the apparently out-of-character behaviour of Benjamin Blake.

"Russell here thinks there's more to it, fancies himself as fuckin' Inspector Morse," Newman stated with a derisory laugh.

"Maybe there is more to it," McLelland said. "You've got to admit that this is not a normal day and for two incidents of this nature to happen within a couple of hours of each other, less than a mile apart is a strange coincidence."

"And Burgess and Magowan have been sent to a suspected suicide at the uni," Russell said, pleased to have some support.

"Don't be daft. What do you think there's some big conspiracy in play? The KGB is bumping off Glaswegians or maybe it's MI5 taking care of subversives or maybe they're silencing UFO abductees. A load of shite." Newman dismissed the notion with a wave of his hand.

"Sometimes I forget what a prick you are Newman, and then you open your mouth just to remind me," McLelland replied.

There was real enmity between the two detectives. Newman thought that McLelland's meteoric rise was based on his ability to cosy up to the senior management team, while McLelland thought Newman was a lazy copper who was working his time until he could claim his pension.

McLelland reached into his pocket for his cigarettes while he placed his feet on his desk. He lit one and blew the smoke into the air, His whole attitude showed how little he cared what McLelland thought.

Russell and Stephens kept their heads down, unwilling to become embroiled in the argument but Tom Russell was sure that there was more to the situation than was obvious by the cursory investigation they had so far performed.

The following day would reveal whether his gut was correct.

CHAPTER 3

The post mortems in the Blake case were the first of the day and Tom Russell was ordered to report directly to the city mortuary at eight o'clock. The roads were busy as rush hour began to ramp up, and it took him a bit longer than he had expected to travel from his flat in Shawlands to the building adjacent the High Court in Jocelyn Square.

Constructed from a combination of blonde sandstone and red brick, the mortuary was a relic from another era. Inside it was dark and cold due to ancient tiles on the walls and floor, lighting that always seemed inadequate and a heating system that was erratic. It all contributed to a general air of dilapidation. Russell hated the smell of the place that was a combination of disinfectant undercut with the slightest hint of decay.

Newman was waiting in the autopsy room with Professor Marriot and a female technician who was introduced as Lynda Ryan.

"We're just waiting on Dr Dent and then we'll get started. Special bargain today gents, three for the price of one," the pathologist said cheerily.

When Dent arrived he didn't even bother to acknowledge the other people in the room. Dent was a solemn, sullen individual and the only time he spoke to any police officer was when he was performing a post mortem or when he required some information from them. He was about five feet five inches tall, stick thin and going prematurely bald. Russell guessed he was in his early thirties but he carried himself like an older man. He was a stark contrast to his effusive boss.

The bodies of Mr and Mrs Blake were already laid out on two metal tables, while Benjamin's remains were off to one side on a trolley.

Professor Marriot began the formalities by approaching the body of Agnes Blake and conducting a preliminary visual examination of the corpse before Lynda Ryan washed it carefully. When the Y-incision and the removal of the ribcage was complete the professor said, "Let's get to the heart of the matter."

He removed Mrs Blake's heart and said, "As we thought the knife punctured her left ventricle, which would have killed her instantly." There were no surprises as the process of examining and weighing the organs was completed and everything looked like their assessment at the scene had been correct.

The first of the three examinations over, it was now the turn of the older of the two men. A new set of instruments were brought on a tray from a sterile cupboard.

The same procedure for Abraham Blake confirmed that he had bled out due to the severing of his carotid artery when the knife was drawn across his throat. The only other thing of note was that the man had a congenital heart problem, which according to his medical records had apparently gone undiagnosed.

While the professor worked on Abraham, Lynda Ryan had returned the body of Agnes Blake to a condition that would be suitable for burial. She wheeled the trolley that supported the body of Benjamin Blake over to the table that was occupied by his mother. The pathologists lifted Agnes Blake on to another trolley, the table was cleaned and then they slid Benjamin across to take his mother's place.

The autopsy process began again while Newman looked bored. The professor reiterated what he believed had happened in the flat as he confirmed that Benjamin's wounds were consistent with a knife being plunged into his stomach by his own hand and then drawn across his abdomen to complete the ritual suicide.

When it was over the professor said, "We'll get the blood work done but I think you can take it as read that this is just as it appears. A case of Mat, Pat and Sue."

"Eh?" Newman looked puzzled.

"Matricide, patricide and suicide," the professor laughed as if he had found the perfect joke.

Newman said to Russell, "See, there ye go Miss Marple, nothing other than murder, suicide. Wrap up the paperwork and head for the pub I would say."

Russell stood pensively, convinced by the gnawing feeling in his gut that there was more to this than was obvious but he could do nothing other than obey his superior officer.

When they got back to the station, Russell could hear Newman across the corridor in the drug squad office, full of his own self-importance as he slagged off Russell as a prima donna looking to earn a career by creating a case where there was none.

Russell sat at his desk preparing his evidence for a trial that was due to start on Monday. He kept his own counsel knowing that Newman was deliberately trying to goad him into a reaction. The more he worked with Newman the less he held him in any regard, and based on their first meeting, that was from a very low starting point. The detective inspector was both a bully and clown; Russell vowed to himself that he would never be the kind of boss that thought it was acceptable to treat with disdain his colleagues and those under his command.

He tuned out Newman and concentrated on reviewing what was going to be said in court on Monday, if he was called. For the police the court system could be a notorious waste of time. An officer could be called to give evidence only to sit all day while lawyers debated some obscure point of law. Russell hated it but he knew it was an important part of what the police did: he just wished that it were a little more efficient.

The detective constable spent the rest of the day in preparation for his court appearance and finishing his data input from the Blake case. At five thirty it was time to head for home.

***

After a quick shower and meal of fish and chips, Russell decided to visit his father in Paisley. He liked to check in on him from time to time.

His father lived alone in a small semi-detached house in a quiet part of the town. When his son arrived Stuart Russell was in the garden, removing small plants from pots and placing them into a patch of bare earth. He was fifty-three, a fit man who enjoyed keeping himself busy. He had recovered from the disappointment of losing his job in a textile firm five years earlier and was now content to work at night and then when he could, garden or golf during the day.

"Hi, Dad."

The older man looked up. "Oh, it's yourself. How's things?"

"Busy. I'm working that weird murder, suicide thing that happened yesterday."

"I seen that in the paper, poor folk. What made that boy do that?"

"Not sure yet, there doesn't seem to be anything in the lad's history that would suggest he was capable of it but I've already seen that people can do the most horrible things for the weirdest of reasons. What have you been up to?"

"I've got a night shift later, so I thought I'd get a bit of gardening done while the weather's nice and we've got some light."

"Do you need a hand?"

"If you don't mind that would be great."

The two worked side by side, Russell created the hole for the seedlings, and his father placed the plants into their new home.

"Have you had your dinner?" his father asked.

"Aye, I had a fish supper."

"You not seeing Karen tonight?"

"No, we're supposed to be going to the pictures tomorrow. Something with Robert De Niro and Bill Murray. 'Mad Dog And Glory' I think it's called. Anyway it's a night out I suppose."

"Is this one serious, d'ye think?" Stuart Russell was keen to see at least one of his sons settle down.

"Maybe." In truth, Russell wasn't sure what was going to happen with Karen Blackmore. They had been going out together for six months but it was difficult to get into a regular pattern of dates due to his job. That meant they still didn't know much about one another but he did think she was a little strange sometimes. She would question him about the women he worked with, quizzing him with a little more intensity than he thought was appropriate for where they were in the relationship. At other times, he felt he should be flattered that she was taking such a keen interest in him. 'Time would tell' was his basic philosophy; he wasn't going to be the one making any moves to change their current status of casual tenderness.

"You heard anything from Eddie?" Russell said.

"No, not a peep since his business went belly-up. You know what he's like. The last time I saw him, when he was here for the money, he said he was going to London. Some mate had a business proposition for him. I've not even had a phone call since."

"He's a waster, Dad."

His father sighed, "I know, I know but what can you do?"

The two men worked away together for an hour, discussing the merits of the local football team, St. Mirren, who had a chance of promotion to the Premier Division. They also talked about one of Stuart Russell's neighbours who had suffered a heart attack. Passing time the way men do, discussing nothing of consequence but comfortable in each other's company.

When the planting was done, it was time for the older man to get ready to go to work. Russell worried about the fact that his Dad worked as a security guard at a building site, but his father had reassured him that he was never going to be a have-a-go hero, and if there was ever any trouble the only thing he would do was to call his son's colleagues.

They exchanged a warm handshake and Russell drove back to the city.

CHAPTER 4

Russell arrived at the court building on Monday morning at the appointed time, having spent the previous day going over his notes and the evidence once again. He was always paranoid that someone might get away with a crime because a clever, smooth lawyer found a way to trip him up.

The movie on Saturday night had been fairly entertaining but Karen had once again been in a strange mood. She would swing between stony silence and being so talkative he couldn't get a word in. When she was speaking to him she would throw in subtle questions about Alannah: What did she look like? Did he think she was attractive? Did she have a boyfriend? He had mumbled vague answers in an effort to steer the conversation into less troubling waters.

Now as he sat in the courtroom waiting area, he watched the lawyers racing by, wigs and cases clutched in their hands, robes flapping behind them like superhero capes. He couldn't understand the bizarre need to dress like it was the eighteenth century: why did anyone think those wigs gave the court gravitas? He thought it made them look like actors in some ancient farce.

Hours ticked by with no indication that he was going to be called. The Clerk of the Court visited him twice to apologise for the delay because the prosecution witness on the stand was being cross-examined vigorously by the defence lawyer and it was causing frequent delays as the two sides met with the judge to argue what the law would allow to be asked and answered. Eventually, after five hours of Russell's boredom, then frustration and then anger, the clerk returned to thank him for his attendance but that he would not be required as the accused had changed his plea. He had to check his response, realising it wasn't the poor woman's fault that the justice system was a mess. He thanked her for letting him know and walked out of the court building.

As the mortuary was right next to the court, he decided to see if the blood results for the case had been processed. Linda Ryan was the only person in the untidy office when he arrived.

"Hi, Linda."

She smiled warmly. "Detective constable, what can I do for you? There's no P.M. scheduled for you, I don't think."

"No, I was wondering if the blood results were in for the Blakes, the three people from Friday."

"I'm not sure. There was a delivery from the lab a short time ago, I'll check it for you." The heavy-set woman walked out leaving Russell to stare at the disorganised contents of the room; he wasn't sure how the mortuary staff could ever find anything among the piles of reports, photographs and files.

She was gone about five minutes. "Got them," she said brightly as she returned.

She placed a number of envelopes on the desk and began flicking through them. "This is the father, Abraham," she announced. She studied the documentation for a short time before saying, "Nothing out of the ordinary there." She lifted the next file but Agnes Blake's results indicated nothing other than medication she had been taking for her asthma.

However Linda's reaction to Benjamin's results was very different. "Oh, this is interesting."

"What is it?" Russell moved forward in his seat, anticipating and hoping that his instincts were correct.

"That young man had enough psychotropic drugs in him to send a horse on a mind-expanding trip," she replied.

"What kind of drugs?"

"There are substantial traces of LSD, mescaline, psilocybin and cocaine."

"These could alter someone's perception of reality, couldn't they?"

She nodded vigorously, "In a big way. I've never seen anything like this. One of these drugs may be present in a user's bloodstream and at the very most two but never four. Talk about overkill."

Russell was keen to prove his theory went beyond the Blake case. "There were two other cases brought in on Thursday night, a suicide and a couple who fell from a window."

"I heard about those but I didn't deal with them."

"I know they are not my cases but could you check the results on them? It would save some time for my colleagues."

"Sure," she said as she began to shuffle the files again.

She expressed surprise as she announced that both Debbie Carlisle and John Morrison had an identical blend of hallucinogens in their bloodstream.

"It can't be a coincidence can it?"

"Definitely not," Russell replied. "I'm just not sure what it means. I'll need to get back to the station and let my colleagues know. It's up to the senior officers what happens next. Thanks for your help."

Linda flashed another flirtatious smile as she brushed her hair from her face. "You're welcome." Russell was completely oblivious to the interest that the technician was taking in him. He hurried away with a quick wave, leaving Ryan to her fantasies of romantic entanglement.

***

Russell arrived back at the station at around three o'clock. Newman was sitting with his feet on his desk nursing a cup of coffee in his thick hands when his D.C. walked in.

He said with customary sarcasm, "It's the world's greatest detective. How was court?"

"A waste of time, the bastard changed his plea."

"Wee fucker, you should have given him a kickin' when you had a chance."

"Not really my style, sir."

"That's your problem, Russell, you think that catching villains is only about the brain. Sometimes you need to let them know who the boss is."

Russell ignored the D.I.'s antiquated philosophy of policing. "I went into the mortuary. The blood tests were in for the Blakes. Benjamin Blake was drugged with a mixture of hallucinogens that would have a pink elephant seeing grey humans."

"A fuckin' druggie. I might have known."

"He wasn't the only one with those drugs in his system."

"The Blakes were old hippies?" Newman laughed.

"No, the blood analysis from Debbie Carlisle and John Morrison had exactly the same results. I think someone poisoned them."

Newman couldn't hide his derision. "What? Are you tripping as well? It's probably some bad batch of shit that's on the streets."

"Benjamin Blake had no history of drug abuse, Debbie Carlisle likewise and John Morrison was a fifty-one year old man. How many men of that age are out buying dodgy LSD on the streets?"

"What's this about LSD?" Mark McLelland asked as he entered the room.

"This clown thinks somebody poisoned three people with hallucinogenic drugs," Newman replied.

"What?"

Russell told McLelland the same story that he had related to Newman and then laid out his theory. "I think someone poisoned these people with a potent mixture of drugs: potent enough for them to be terrified into committing murder and suicide."

McLelland listened intently before replying, "Do you think they were targeted?"

"I honestly don't know."

Newman sat shaking his head, although even he was wondering at the likelihood of the alternative he had proposed. This was going to turn into a long, complicated investigation if Russell was correct.

"How would the drugs get into their system?" McLelland asked.

"Injection or ingestion would be the two alternatives," Russell suggested.

"Are the results back on their stomach contents?"

"I didn't ask, sorry," Russell replied.

"No problem. You've done a good job, Tom. Your instincts were bang on. We better tell the chief super, we're going to need more bodies." McLelland moved in the direction of the chief superintendent's office. "What are you waiting on Russell?"

"Sorry, sir?"

"You know more about this than me, you're in a better position to give the details to the boss. Come on."

Russell followed his colleague, leaving Newman stewing in his own rage.

Chief Superintendent Brian Woods was a copper of a very old school. At six feet two inches tall he weighed in at eighteen stone. His huge head sat atop a muscular body, arms like branches of an old tree were attached to his broad shoulders and his hands looked as if they could crush a man's head. So large did he appear, the desk he occupied looked like he had borrowed it from a primary school.

Tom Russell hadn't had too many dealings with Woods but he always felt intimidated in his presence. He thought that his superior probably did not suffer fools gladly and Russell did not want to look like an idiot in front of him.

"Mark, what can I do for you?" Woods growled.

McLelland invited Russell to tell the story and his theory one more time. Russell was close to wilting under the stern, scrutinising gaze of the superintendent but he laid out the facts and the reasons for his theory.

"Right, we need to get a team together. Who's about?"

"Just D.I. Newman and us at the moment, sir." McLelland replied.

"Briefing tomorrow at nine. Get Alannah to spread the word," Woods commanded.

"Yes, sir." McLelland was accustomed to Woods's brusque manner, which had more to do with his belief in getting his message across in simple terms than any natural rudeness.

The conversation at an end, Russell and McLelland moved to the door.

"D.C. Russell," Woods barked.

"Sir?" Russell turned fearing the worst.

"Good job."

"Thanks, sir." Relief rather than delight formed the expression on Russell's face.

"What did he say?" Newman asked when the two men returned to the C.I.D. office.

"We're rolling the three investigations together," McLelland responded. He was glad that Russell had proved the older detective was wrong, he took great pleasure in Newman's apparent disgust.

McLelland initiated the procedures to formalise the rolling of the three investigations into one, instructing Alannah to organise the briefing for the following morning. The dynamic of the investigation and indeed the station was about to change until the poisoner was caught.

CHAPTER 5

A swarm of detectives and uniformed P.C.s packed into the C.I.D. room the following morning. The air was uncomfortably warm and sticky as they sat or stood listening to the bizarre tale of three people drugged into deadly delusions. Even the most senior officers present seemed to be baffled by the details of the crime.

McLelland led the discussion, guiding them through each of the three scenes and describing what they believed had happened at each locus. The details of the bloodbath at the Blake residence was by far the worst, the one that held the most horror for every one in the team but each of the crimes had their own bitter poignancy.

When McLelland was finished, a fresh-faced P.C. in the front row asked, "Sir, could it be an April Fool's joke that went wrong?"

"Judging by the amount and number of hallucinogens used, I would doubt it. This appears to be a deliberate attempt to drive these people insane. Whether the killer expected Benjamin Blake and Debbie Carlisle to kill other people is anybody's guess. However, I do believe that the perpetrator had a fair idea that there would be deaths related to this crime."

"Ha," D.I. Newman, who was standing beside his colleague, vocalised his doubt of the theory.

"D.I. Newman is not convinced that I am correct and as he is in joint command of this investigation, he can tell you his thoughts." McLelland knew that the antipathy between the two detectives was not something that they should be displaying to the team but Newman wasn't prepared to put on a mask of professionalism.

"Ah think it's mair likely that whoever did this fancied it was a bit of a laugh. Maybe experimenting to see what would happen if he mixed the drugs but wisnae man enough to try it himself. It'll be some wee druggie student bastard that's behind this, mark my words." He waved a pointing finger in emphasis.

Tom Russell was standing close to the back of the gathering and hoped that his superior couldn't see the shake of his head. At the end of the previous evening, Newman had lectured Russell on his theory but it didn't sound any more convincing on a second rendition.

"At the moment the motive behind this is irrelevant. We have to establish any possible links between these people. Were they deliberately targeted or have they been victims of a random attack? Both John Morrison and Debbie Carlisle have links to the university, it might be that the killer presumed Benjamin Blake was a student. We'll need a team to go to the uni and see if there's anything there. The relatives of each of the victims should be interviewed. We need to find out if there's another link that the victims may have mentioned to their loved ones or any drug connections that exist. Is there a rogue supplier out there? Any questions?"

"Do we know how the drugs got into their system?" Ruth Stephens asked.

"Not as yet. I've asked the pathologist to take another look at the bodies for possible injection marks which may have been missed during the P.M.s. We've also asked for the tests of the stomach contents to be made top priority at the lab. Anything else?"

There were a number of mumbled negative responses and gestures.

"D.S. Hendricks will allocate your detailed jobs for the day. Report anything significant to D.I. Newman or myself as soon as you have it. Get to work."

***

Gladys Carlisle sat on a suede sofa, a broken fragment of the woman she used to be. Her thin grey hair hung weakly; unwashed and untended since the news of her daughter's death. Her red-rimmed, green eyes peered morosely from behind her thick-lensed spectacles. Although she was looking straight at the two detectives, her gaze seemed to be off in a previous, better version of the life that had been thrust upon her. In her hand she clutched a paper tissue that found its way frequently to her eyes to wipe away her tears. Her elder sister sat beside her, a heavier edition of the distraught mother, she was providing the familial strength that every grieving parent required. She had been the one to offer Russell and Newman that traditional Scottish comfort in times of trouble - a cup of tea. Frank Carlisle was in his bedroom, unable to face the questions about his daughter's death, unable to face the fact that she was gone and wasn't coming back.

Russell was unhappy when Newman had opted to join the questioning of the family, telling McLelland that he thought the younger inspector should co-ordinate the investigation from the C.I.D. office. McLelland would have been a much more sympathetic voice to listen to the story the Carlisles would tell. The family of any victim may hold the key to a murder whether they were aware of it or not. Newman's blunt delivery and opinionated approach could alienate them and make them less cooperative.

When the two women were settled and Debbie's mother's sobs had stilled, Newman said, "Mrs Carlisle, It's important we get to know as much as we can about Debbie. There may be some aspect of her life or character that could open up an avenue of investigation for us."

"I understand," the younger of the two women replied.

"Can you tell us about her?"

"She was a lovely girl. Very bright, I don't where she got it from, no' from me that's for sure. She was a hard worker all the way through school, determined she was going to go to university. She was the first to get there from either our family or Frank's, we were so proud." Russell sat with a pen poised over his notebook while he listened intently.

"Frank. That's Mr Carlisle?"

"Aye, he's no doin' too well. They were awfy close, the two of them. We were a close family but you know that men find it tougher dealing with these things."

"We'll need to speak to him at some point," he said abruptly.

"I know, he's just not up to it at the moment."

"You said Debbie was very hard working at school. Surely, she must have went through a rebellious phase, you know the way most teenagers do?" `Newman was blundering towards the tougher questions, asserting his belief that Debbie couldn't have been as innocent as the stricken mother was painting her.

"Eh... nothing too bad. Stayin' out later than she was supposed to, general hormonal moods but nothing that we couldn't cope with."

"She must have been involved with alcohol or drugs, every kid does," he said more aggressively than he should have.

Mrs Carlisle's face betrayed a curious mixture of dread, disbelief and disgust. Her sister voiced her own anger, "That lassie wis nae druggie."

Newman pressed on. "Look, we need to establish if she had ever dabbled, maybe knew somebody that was involved in drugs in some way. You do want us to catch who did this don't you?"

"Of course we do but she was not involved in drugs," Gladys Carlisle replied firmly and with a finality that brought that line of questioning to an end.

Russell could see Newman's disappointment but even he wasn't stupid enough to pursue it when Mrs Carlisle was clearly convinced of her daughter's avoidance of drugs. No family, particularly one as respectable as the Carlisles could imagine their sons or daughters being involved in drugs or any criminal activity. The police knew the reality: there were increasing numbers of young people who were tempted by marijuana at the very least. It would take a little longer to discover if Debbie Carlisle was one of them.

When the two detectives were clear of the Carlisle house Newman said, "Why do they aw think that their weans are perfect?"

"None of Debbie's friends thought she was involved in drugs either."

"Aye, you can trust a bunch of fuckin' layabout students to tell us the truth," he replied with a heavy coat of sarcasm on every word. "And her Da', couldn't speak tae us. He's the one that'll know the truth for sure. I widnae be surprised if he was involved in some way."

Russell decided not to respond - Newman would have charged his grannie with the murder if it meant getting a quick conviction. The journey back to the station was another bore fest as the senior officer listed, in minute detail, the technical specifications of the car. It was all Russell could do to stifle a yawn.

***

The rest of the detectives who had visited the families of the victims had met a similar degree of shock at the suggestion that the people involved would have been connected with the world of illegal drugs in any way. McLelland felt confident that the deceased weren't intended targets but unfortunate, random recipients of a psychotic act.

A loose collection of around eight of the investigating team were gathered in the C.I.D. room, each with a mug of something hot, sitting around a table that had a plate of digestive biscuits in the centre, when one of the office phones rang. Alannah answered it. "It's the lab, they want to speak to the officer in charge."

McLelland motioned to stand but Newman stopped him before he could finish pushing back his chair. "Three victims, I'm the senior investigation officer."

"Shouldn't we let the chief super decide that?" the younger man replied.

"He'd agree with me. First scene, largest number of victims and I've got seniority in terms of time served and age." He took the phone from Alannah.

"D.I. Newman," he said into the handset.

The conversation in the room had faltered into silence as the detectives tuned into one half of the call.

"Right… OK… aye." Newman was taking notes while resting his considerable bulk on the edge of the desk.

Without any further acknowledgement of the caller he put down the phone and walked with an important swagger to the end of the group of desks.

"That was the techs with the stomach content report. All three of the poison victims had been eating some kind of cake. The boy ate a doughnut, the lassie had some kind of bun and the suicide guy had an éclair. Anybody remember if there wis any baker's boxes or something similar?" Blank looks and heads shaking in ignorance were the only reply.

"We need to see where they got the cakes from. Volunteers to visit the scenes?"

Tom Russell and two other D.C.s put up their hands.

"Russell you go to the Blakes, Stephens get across to the student flat and Jenkins check out the uni. Make it quick, we don't want any mair crazies running amok."

No one moved and Newman shouted, "Well, what are ye waiting for? Get yir arse in gear."

Russell and his two colleagues - who had paused thinking that there would be more information or precise instructions - headed to the door. They could hear Newman saying, "Where's ma tea?"

CHAPTER 6

Russell unlocked the door to the Blake flat and stepped under the crime scene tape that was covering the entrance in the shape of a St. Andrew's cross. The coppery, metallic smell of the blood permeated the hallway. Death lingered, unwilling to escape the confines of the house, an unwelcome visitor who refused to leave. Russell could feel the revulsion and nausea grip him but he tried to desensitise himself to what he was about to face and walked into the living room.

The crime scene, if anything appeared even more awful. The blood had dried to a characteristic tawny brown colour and the voids in the pattern where the bodies had been told their own melancholy, macabre story. Some day soon a cleaning squad would arrive and remove all trace of the terror that had occurred in the room, leaving it ready to accept new owners. Russell wondered how many of the houses in the city had been cleansed of tragedy in a similar way and how many people lived in rooms with the hidden truth of murder or suicide that had once visited their homes.

He turned his attention to the galley kitchen that formed one part of the larger room. There was a good chance of finding where the tainted cake had come from, unless it had already found its way to the rubbish dump. He checked the cupboards and found tins, packets and bottles, many of them branded as Valushop produce. Russell knew there was a Valushop supermarket within a mile of the flat and it looked like the Blakes were regular shoppers but it didn't necessarily prove anything about the origin of the doughnut. He then moved to the tall pedal bin that sat under the breakfast bar that divided the kitchen from the living area. When he removed the lid he was engulfed in the smell of rotting food that, combined with the smell of the blood gave him an overwhelming urge to throw up. Russell stood back and gulped at the air but there was nothing fresh in the room, least of all the air. He managed to force down the sickly feeling before emptying the bin's contents on to the tiled floor. It didn't take him long to find a Valushop branded paper bag with traces of sugar and grease on the inside. It took a little longer to find the receipt that confirmed Benjamin Blake's purchase on the day of his death. Russell wasn't sure if the shop in question had their own bakery but he was now sure that it was the source of at least one of the contaminated cakes.

***

The consensus among the C.I.D. team was that Valushop was indeed the best place to continue the investigation into the freakish series of deaths. D.C. Stephens had recovered the box that had held the iced buns and Jenkins had discovered from the staff in the university that a cake run had been organised to celebrate the birthday of one of the students. Dr Thomson, the lecturer who was taking the class on the fatal day had blanched when he realised it could have been him or any of his students who could have chosen that particular pastry. The thought of what a victim could have done with the selection of chemicals available in the room had made him ill enough to finish work early and go home.

Newman and McLelland listened to what the junior officers had to say. Inevitably it was Newman who was the first to speak. "Sounds like we've got somebody with a grudge against the supermarket. Probably some disgruntled ex-employee, thought he would get his own back."

McLelland was a little more considered as he said, "It's possible but it could be anybody in the supply chain. The bakery, the drivers or even a member of the public with access to the shelves."

"I'm tellin' you, it'll be some wee spotty herbert who got the sack for dipping the till."

The other D.I. stayed silent.

"Right, we'll go in heavy handed and shake the culprit loose. He's probably got some sympathisers within the staff; one of them is bound to crack. McLelland, Russell and Stephens you're wi' me."

Mark McLelland wasn't happy about the tone Newman had used but felt it was necessary to be present at the supermarket to ensure that D.I. Newman didn't decide to short cut established procedure in an effort to secure a quick conviction. For his part, Russell was glad that he wouldn't be the only one to join Newman on his crusade.

He was disappointed when he couldn't avoid the car journey with his superior and was relieved when they finally pulled into the car park of the supermarket. McLelland and Stephens were waiting at the automatic doors and all four entered together. This particular store wasn't one of the huge shops that were beginning to pop up around the country; there were only six checkouts servicing fifteen rows of groceries.

Newman marched up to one of the checkouts and demanded of the assistant, "Where's the manager?"

The woman who was placing her shopping on the conveyor belt said indignantly," Hey, whit's your gemme? Ah'm gettin' served here."

"Polis, hen. Shut yir geggie, this is important. Manager?" he said to the young woman who responded by turning to a microphone, pressing a button and announcing, "Mr Braben to checkout one."

"Satisfied?" she asked the policeman sarcastically.

"Watch yir lip, hen."

Newman turned away and Russell saw the women muttering to each other, sure that he saw the customer mouth 'arsehole' and the assistant nod her head. He couldn't fault their assessment.

About a minute later, a short man in a dark blue suit, white shirt and a fire engine red tie - that matched the colour of the supermarket's logo - walked towards the checkout. He said exasperatedly, "What is it, Sharon? I'm very busy you know."

"P.C. Plod there wants to talk to you," she replied indicating the detectives with a head movement.

"Oh, I see. I'm Donald Braben, the store manager. Can I help you?" he asked politely.

Newman brandished his warrant card. "Detective Inspector Newman. I'm here because there's a link between this place and the deaths that occurred in and around Partick last Thursday."

"Brilliant. What a dick." Russell heard McLelland mutter.

Braben's pale face flushed to the roots of his immaculately styled black hair. His jade green eyes began to flutter and he appeared to be gasping for air. "Oh... oh dear... no that can't be true. Goodness me what will head office think."

"You've got mair than your bosses tae worry about, pal. Is there somewhere we can talk?"

The manager was obviously flustered, but he composed himself enough to lead the detectives towards his office.

Before they went through the door Newman said, "Stephens, have a look around the store, see if it's possible that it was a customer that laced the cakes and check if there's CCTV tapes from Thursday."

"Yes, sir."

The manager's office was a compact grey box of a room, packed with equally grey filing cabinets and an occupant whose face was rapidly changing to match the decor. There were only two chairs for visitors, so Russell stood while the two inspectors settled down opposite the fidgeting manager. Braben rearranged paper on his desk, straightened the same pencil about twenty times and ran his fingers through his hair while Newman talked.

"We've got a serious situation here. We have reason to believe that cakes that had been tampered with caused the deaths in this area on Thursday. Those cakes originated in this shop. What have you got to say to that?"

"I don't understand, in what way were they tampered with?"

"We can't reveal the details but we believe that it may be the result of either a disgruntled ex-employee or sabotage by a current employee with a grievance."

McLelland interrupted, "Those are just two of the possibilities we are investigating."

Neither Russell nor Braben missed the look of annoyance that Newman fired at his colleague.

"As I was saying, is there anyone you could think of that would fall into either of these categories?"

The manager's fidgeting moved into overdrive. "No, no, I don't think so."

"We'll need to see your personnel records."

"I would need to ask head office," Braben replied weakly.

"Mr Braben, it's vital you cooperate. You don't want to be responsible for any more incidents like this do you?"

Tom Russell thought the poor man was about to burst into tears.

"No, but all our employee records are held at head office these days," the manager whined defensively.

"We'll get the details but it would be helpful if you let your head office know what we need and that officers will be round to collect the information. Hopefully, we won't need to waste our time getting a warrant, that might irritate us a little."

"I'll do my best."

"We'd like to speak to the staff. How many people work here?"

"We've got twenty seven part-time and full-time staff split over two shifts plus another three casuals at the weekend."

"I think we can presume that the weekenders aren't involved for the moment. Is there somewhere we can interview the people who are currently working?"

"There's the smokers room."

"That'll need to do. I'll stay here with you and my colleagues will begin interviewing everyone. Organise a list and pass it to D.I. McLelland here."

"It's not very convenient when the store is open," he said, his consternation writ large on his face.

"We could close it, if that's better." Newman's voice carried enough of a threat that it prompted a panicked response from Braben.

"No, no, I'm sure we'll manage."

"You can show Detectives McLelland and Russell to the room. Oh and bring me a tea on the way back."

Braben led an angry McLelland and a disconsolate Russell to a gloomy room close to the area that the staff used for breaks. Despite a whirring extractor fan, a pall of blue smoke hung in the air and every surface was covered in an oily brown residue. There was a Formica-covered table at the centre of the room with an ashtray that contained a small mound of cigarette butts. Around the table were a group of ragged and dirty chairs of varying designs and colour.

"Lovely," McLelland observed disdainfully after Braben had left the room and had gone off to organise the interviewees.

When the manager returned with a middle-aged woman, McLelland pointed to the ashtray and said, "Can you please dispose of that?"

"Yes, of course." He lifted the ashtray before he said, "Initially I've chosen the staff that were on duty on Thursday, I thought they might be the most helpful." He passed the piece of paper to McLelland.

"That's great, Mr Braben, thank you."

He left the two detectives with the woman whose name was Sharon Derrick. She proved to be a completely useless witness, unable to remember what had happened the previous Thursday, nor could she recall a single ex-employee who might be nursing a grudge. It wasn't uncommon for Glaswegians to be deliberately uncooperative with police officers but Russell thought Mrs Derrick was genuine in her lack of knowledge.

She set the template for the afternoon as staff member after staff member stated their ignorance of the crime and their inability to identify a possible suspect.

When he was satisfied that he had eliminated Braben from the inquiry, Newman joined the others in the smoking room. Ruth Stephens was also there as the final three people on the list were interviewed. After two more fruitless interviews, Newman said, "Bloody hell, I need a fag." He had just finished lighting up the cigarette when Braben showed the final staff member in.

Sammy Cowan blanched when he realised who was in the room, the faces of Newman and McLelland were both very familiar. Sammy was a career criminal with a record of failure.

"Sammy Cowan," Newman said with a smile of undisguised pleasure.

"Mr Newman, sir," Cowan replied.

"Take a seat, Sammy. I'm sure this won't take long if it's anything like our previous meetings."

Cowan sat down heavily in a rickety wooden chair. He was in his mid-fifties with thick, curly greying hair. His face was lined with a map of deep wrinkles that looked like someone had chiseled them in. His opal blue eyes were wide in fear and his nicotine-stained right hand drummed a nervous rhythm on the table. He was dressed in the standard supermarket uniform but it looked like it hadn't been in contact with an iron in some time. Tom Russell thought he cut quite a pathetic figure.

"Sammy, this is a big one. You were a bit out of your league when you tried to pull this off."

"Ah don't know whit you mean, Mr Newman."

"What was the plan, Sammy? A wee bit o' blackmail maybe? Thought you could get the supermarket to pay out to stop it happening again?"

"Ah don't know whit you're talkin' aboot, honest."

"Sammy, you're a career loser. Failed at burglary, as a conman and as a drug dealer. What made you think that you would make it as a blackmailer?"

"Please, Mr Newman, ah've goat nae idea whit you're oan aboot. Ah've been straight fur seven year and this is the longest ah've ever hud a joab. Why wid ah throw that away?"

"Cos you're a wee arsehole. You got tired of being a good citizen and decided that it was time for you to make a big score. D'ye honestly think we don't know how people like you think?" Newman shook his head. "You're going away for good this time, Sammy boy." He drew in a lungful of smoke and sighed it out as if satisfied with his conclusions.

"Naw, naw. Ah've no done anythin'. Please, ye've goat tae believe me." He stood up abruptly but Newman's voice was enough to make him respond like a well-trained dog. "Sit," the detective growled.

"Now Sammy tell us where you got the stuff. You probably thought it was something harmless, maybe you didn't think that people would die. Cough up a name and it might not be just as bad for you."

"Deid? What stuff?" Cowan was now on the edge of hysteria, his voice racing up the scale with each accusation.

"I've got six people dead, Sammy. Even if you only meant to give them a fright, it's still a serious crime."

Before Cowan could respond McLelland said, "D.I. Newman, a word." He indicated the door with his head.

When he couldn't see an ashtray, Newman threw the butt of his cigarette on the floor and stubbed it out with his foot. "D.I. McLelland is going to tell me how you're a poor innocent but dae yirself a favour and give D.C. Russell your statement, it'll save us all a lot of time.

McLelland moved into the staff break area, away from the door of the room. "What the fuck are you playing at?"

Newman laughed. "Ah knew it, you don't like him for this."

"You're kidding, right? Sammy Cowan can hardly work out what socks to put on in the morning, never mind come up with some complicated plan to blackmail a supermarket. There's been no contact from anyone at Valushop saying they're being blackmailed. You would think that would have been the first thing to happen after Thursday. This isn't about somebody trying to make a fast buck and certainly not a petty criminal who's not been in bother for over eight years. I know you like everything to be wrapped up in a nice wee bundle but this isn't some stabbing outside a chip shop with twenty witnesses. The person behind this has intelligence, the ability to plan and a sadistic streak the width of the Clyde. None of that describes Sammy Cowan."

"Fuck off, McLelland. We know you want to be on the fast track to some braid and you think if you get a big case that will speed things up but this is Glesga. We don't huv master criminals; we huv hard men and wee arseholes like Cowan. A hard man disnae use poison, it's pathetic losers like Cowan who don't have the guts to chib somebody or put a bullet in them that pull off a stunt like this."

"I'll contact the chief super if need be, but I'm not wasting time and resources on this. Whoever did this could decide to try again and we could end up with an even worse body count.

I'm not going to let you fit Cowan up because you're too lazy to do the job right."

"Listen tae yirsel. Like some wean running tae his mammy."

"It's up to you but I'll have no part in this."

Newman marched away in the direction of the smoking room while McLelland headed for Braben's office.

"Did he confess all, D.C. Russell?" Newman asked as he entered.

"No, sir." Russell replied.

When Newman took his seat again, Sammy Cowan was a little calmer but his fear was still evident.

"Please Mr Newman, ah've built a life for masel'. Ah cannae go back tae prison. Ah've no done anythin' wrang."

"You were here on Thursday, tell me about your day."

"It wis jist a normal day. Ah stacked shelves, helped with a delivery and did an hour on the checkout."

"What about cakes?"

"Cakes? Whit aboot them?"

"Did you put the cakes out on the shelves? Did you handle them at any time?'

Cowan paused before replying, "Ah don't think so. I was stackin' the soup and beans an' that. Then the dairy van arrived and ah helped organise the delivery in the refrigerated stock room. Ah wisnae near the cakes oan Thursday."

"I think yir lying to me, Sammy. I think you thought you would try a bit o' blackmail and make yourself enough cash to retire oan. I think we should take a wee trip to the station."

"Naw, naw Mr Newman. It wisnae me honest, it wisnae me."

"Take him," Newman ordered Russell and Stephens.

"Sir, are you sure about this?" Russell asked.

"Are you questioning my orders, Mr Russell?"

"No, sir," Russell replied reluctantly.

It was close to six o'clock before the interviews were complete. McLelland thanked Braben for his help - Newman had walked out without even an acknowledgement of the manager. A relieved Braben promised that he would get in touch with the supermarket's human resources department and urge them to help the police as much as they could.

Newman waited until they were back in the C.I.D. room before initiating the discussion about what they had discovered.

"There's a chance that a customer could have injected something into the cakes," Ruth Stephens said. "The cakes that were poisoned are on display on shelves, so someone could have added the drugs but they would have had to be careful to avoid being caught."

"CCTV?" McLelland asked.

"I've got the tapes for Wednesday and Thursday, although according to the supervisor the cakes should have been delivered on the Thursday morning but I thought I would check both just in case. I'm not holding out too much hope even if they were caught on camera, the images are black and white and pretty crappy resolution."

"Do yir best, hen. Look out for Cowan, I'm sure he's the one," Newman said.

Ruth Stephens looked like she was going to respond to his patronising attitude but bit her tongue.

"Newman, try treating your officers with a little more respect," McLelland said.

"Whit?" Newman asked innocently.

McLelland shook his head. He changed the subject. "I think we have to look at the delivery driver and the bakery," he said.

Newman replied, "Wait 'til we've checked wee Sammy oot. It'll save a lot of work."

***

Sammy Cowan was so desperate to prove his innocence that he insisted that the police search his flat without the need for a warrant. He gave Russell the keys and told him, "It disnae matter what yir lookin' fur, ye'll no find it in ma flat."

Newman decided to put the petty criminal in a cell until a full investigation of his work records and the search of the flat was complete. After two hours and a thorough inspection of the flat, Russell and the team returned with no evidence that might have indicated Cowan's involvement.

"He's probably got it stashed somewhere else," was Newman's dismissive reply when Russell told him.

The pressure to let Cowan go increased when Stephens had finished analysing the tapes. She went over the full day's CCTV and at no point was Cowan shown to be anywhere near the cakes either in the store room or the bakery counter in the shop.

"It wasn't him," McLelland asserted.

Newman stood firm. "Ah still think we should question him."

"You're the S.I.O. but you're wrong. I will see what the chief super thinks." McLelland went to talk to Woods with Newman marching angrily behind him.

The detectives who were left in the C.I.D. room laughed at the sight.

"A pair of weans," Ruth Stephens commented. There was no disagreement from anyone.

They returned twenty minutes later. "Cut him loose," McLelland told Tom Russell. "Tom, make sure you apologise to him, " he added.

"Apologise to that wee shite." That was rubbing salt into the wound as far as Newman was concerned.

"We made a mistake, we should say sorry. Well technically it should be you that says sorry," McLelland said.

"Fuck off," Newman replied. "Ah'm going home." He stormed off.

When Tom Russell returned having done as ordered, McLelland said, " That should do us for tonight. Tomorrow we'll have a look at the delivery drivers and the bakery."

The detectives finished their various tasks and drifted off one by one.

CHAPTER 7

T he following day Russell was assigned to accompany the two feuding detective inspectors as they travelled to the south side of the city to visit the Perfect Delicake Bakery. The three-storey, red-brick building was built in the thirties; it comprised a suite of offices at the front with distinctive white-framed windows and behind the office block was the production area that included vast storage bins and lots of pipes. When Russell opened the door of the car, his nose was filled immediately with the warm, inviting smell coming from the ovens.

"Mmm... we might get some good freebies out of this," Newman said as he walked towards the building.

"Shouldn't we wait for D.I. McLelland?" Russell asked.

"We'll get him inside," Newman replied as he strode on.

They walked into the reception area that Russell imagined hadn't changed since the building was opened, other than the new corporate logo on the wall. There was a low wooden desk for the receptionist; some faux leather chairs for visitors and the walls were covered in teak-coloured panelling on which was a series of framed photographs that showed the evolution of the bakery since its foundation.

Newman approached the desk where a heavily made-up woman was waiting.

"Can I help you?" she asked, smiling sincerely.

"Detective Inspector Newman and this is Detective Constable Russell. We need to speak to your head man."

"Can I ask what it's regarding?"

"It's police business, that's all you need to know," he replied rudely.

"Yes, of course. I'll contact Ms Nichol."

"I said I want to speak to the organ grinder not a monkey."

"Ms Nichol is the chief operations manager and a director of the company. She is the senior member of staff at this facility," the receptionist said haughtily. "Could you please take a seat and I'll see if she's available?

Russell smiled as he walked behind his boss to the low seats that were arranged at the window. The spring sunshine streamed in through the glass and Russell was soon uncomfortably warm. Newman seemed non-plussed by his earlier embarrassment and kept looking at his watch to indicate how precious his time was. McLelland arrived when they had been waiting five minutes and it was clear that he was unimpressed by Newman's decision not to wait for him. After the morning briefing had finished, he had been allocating work to the other officers in the investigation. A task that technically should have fallen to the senior investigating officer but that had been delegated to him by Newman. A team was assigned to collect personnel records for the supermarket's current and ex-employees, a uniformed P.C. was allocated as an extra resource to help Ruth Stephens take a closer look at the video tapes and enquiries were continuing into possible connections between the victims.

After ten minutes a heavy-set woman, who Russell reckoned to be in her mid-thirties, arrived to greet them.

"I'm Deirdre Nichol, welcome to the Perfect Delicake Bakery," she said in a friendly but formal way.

As the detectives introduced themselves in turn, Russell observed the woman. She had a square, almost manly face but her striking blue eyes and fine cheekbones gave her a handsome appearance. She was dressed in a well-cut business suit with a plain but expensive blouse and a single row of pearls around her throat. Her flat shoes matched the navy blue of her suit and were trimmed with cream.

"I'll take you up to my office," her annunciation was clipped and precise.

Her office was on the top floor and overlooked the car park. The same wooden panelling covered the wall and behind her desk was an oil painting of a stiff, stern-looking Victorian gentleman with a bald head but impressively thick bushy beard.

"My great, great grandfather Thomas Macintosh, the founder of the company," she said to Russell when she noticed him staring at the picture. "The Macintosh bakery was founded in the late nineteenth century in Pollokshields. He baked bread, cakes and pastries from a shop in Paisley Road West. The company expanded and grew to include three shops across the city until this building was constructed in 1933. We've been through a series of takeovers and mergers since the early eighties and we're now part of the Perfect Delicake Bakery family." It sounded like a speech she had given frequently.

"I see." Russell said.

She invited all three detectives to sit and pressed a button on an intercom to ask for some tea and coffee to be delivered. Newman was itching to get started but waited impatiently for the drinks to be brought in. His mood improved immensely when he noticed the iced buns that were offered as an accompaniment.

Ms Nichol was insistent that the detectives accept her hospitality and persuaded a reluctant Russell to have a cup of tea. When everyone was served she asked, "Now gentlemen, what brings the members of the constabulary to our little bakery?"

Newman launched into the now familiar description of the events of the previous week. As he had been with Braben the previous day, he was very direct as he told the woman that he believed that one of her employees may be involved in the deaths but there was none of the callous, haranguing tone he had used with the supermarket manager. In his time with Newman, Russell had noticed that the older man was in awe of rank and position, becoming like Uriah Heep when he was in the company of superior officers or those in position of power.

"I'm sure that you weren't aware of any connection Ms Nichol, but the evidence points to someone within the supply chain being responsible for this terrible crime. The company supplies cakes to the Valushop supermarket, is that correct?"

"Yes, we supply freshly baked goods to about thirty of their stores in the West of Scotland from this bakery."

"How are the deliveries organised?"

"We have our own drivers that visit all the supermarkets we supply, it's not only Valushop."

"Are all of the drivers employed by the company?"

"Except at Christmas when we have to use outside contractors to help us fulfil our obligations at that busy time."

"Ms Nichol have you had any threats against the company? Maybe from ex-employees?"

She bubbled a laugh, "We're hardly a multi-national oil company, inspector. I think you'll find that most people like a cake or two. And no, we've not had any disgruntled employees threatening a rampage with loaded pastry."

"I hope you don't mind but we will need access to your employees records, recent past and the present."

"Of course, we will do everything we can to help."

"We will also need to see the packaging area and to speak to the people there."

"As I said, I will instruct everyone to cooperate fully."

"D.I. McLelland, I think you should have a look at the staff records while D.C. Russell and I interview some of the workforce." Newman was continuing to be deliberately provocative but McLelland was stoic in his agreement to the request.

Mrs Nichol arranged for her production manager, whose name was James Dickinson to lead the two detectives to the relevant area of the building while a bubbly woman from the Personnel section accompanied McLelland to the records department.

Newman and Russell were required to dress in white coats, paper shoes and hairnets to pass through the food preparation areas. It was obvious that the processes used would make it unlikely that the hallucinogens had been added during the mixing or baking of the cakes. It would have been impossible for the chemicals to be targeted precisely due to the random nature of the preparation, and the time in the ovens would have made the effects of the drugs unpredictable if not inert.

The packaging of the baked goods was done in a relatively modern extension to the original bakery. There were five lines that dealt with specific products, one for savouries, two for bread and two for cakes. The two detectives stood in the cacophonous noise of the machines watching one of the cake lines. It was currently running for iced buns that came from the icing area and were placed on a conveyor belt. As the buns passed down the line, a group of workers was lifting four buns at a time and placing them into open-topped boxes, which were then placed on another line where the boxes were wrapped in a thin cellophane covering. Although it may have been difficult, there was definitely an opportunity for one person to inject the drugs into a single cake during the process as each of the packagers were well spread out on the line.

"I'll take you to the locker room and you'll be able to speak to the staff there," Dickinson shouted above the bangs, clatter and hum of the line.

He walked to a door that led to a long narrow room where two rows of lockers stretched out towards a break area. The two detectives dumped their protective clothing in the large bins just inside the door and followed Dickinson down through the narrow passage between the lockers.

There was a group of seven people around a table with tea, bottles of soft drinks and sandwiches in front of them. The conversation stopped immediately.

"Folks, this is Detective Inspector Newman and Detective Constable Rus…" Before Dickinson could finish the sentence a young man sprang from his chair and bolted for the exit.

"Get after him," Newman bawled at Russell who had been slow to react.

Russell burst out of the door, looked left and right before spotting the man running across the car park. The detective set off in pursuit. The suspect had a decent lead on him as he charged out into the street. Russell pumped his arms and legs in the way he had been taught by his P.E. teacher back in school. Back then he had been a decent sprinter, but it had been a long time since he'd had to use those muscles to propel him at such a rate.

He had to slow, struggling for traction as he turned on to the street; his dress shoes were inadequate for running at high speed. He spotted his prey and picked up the pace. The man looked over his shoulder and darted to his left, which took him out into the road and across to the opposite pavement. Russell had to wait for one of the bakery vans to pass before he could follow. He watched as his target turned into a narrow alley that ran behind a street of old tenements. He was gaining and the young man appeared increasingly desperate, glancing over his shoulder more frequently as his feet pounded the tarmac. After one such glance, his hip caught the edge of a rubbish bin, knocked him off balance and spun him into a painful fall. Russell gained quickly but before he could lay hands on him, the man was up and off again but the collision had injured him. As a result it wasn't long before Russell completed the chase and pounced on the runner. They tumbled to the ground and the breath was knocked from the young man.

The detective secured the suspect's hands and hauled him to his feet. He read him his rights and the now disconsolate runner nodded to say he understood. When he had steadied his breathing, the detective constable used his radio to call for a car to pick them up. The prisoner said nothing as they waited for the transport but he wept openly. Tom Russell was pretty sure that he had caught the poisoner.

***

The bakery worker's name was Nicky Petterson. He was twenty years of age and had no previous record of criminal behaviour. He cried all the way to the station, he said nothing but did manage to irritate Newman with the sound of his sobs.

Russell was surprised at how upset the suspect was; it didn't fit with the profile of someone who had carefully planned a crime this awful and it did make him wonder if the deaths had come as a shock to the man but then guilt can have strange effects on people.

Newman decided to lead the interview and told McLelland he could listen in to the recording while Russell took the notes.

Petterson was long-limbed, blue eyed with blonde hair and looked every inch the Scandinavian that his name suggested, but he had been born in Edinburgh.

"It is 11:55 am on Wednesday 7th April, 1993. This is the first interview with Nicky Petterson in connection with the six deaths on Thursday 1st April 1993. Present in the room are Mr Petterson, Detective Inspector Newman and Detective Constable Russell. Mr Petterson has been informed of his rights but has not asked for the presence of a lawyer for this interview. Can you confirm that for the tape please, Mr Petterson?"

He lifted his chin from his chest and said, "That's right."

"Mr Petterson would you care to tell us what happened?"

"No one was supposed to get hurt, he said it was just a practical joke."

"Well six people are dead so you better tell us the whole story as it will make things easier in the long run for you, son."

"This guy approached me last week and offered me £250 if I would put a laxative in the cakes. He was very specific and said it had to be on April Fool's Day. He said it was just a practical joke, an April Fool prank. He said the bakery had sacked him and he wanted to get back at them."

Newman's wafer thin patience was already close to snapping and he sighed as he said, "What did this man look like?"

"I don't know. He wore a mask."

"Oh, how convenient, a bloody mask. How did he approach you?"

"He came to my door. He said he had followed me home as he didn't want anyone at the bakery recognising him and that he didn't want me to be able to describe him."

"With all due respect, that sounds like a lot of bollocks, Mr Petterson," Newman said with no trace of respect.

"But it's true. You don't think I did this on my own? I wouldn't do that."

"Look at it from our perspective. What's more likely? You thought you would play a practical joke that went wrong or that some mystery man asked you to place a cocktail of drugs in some cakes to take revenge on an ex-employer. What a load of shite."

"Look he was well spoken, short maybe five feet five or six. He wore one of those carnival masks you see in Venice or somewhere. It was one of those multi-coloured clown costumes. A... a harlequin that's it."

Newman's exasperation began to show. "I'll give you ten out of ten for imagination but there's no way that any jury in the land is going to believe that load of old cobblers," he growled.

"It's true, I swear it's true."

"How did he pay you?"

"He gave me half up front and then there was an envelope with the balance at my house when I got back from work on Friday."

"Where's the cash?"

"I spent it on a new hi-fi."

"All very convenient. Putting aside your fantasy friend, how did you get the drugs into the cakes?"

"He's not a fantasy!" Petterson shouted.

"Calm down, son. You're in enough trouble tae last a lifetime so don't make it worse. Now how did you get the drugs into the cakes?"

"He gave me three small hypodermic syringes. He told me to inject the stuff into three cakes, he said he wanted to create a scandal that would embarrass the bakery when people realised where the cakes had come from. He was offering £250 and I didn't think it would do any harm."

"Why didn't you come to us on Friday with this story? You must have realised that those deaths were related to what you did."

"I was hoping they weren't, I thought it was just a coincidence. I honestly didn't think anybody would get hurt."

"Aye, ah believe that bit but I think the reason you didn't come in on Friday was that the whole idea was yours and you realised that your prank went too far. Tell the truth, the mysterious masked man doesn't exist, does he?"

"He does, he does. I swear he does."

"Bollocks! Tell the truth or it's a murder charge you'll be facing."

"I want a lawyer."

"Interview terminated at 12:00pm." With obvious disgust Newman battered the stop button on the recorder.

"You're an idiot, son. They'll throw the book at you."

Russell followed the senior officer out of the room while a uniformed constable arrived to take Petterson to the cells.

"I've heard some amount of crap in that fuckin' interview room but that takes the biscuit. A masked man, holy hell."

Russell wasn't as convinced. "It does seem a strange story to make up though. He's been caught, why not just tell the truth?"

"Oh, gonnae no gies that crap. Maybe he's a loony, maybe he's hoping to go for a diminished responsibility defence. How the fuck should ah know? But he's lying, I'm sure of it."

Over the course of the afternoon the case against Petterson strengthened. The three syringes were found in his house and forensics could find no fingerprints other than those of the suspect. A warrant was issued to check his medical records, which confirmed that he had been under the care of a psychiatrist and had been diagnosed as being bipolar. The forensic team could find no evidence of anyone else being involved in the crime.

Russell was back in the interview room with Newman at five o'clock. Petterson's lawyer was now sitting, grim faced beside him whispering her advice into his ear. Initially, he kept up the story of the Harlequin but after a short recess she advised Newman and Russell that her client would plead guilty due to diminished responsibility.

"The prick'll get away with it. Mental problems, my arse." Newman had grumbled when they returned to the C.I.D. room. "Anyway, that's a job well done boys. Who's for a pint?"

There was a loud cheer from the assembled officers.

Tom Russell didn't join the celebrations, the six dead people played on his mind and there was something that continued to gnaw away at his gut and refused to let him believe that there wasn't more to this case than they had so far uncovered.

CHAPTER 8

O ver the next month the case against Petterson became rock solid and at no time did he deny that he was responsible for the action of placing the drugs in the cakes. He did continue to claim the existence of the masked man and the defence hired a psychiatrist to examine him. The doctor claimed that the suspect was suffering from paranoid delusions and persuaded a judge that the young man should be confined to a secure psychiatric unit for further analysis and his own protection. Newman railed at what he saw as a weak decision, convinced that the man should be facing charges of culpable homicide but the Procurator Fiscal's office was simply relieved to have Petterson off the street.

The murder team dispersed back to their more mundane duties. Tom Russell dealt with domestic abuse, a pub stabbing and a series of related burglaries. Newman had taken the lead on the stabbing, as it was exactly the kind of case he loved. There were ten witnesses as well as CCTV footage, the killer was caught literally red handed as he tried to flee the scene leaving behind the murder weapon which had his fingerprints, as well as the victim's blood all over it.

As spring edged into summer, a call to Partick police station one Monday morning changed the complexion of the hallucinogen deaths. Tom Russell had just finished writing up the most recent burglary - plodding through the online form at the rate of about three words a minute - when the phone rang.

"Partick C.I.D., Detective Constable Russell speaking."

"Tom, it's Mark McLelland. Is Newman there?"

"No, he's on lunch."

"When he gets back, grab him and get both your arses over here now."

"Where's here, sir?"

McLelland gave him an address in Kilbarchan.

"What's up?"

"We've got a body that you both have to see. Be here A.S.A.P., that's an order." Before he could ask any further questions, McLelland hung up abruptly.

Newman arrived back with a trail of crumbs decorating his suit jacket and tie.

"Sir, we've got to go to a crime scene. D.I. McLelland says it's important."

"What? Who the fuck does he think he is?"

"Sir, he told me to tell you that it was an order."

"He's a comedian. An order?"

"Yes sir," Russell said plaintively.

"Fine. Have you got the address?"

"Yes, sir."

Russell followed Newman as he stormed out the station to his car.

The drive to Kilbarchan took twenty-five minutes and when they pulled up in front of the house, the full crime scene procedure was already well underway.

The house was an early Victorian villa, gleaming white in the strong summer sunshine. The main door was on the right of the house and a multitude of people was mulling around the entrance as Newman and Russell approached.

"Who the fuck do you think you are?" Newman shouted to McLelland who was standing away from the door, smoking and chatting to a forensic technician.

"This is Deirdre Nichol's house. Go inside and you'll see why you needed to be here," McLelland replied with quiet resignation.

As they walked into the hall Professor Marriot was on his way out having completed his initial findings. Newman said, "How's it going Prof?"

"Not good, Harry. This is a bad one." His reply contained none of his normal levity. Russell noticed how quiet the other officers and technicians were, the atmosphere was more sombre than usual.

Inside the front room the crime-scene photographer was packing his camera and lenses into his equipment bag. Another technician was dusting for prints on an oak sideboard. Everyone was doing their best to ignore the reason for them being there.

"In the name of God," Newman exclaimed while his colleague gasped simultaneously.

On a green sofa lay sprawled a little girl who was about four years old. Her throat had been cut deeply, the blood had stained her white dress a deep pink and found it's way on to the cushion below her. On the floor underneath her hand was a small, very worn brown teddy bear. In the middle of the floor on a Persian rug, the girl's mother rested face up. Her arms were strapped to her side due to the clear cellophane film that wrapped her naked form. Her thick neck had been brutalised in a similar way to her daughter, the blood still not completely dry where it had landed on the cellophane. She was ice white and on each of her eyelids was a little sticker complete with tiny printed writing.

The two detectives approached her still form and bent over. The printing on each of the stickers read 'Best before 1st April 1983.'

McLelland walked into the room and said, "Ms Nichol was wearing this when she was found." In his gloved hand he held up a Venetian mask, painted in the style of a Harlequin. The mask was designed to cover both the face and the neck of the person wearing it. The white face was adorned with a clown's make-up of red, blue and gold paint. The face was topped with a sculpted hat painted in four colours arranged in the familiar diamond pattern; the collar was a motley of the same shades. Between the face and the collar, a red line had been painted to match the fatal line that crossed the victims' throats.

"What the hell is this?" Newman said.,

"We also found this," McLelland said as he handed Newman a business card.

The same Harlequin design appeared at the bottom right of the white cardboard. In the centre was a single word, 'FOOLED'.

"It looks like Petterson was telling the truth." McLelland said sadly.

"He could have arranged this, " Newman said but he was well aware that Nicky Petterson's story was beginning to look less like the ravings of a lunatic. There was however another form of lunacy in these acts.

"I don't think even you believe that Harry. He was stupid and greedy but he's not capable of doing this to cover his tracks.

Somebody else really hated Deirdre Nichol." McLelland's tone was non-confrontational; the sight of the two bodies was enough to put their petty spat into perspective.

"But why the kid?"

"The poor wee thing was probably just in the wrong place at the wrong time."

"Could it be somebody else picking up on the Harlequin thing?" Russell suggested.

"No, we managed to keep a lid on that, there was nothing in the press." McLelland replied.

"The husband?" McLelland said.

"Ex. We'll need to have a closer look at him but I really hope he's not the kind that could do that to his own daughter."

"This is a fuckin' mess. What's the Fiscal say?"

"Let's just say he's ready to read the riot act. He'll be gunning for us."

"Who found them?" Russell asked.

"The cleaning lady. She came in this morning for her normal shift and found them like this. She's been taken to the Royal Alexandria suffering from shock."

"I don't blame her, " Newman said.

"What did the professor say?" Russell asked.

"He reckons they were killed sometime on Saturday. The post mortems will be this afternoon, he is putting everything else on hold. I don't think I've ever seen him so affected by a scene."

"Aye, he looked a bit shell-shocked when we arrived." Newman's observation could equally apply to him.

"We need to get a team together right away.

***

The mortuary was grimly quiet as Professor Marriot and Dr Dent conducted the post mortems. There was nothing unexpected in their observations and deliberations; the two bodies told the story of their deaths in exactly the manner that the detectives expected. The pathologists confirmed death as being sometime on the Saturday, which at very least gave them a timeline to begin the investigation. Russell noted that despite Marriot's obvious distress, Dent continued to work as if the murder of a child and her mother was simply part of the routine. There was an undeniable gap in Dent's character.

It was five-thirty when the police officers returned to their base. Thomas Nichol had been told of the deaths and had agreed to come to the station.

Mark McLelland insisted on doing the interview, not that Newman put up much of a fight. Some of his usual arrogance and stubbornness seemed to have been knocked out of him by the revelations of the day. McLelland gestured with his head, indicating to Tom Russell that he should join him.

The interview was to be conducted in the less intimidating atmosphere of the family room that had been created recently in the station. The pastel-decorated space had Monet prints on the walls, two low couches and a plain coffee table with a small vase of flowers. There was still the hint of the smell of new paint and wallpaper paste in the air.

Thomas Nichol was a thin, bespectacled man who looked to be approximately the same age as his ex-wife. Russell thought he looked fragile and wondered if the bereaved man was up to the questions that were about to be asked.

"Thanks for coming in, Mr Nichol. We're very sorry for your loss. I know how difficult this must be for you but if we're going to get the person who did this we need to move as quickly as possible."

"Did they suffer?" was the worried response.

"No, it was over very quickly we believe." McLelland told a customary lie that was used to spare the feelings of grieving families. It was a small crumb of comfort to people who feared that their loved ones had died a long painful or terrifying death.

"When did you last see your daughter and your ex-wife?"

"I dropped Charlotte off about nine-thirty on Friday at Deirdre's house. It should have been earlier but Deirdre's flight was delayed. She had been at a meeting in London." His voice was flat, almost monotone. He appeared to be in the numb stage of grief before anguish and anger would grip him. Russell had discovered that no one was capable of dealing with their emotions in the period immediately after they discovered their loved ones had been murdered; they simply disconnected from the emotional reality.

"Was that a regular arrangement?" McLelland kept his voice modulated and steady. Providing an anchor for Thomas Nichol to fix on.

"Charlotte was with her mother every other weekend. She stayed with me the rest of the time."

"So you had custody?"

"Yes, it made more sense. Deirdre worked long hours and I can do a lot of my work from home."

"Your divorce was amicable?"

"Yes, we just drifted a part. We thought that Charlotte might have brought us closer together but a child can only paper over the cracks for a short time before they begin to show again. We were still friends," he said softly.

"Was there a third party involved?"

"No."

"What is it you do for a living?"

"I'm a computer programmer."

"Do you know of anyone who would want to harm your ex-wife? Had she received threats or abusive mail recently?"

"No, she was a very kind person. No one would want to hurt her. Even if she had received anything like that she would probably have kept it from me. She wouldn't have taken it seriously."

"Thanks Mr Nichol. I have one last question, does the April 1st 1983 mean anything to you?"

Nichol looked confused. "No, why?"

"That's fine, it's just something that has come up during the investigation."

Russell led the little man out of the room. "Do you need me to get someone to run you home?"

"No it's fine. My sister is waiting for me."

The detective thanked him for coming and expressed his sympathy once more.

Back in the C.I.D. room the detectives gathered round McLelland to hear what had happened. He went over the details of the crime scene for those who hadn't been in attendance. He told them that there was little or no chance that Nichol was the guilty party. He believed that Nichol's grief was genuine. Ruth Stephens suggested that he may have hired someone but McLelland was convinced that he had nothing to do with the murder. However, he did agree that Thomas Nichol's financials should be checked just in case."

"Where's D.I. Newman?" the senior officer asked having just realised that Newman wasn't present.

"Went into see the chief super about an hour ago. I've not seen him since," Stephens said.

"Did Mr Nichol know anything about the date?" Gary Magowan asked.

"No. Any ideas?"

There was a period of quiet but no one had any concrete suggestions.

"It's obviously relevant to the murderer. It also explains the drugs in the cakes. Ten years to the day." McLelland was vocalising his own thoughts.

"Was the killer hoping that the scandal would break the bakery or get Ms Nichol the sack?" Russell said.

"I think you're right but this escalates it way beyond death by remote control. I can't quite get my head around what's happened, what the hell way does the killer think?" McLelland asked.

Ruth Stephens threw out some rhetorical questions.

"If it was simply revenge, why wait ten years? Why not take revenge on Ms Nichol directly?"

There were nods of agreement around the table but no offers of possible answers.

"We'll get the full team assembled tomorrow and take it from there."

Harry Newman arrived and walked to his desk. He took a polythene bag out of one of the drawers and began to put items from the surface and the drawers into the bag.

"What's up?" McLelland asked him.

There was no reply and when he was finished packing the bag, Newman walked out without a word.

"What the hell was that all about?" Ruth Stephens asked.

"Harry's going to be taking some leave." Chief Superintendent Woods answered as he entered the room.

"But we're going to need as many bodies as possible for this harlequin thing." McLelland said.

"Harry feels responsible for what's happened and he's asked to be put on sick leave. He wanted to resign but I persuaded that he maybe just needs some time to think it through. I'll get another D.I. if you need one but I'd rather you lead the team and I can bring in another D.S. or two. If you think you're up to it?"

"Eh… of course. If you think it's for the best."

"Keep Harry out of it. You all know the background, we don't need anybody pestering him for further information," Woods warned. He returned to his own office leaving his team both shocked and silent.

CHAPTER 9

The full investigation began the following morning. A team of thirty detectives was assigned to investigate the death of Deirdre Nichol and her daughter, as well as taking another look at the original crimes. With the horrific murder of the child at the forefront of their minds, the coppers were primed and eager to get started.

Among the early tasks were forensic checks on the Nichol house and comparisons with Petterson's home; they were the two places that the killer would definitely have visited.

The neighbours who had properties adjoining the Nichol house were quizzed but it was the kind of street where people kept to themselves which, combined with the size of the grounds, meant that no one had seen anything that was relevant.

Deirdre Nichol's phone records, office computer and correspondence were all subject to thorough checks but once again there was nothing significant.

Tom Russell joined Mark McLelland when he visited the secure psychiatric unit to tell Nicky Petterson that he wasn't mad and that he was now facing charges of culpable homicide that would probably see him jailed for a significant chunk of his life. Petterson greeted the news with relief and did all he could to remember exactly what the Harlequin looked like but the disguise was near perfect. All he could tell them was the killer's height and build. Petterson's lawyer wasn't so pleased to hear the news and was quick to point out how cooperative his client had been and how she hoped that it would be taken into consideration. McLelland told her that was a matter for the Procurator Fiscal and the court. They took Petterson into custody from where he was transferred to a remand centre awaiting sentencing. There would be no trial, just an appearance before a judge to confirm the time he would spend in prison.

"I wonder if he still thinks that it was worth £250?" Russell asked after they had handed him over to the custody sergeant.

"I've never seen anyone so happy to hear they were going to jail," McLelland observed.

"Aye, so much for the expert psychiatrists."

When they returned to the office, Ruth Stephens gave McLelland the toxicology report. He read the findings with horror. It confirmed that Deirdre Nichol had been injected with the same hallucinogens as the earlier victims. The pathologists and forensic technicians reckoned that the little girl had been killed first while her mother watched. She had been wrapped in the cellophane and then injected with the drugs. She would have suffered a horrific period of terrifying visions before the killer finally put her out of her misery.

"Poor woman," he commented when he finished reading it.

"What does it say?" Stephens asked.

McLelland read the details to those present. It served to strengthen their determination to find the killer but in truth there was little in the report that would move the investigation forward.

***

Despite the best intentions, vigilance and dedication of the investigation team, the days passed and the inquiry began to stall very quickly. The press was all over the story and when someone leaked the information about the mask, the newspapers had a field day.

On the Friday after the discovery at the Nichol household, one paper focused on the failure of the earlier investigation and in particular the role of Harry Newman. It was as comprehensive a hatchet piece as anyone had ever seen; it even included an interview the woman who had been upset by Newman in the supermarket.

Although Tom Russell didn't rate Newman as a detective or even as a human being, he felt the attention he was getting was unfair. The failures weren't only his, everyone in the team had to take responsibility for the inability to find the real killer. When his shift was finished, he decided to visit the D.I. to make sure he was alright.

He drove to Newman's house in Clarkston. The Mondeo was parked in the drive, so it looked like Newman was home.

Rain was pattering down on Russell's head as he stood knocking on the large brass letterbox. He knew that the older man was divorced and lived alone. He had rapped the door a couple of more times with no reply. The D.I was not a man who was fond of exercise and Russell couldn't imagine him leaving the car to walk anywhere. He made towards the window, inside the curtains were closed, but there was a gap that allowed Russell a view into the interior. In the dim light he could see a figure in an armchair, head back, arms hanging limply.

"Crap." Russell ran back to the door but there was no way he would be able to break the substantial storm door on his own. He ran down the drive and managed to vault over the fence between it and the back garden. The back door was double glazed with a PVC surround. Russell thought that he would need to break the glass but was surprised when the handle moved and the door swung open.

He ran through the large kitchen into the hall and then into the living room. Harry Newman was prone on the chair; two empty bottles of whisky and an equally empty bottle of prescription drugs lay on a small table. Below one of the whisky bottles was a hand-written note that, in a jittery hand Harry Newman had managed to write, *'I'm sorry. H.N.'*

Under the table was a copy of the newspaper that had so savagely destroyed him as well as a postcard. His name and address was typed on one side, but there was no stamp.

Russell placed his fingers at the man's throat but the temperature of Newman's skin and the lack of pulse proved his worst fears were correct. He reached for his radio and called in the tragedy. When the call was over, he opened the front door and walked back to his car where he lifted a pair of crime scene gloves from the boot

Back in the house, he pulled on the gloves and lifted the postcard. On the other side was a single word with the now familiar Harlequin mask in the corner. The word was printed in a large typeface and in capital letters; it read simply, *'FOOL'*.

Within fifteen minutes the house was crawling with technicians, uniformed officers and the detectives from Partick as well as the local station. There was anger in the air but Lionel Marriot could only say that he believed it was suicide and that no one else had been involved. It did little to dispel the fury and frustration the detectives were feeling.

***

The following week all the evidence backed up Marriot's assessment. When the note was compared to Newman's handwriting it was obvious that it was his despite the lack of control brought on by the alcohol and fear he was feeling. Everything pointed to a combination of guilt at the Nichol deaths, the humiliation of the newspaper and the killer's postcard had pushed the distraught detective over the edge.

Within another week the leads in all cases dried up. There were no fingerprints on any of the items the killer had left at the crime scene, there were no eyewitnesses to the delivery of the postcard, there was nothing new and the chances of catching the murderer seemed more distant with every passing day.

After four weeks the team was scaled down as the criminal element of Glaswegian society continued to go about their trade and officers were needed on more pressing cases. When the case was officially declared cold six months later, Tom Russell was one of only two detectives who were still officially assigned to the Harlequin deaths.

On April 1st 1994, Detective Constable Tom Russell arrived at Partick police station aware that one year had passed since the first bizarre deaths. He walked into the C.I.D. room, before he could sit down his eye was drawn to a billboard across the street at the back of the station. A grinning Harlequin mask stared back at him and under it was a sign which read *'IT'S NOT OVER YET'*.

PART TWO
April 1st 2003

CHAPTER 10

A t midday, they began to emerge like butterflies spreading their wings to soak up the rays of the sun. They came in pairs, running joyfully from the streets around George Square to assemble at points across the wide expanse of public space at the heart of Glasgow. They were dressed identically; loose one-piece costumes that were patterned with pastel-coloured diamonds. On each head was a three-point fool's hat with that same pattern and on their feet a pair of oversized white shoes. Every face wore an identical clown's makeup of white greasepaint with spots of black and red to emphasise certain features. Some of them juggled, others performed gymnastics while the rest just clowned with buckets of water and other props. The office workers, students and shoppers began to form small crowds around them, watching with delight in the warmth of the spring sunshine. The mood was festive and the banter that the city's natives are renowned for bounced around the little groups as they heckled the performers with good humour.

The atmosphere shattered in an instant when a scream crashed through it, laced with fear and shock it travelled across the large open space and bounced in multiple echoes from the buildings. The performances stopped and people began to congregate in one corner of the great square where three men lay in an ever-extending puddle of blood. On top of one of the bodies, a small white piece of card was gradually being turned a deep crimson but the design and text remained visible. Printed in the middle were two words and a simple graphic that would bring chills to the city's detectives. The Harlequin was back.

CHAPTER 11

Tom Russell sat outside the changing room, failing hopelessly in his attempt to not appear too bored. He knew what kind of day he was in for when Karen had told him that she wanted to go shopping and he had to go with her. An invitation to a wedding in June had prompted the trudge around the shops as Karen searched for the perfect dress for the occasion. Russell thought there was plenty of time to get what she needed, but his wife was insistent that she could never be sure when the two of them would be available on the same day between now and the day of the wedding. So Russell had applied obediently for a day off and was 'enjoying' it by visiting every dress shop in the city. The trip had begun at nine that morning and by half past twelve his stomach was telling him it was time for some lunch, and a break from the endless parade of designs and colours.

Karen came out of the changing room wearing a cerise dress that was fitted around her bust and torso before flaring out at her hips.

"Well?"

It was the tenth dress she had tried on so far that day and with the exception of one, they had all looked fine to her husband. "It's nice," he said for the ninth time.

"You can't just keep saying that. Help me out. Do I suit it?"

"Aye, I like the colour," he replied with as much enthusiasm as he could summon.

She walked to the mirror, turned and looked over her shoulder. "No, it makes my hips look too broad and I don't think that it's right for a wedding. You need to be honest with me, Tom." She walked back into the changing room and Russell groaned; he knew all too well the perils of being honest with Karen when it came to helping her choose clothes.

"I think we should go for a bite to eat," he shouted into the curtained area.

"After I try this last one," she replied and Russell's stomach gurgled its disapproval.

He sat trying to ignore one more of the turgid tunes of another bland boy-band that seemed to be pumped into every store, when the distinctive ring of his mobile phone startled him.

"Hello, Detective Inspector Tom Russell speaking."

"Tom, it's Mark McLelland. I know it's your day off and I'm sorry to disturb you but I need you to come in."

"That's fine, sir. What's up?"

"The Harlequin's back," the chief superintendent said quietly.

"First of April," Russell muttered. He wasn't really replying to McLelland, he was lost in his own initial horrified thoughts and the implications of those three words.

There was a period of shocked silence, which was punctuated by McLelland saying, "Are you still there?"

"Sorry sir, yes. What happened?"

"It's better if you see it for yourself. It happened in George Square just after twelve."

"I'm not far away, I'm in Debenhams in Argyle Street. I'll be there in five minutes."

"OK. See you soon."

With his phone back in his pocket, he stood up and walked to the changing room. "Karen, I'm really sorry but I have to go to work."

"But you're on holiday," she replied with annoyance.

"The Harlequin's back."

She realised immediately what that meant to her husband and replied, "Oh. You better go then. I'll see you later." There were times when she hated her husband's dedication but today was not one of them, she knew exactly what was at stake.

"Sorry love. Bye."

His brisk walk up the length of Queen Street took him to the blue and white crime scene tape of an outer cordon that surrounded the whole of the square. He flashed his warrant card at the female constable who was on duty at the cordon and ducked under the flimsy barrier. A path had been marked out with more tape and Russell followed it to the inner cordon that surrounded the flashing lights, forensic tent and a crowd of busy people. He gave his name to a detective who was controlling access to the scene. Close to the edge of the cordoned off area Chief Superintendent Mark McLelland was waiting with an anxious expression on his face.

"Thanks for coming, Tom. I thought you would want to be involved. We could do with some continuity."

"What happened?"

McLelland gave him a brief report about what little they knew. "We've got a couple of eyewitnesses, but I don't think they're going to be much help. I'll let you speak to Mr Gregson first; he was closest to the incident.

Robert Gregson was sitting in an open ambulance just outside the inner cordon, a cup of sweet tea in his hand as McLelland and Russell approached. He was dressed in dark grey trousers, a white shirt that was stained with blood and a red tie that he had loosened at the neck. His suit jacket lay at his side scrunched into a ball, it had been dyed a dark maroon due to the amount of blood it had absorbed. The witness was in his late forties with receding hair and a greying goatee beard. He seemed calm but detached from his surroundings; judging by his pallor he was understandably suffering from shock.

"Mr Gregson, this is Detective Inspector Russell. I would like you to tell him what you saw, if you don't mind."

"Sure," he replied softly. "I was out for lunch, I like to come to the square and sit and eat when the weather's good. When I arrived, there was a crowd of people around a couple of the clowns who were doing a juggling act with rings and balls. They were good and they had attracted a fair number of people. Out of the corner of my eye I noticed another clown in the same costume at the edge of the crowd. I thought he was maybe collecting money for them. I turned back to watch the show when I heard a dreadful gurgling sound. A man close to me fell to the ground clutching his neck. Then I realised there was another guy behind him holding his stomach and then the clown drove the knife into the chest of the man who was standing next to me. I'm sorry but I froze, if I had been quicker I might have been able to catch him. He ran through the crowd and I lost sight of him, then I turned my attention to the injured to see if I could help. The gentleman next to me was dead and I didn't think that I would be able to help the poor soul whose throat had been cut, so I tried to give some first aid to the older guy with the stomach wound. I pressed my jacket against the injury and tried talking to him but he slipped away very quickly." He gulped as if choking back the emotion.

"Mr Gregson, don't worry about not catching the killer. You did the right thing, if you had tried to stop him, you may well have been his fourth victim of the day. What can you tell us about this man?" Russell asked.

"Nothing really, he looked exactly like the other clowns. Sorry."

"Was he tall, short, fat, thin? Anything that might help us to identify him."

"I would say he was slightly shorter than average height, not sure about his build, the costumes were pretty loose fitting."

"I understand. Here's my card. If you remember anything, even if it's the middle of the night, just ring me."

"I will do inspector. I'm sorry I can't be any more help."

Russell and McLelland left the man in the ambulance and walked back towards the main crime scene. They suited up in protective clothing, slipped on overshoes and gloves before moving towards the scene of the tragedy.

Inside the cramped forensics tent, the bodies of the three men lay surrounded by a team of technicians and detectives. It was a sad tableau that looked like the victims had become the subject of some grisly performance art installation. Poised over one of the bodies was the duty pathologist, Doctor Lucy Thompson. She was talking quietly into a portable dictation machine, making her initial observations, oblivious to anything other than the victims and their wounds.

Russell took in the diorama of death. As Mr Gregson had described, one of the men had been stabbed in the stomach, another in the heart and the third had been slashed in the neck. His mind drifted to that very first scene in the Blake's flat, and how it had affected him. Was this a deliberate attempt by the Harlequin to evoke that very image? He wouldn't put it past the sick bastard.

"What do you think doctor?" he asked the pathologist when she had finished recording her notes.

"All three died almost instantly, I believe. The neck and the heart are obvious; it looks like the third man's liver was punctured. He would have bled out very quickly. The knife was quite narrow and extremely sharp judging by the depth of the wounds and how clean the cuts are but that's about all I can tell you until I do the post mortem." Her accent was English, although it was difficult to distinguish any particular regional inflection, there was the slightest hint of Lancashire in it.

Russell had met Lucy Thompson a few times but found it difficult to build a relationship with her. She was always polite but very guarded in her dealings with him; she never gave anything of herself away. Russell didn't even know where her home town was or whether she was married, engaged or single; those subjects either never came up or were rebuffed with a diplomatic charm when he tried to talk about anything other than her work. He wasn't offended as she seemed to be the same with everyone.

"What do you think? Same man?" McLelland asked his D.I.

Russell nodded. "I'm pretty sure it is."

"You've come across this before?" the pathologist asked.

"Ten years ago the Harlequin arranged for a cocktail of psychotropic drugs to be injected into some cakes. The drugs alone caused six deaths but that wasn't enough for him. He then killed the woman who ran the bakery and her four-year old daughter. There were mistakes in the investigation and one of the detectives took his own life as a result."

"I have a vague memory of that, I was at university down south at the time."

"We caught the guy who laced the cakes but not the man who initiated the whole thing. It looks like he's back with another sick April Fool's Day joke."

"Have we got any I.D. on the victims?" McLelland asked Detective Sergeant McKinley who had been one of the first to attend the scene.

"Yes, sir. The man whose throat was cut is Mehmet Ashad, a Turkish national according to his passport. The victim with the stomach wound is Martin Jenkinson who works at a local insurance firm and the third man is Jordan Callender who is a student at the College Of Building and Printing."

As McKinley identified them, Russell studied each of them in turn. Mr Ashad had the olive complexion that characterised many of his countrymen. Russell guessed that he would be in his early thirties. He had thick black hair that topped a handsome face. Above his thick lips he had a thin moustache and on his cheek there was a white scar. Martin Jenkinson was in his late fifties, he was tall and would have cut a debonair figure in a beautifully cut suit, but what had once been finery was now reduced to blood-drenched cloth. His silver-rimmed glasses lay beside his shoulder where they had fallen during the attack. The third victim was in his early twenties, dressed in a thin leather jacket, a designer T-shirt and expensive jeans. White earphones rested across him, and his bag filled with textbooks lay a couple of feet away. His face would never see wrinkles, it was already a cool white remnant of the life and the hope that had filled it earlier that day.

Beside the bag was a little yellow board with a black number three on it. There were many more similar boards dotted around the scene and they would be used at a later date by the forensics team to reconstruct where the evidence they collected had been found.

Russell pinched his nose and then rubbed his forehead. Here were three men; one on a break from work, one in the middle of studies with his whole life in front of him and the third, a visitor to the city. They had arrived at that particular place, at that specific time by a series of decisions and coincidences that had ushered them into the path of someone whose view of the world was so distorted that human life had become an irrelevance. Russell couldn't help but wonder if there was more he and the team could have done to prevent this happening. He made a silent vow; this time the killer's games would end.

CHAPTER 12

McLelland had offered to drive Russell up to the station but as he was still hungry, he told the senior officer that he would walk. It was about a mile up a steep hill from the scene to the station. He grabbed a sandwich and a coffee en route, consuming them as he walked.

An hour after they had left the forensic technicians to continue gathering evidence in and around the locus, McLelland and Russell were standing in a briefing room in Stewart Street Station, a group of around twenty detectives and uniformed officers were waiting to begin the investigations. Many of the younger officers had no inkling of the details of the previous deaths, so it fell to Russell to fill in the gaps in their knowledge. They were astounded to hear the lengths that 'The Harlequin' had gone to initiate his sadistic games. When they were informed of the horrific murder of Deirdre Nichol and her daughter, the astonishment turned to anger. Russell was pleased to see their disgust at what had happened was hardening their resolve to make sure that he didn't slip through the fingers of justice this time. Many of the assembled detectives asked pertinent questions, and some of the details the two senior officers had to recall brought back images from the worst period of their career.

McLelland was granted permission from the assistant chief constable to be the senior investigation officer for the case. This was in spite of the fact that as a chief superintendent his daily role was strictly that of a manager. He hadn't run an inquiry of this scale for over four years but the A.C.C. felt his connection to the original murders would provide a more consistent approach and McLelland was happy to oblige.

When all the questions had been exhausted, McLelland told them, "The first thing we need is a victim profile for each of the three men. If any of these guys has a connection with Deirdre Nichol we need to find it, particularly if that connection relates in anyway to the first of April 1983."

There were nods of agreement and understanding from everyone.

"The second thing is to find the murder weapon. It's highly unlikely but maybe he left something of himself on it and we can use it to identify him. He was very careful to make sure there was no forensic evidence to link him the last time, but ten years have gone by and now we have DNA profiling to help us."

One of the detectives asked, "Sir, why do you think he has let ten years pass since the previous crimes?""

Russell answered, "I think that the date might be a trigger. Somehow, when the clock ticks round to the year ending in three, it ignites something dark in him that he can't resist. With someone this disturbed there's no way to be sure but I think that's a possible reason."

McLelland offered an alternative theory. "It's not something I had considered last time round but what if Glasgow isn't the only place that he has been active in when April Fool's Day comes round. I want a thorough scan of the HOLMES database for any strange incidents on April the first within any jurisdiction across the whole of the U.K. If you have no luck there, check with Interpol. We've been working on the theory that this is a revenge mission but we can't rule out the possibility that this is a nomadic, psychopathic serial killer."

"Wouldn't we have connected the dots before now if that was the case?" D.S. McKinley asked. He was an experienced officer with a keen mind; only his own lack of ambition had prevented him rising further up the ranks of the service. He was both respected and liked by his colleagues and more senior officers always took his thoughts into account.

McLelland conceded the point. "Andy, you're probably right but if he's killing in other countries we might not have made the connection. It's just something to consider that might explain the long gap between crimes."

"Yes, sir."

"The third thing is to get every one of those performers who were involved today in for an interview. Did we get all the names and addresses?"

"Yes, sir the promotions company supplied them," a young female D.C. said.

"Organise as many interviews as you can today and we'll pick up the rest tomorrow," McLelland directed the comment to McKinley.

"Yes, sir," he replied

"Anyone else got any questions or suggestions?"

McLelland felt comfortable that Andy McKinley was a safe pair of hands and that he could be trusted to allocate the tasks to the people who had the appropriate skills. "Andy, can you co-ordinate the assignments please. D.I. Russell and I will need to speak to the press relations people about hosting a news conference. We will have to manage carefully the information we give out as the speculation is likely to be dramatic and probably inaccurate if we don't get a grip of it quickly."

The two senior detectives left the briefing room as McKinley began to bark out orders.

"We'll go to Pitt Street and get this over with," McLelland told Russell in the corridor. The detective inspector nodded reluctantly; if there was one part of his job he hated, it was communicating with the press. He realised that it was an important aspect of what he did, but he always felt the journalists were more interested in tripping up the police than helping to catch a killer.

***

On the short car journey to the Strathclyde Police Headquarters the two men talked about the case. They voiced their thoughts and concerns about the task ahead, and discussed a strategy for the challenges they faced.

Within fifteen minutes they were walking into the press officer's room.

Kelly Ingram was sitting behind her desk peering through a pair of expensive spectacles at an array of newspaper clippings that were strewn across her desk. She remained focused on her task until McLelland coughed discreetly; she looked up and immediately jumped from her seat and rushed over to greet them. "Oh, sorry. I was miles away."

"Kelly this is D.I. Russell," McLelland said.

"Oh, hi. Please come in and have a seat. I believe we have quite the tragedy to deal with."

"I'm afraid so. We're going to have to handle this one very cautiously," McLelland replied.

The two detectives had to remove further bundles of photocopied newspaper cuttings from the visitor's chairs before they could sit down.

"Sorry, we've been asked to compile an analysis of press reporting and reaction to house-breaking over the past three years. I've got cuttings from every local newspaper in Scotland to go through. It's a bit tedious. I'm glad of something more important and interesting to do, even if it is in such terrible circumstances."

Russell had met the woman once before but it was obvious she didn't remember him. She was in her early thirties with untidy fair hair. Her interesting and diverse taste in clothes hung from a tall, fine-boned frame. Her glasses rested on a sharp nose that sat in the centre of a face composed of delicate features. She gave off a nervous energy that some might take for weakness but Russell had heard from many sources that she had a fiery temper and on a bad day, could swear like a bricklayer.

She took out a notebook and pen. "We've already had to field some questions from the press hounds about this. We've batted them away so far but we have to tell them something concrete or the speculation will run riot. With any luck it won't make the evening paper but the television news are running something already. Fill me in," she instructed while looking over her spectacles at the two men.

McLelland began to recite the story, starting with the three bizarre drug-inspired incidents before progressing to the murders at the Nichol family home and the subsequent suicide of Detective Inspector Newman. He asked Russell to supply further detail when needed to ensure that the press officer had as full a picture as was possible in a short time.

"I'll dig out how the team handled it ten years ago," Ingram said. "That should help me understand it."

"If at all possible we'd like to avoid any immediate links being made between the incident today and what happened back then. We kept the Harlequin out of it as much as we could but I doubt that will be possible this time round."

"No, you better tell me what happened today."

As the grisly details of the events of the day were revealed to her, Ingram scribbled furiously on her notepad. Sometimes she would decide that what she had written was wrong and then scrub it out with a series of lines drawn vigorously over the offending words. When McLelland was finished speaking she said, "Mmm... I think we play this very close to our chest and have answers ready should any of them make a connection to what occurred ten years ago. We will give them nothing substantial, just enough to stop the more fantastical and sensational connections being made. How's that for a strategy chaps?"

"I'll be guided by what you say, Kelly."

"Excellent. I'll pull it all together and you pop back in about an hour." She looked at her watch. "That should give us plenty of time for a rehearsal before we brief at half past five."

"I'll see you in an hour," McLelland agreed.

The men left her thumping her computer keyboard as if it were a mechanical typewriter. In the corridor McLelland said, "I'll go back to my office and check my e-mail. I'd appreciate it if you could head back to Stewart Street. I'll get the press conference out of the way and I'll get you back there when I'm done."

"Yes, sir. I'll see how we're getting on with the victim profiles and if there has been any progress with the knife or the interviews. What about the P.M.s, have we got a time yet?"

"Oh damn it. No not yet. Give Dr Thompson a ring and see when they'll be performed?"

"Will do."

"I'll get you a car," McLelland offered.

"No thanks, sir. I'll walk, it's not far and it'll give me some thinking time."

"Ring me when you get the time for the P.M.s"

"Yes, sir. Speak to you later."

***

By the time Russell got back to Stewart Street it was three-thirty in the afternoon and the place was a hive of activity. As he headed towards the main incident room, every door he walked by opened on to a crowded office where dozens of people were collating information from witness statements collected by the officers in the square, and then entering them into the computer; others were performing background checks on those involved in the promotions company. He also knew that some would be trawling the HOLMES and Interpol databases for possible links. This was the less glamorous side of policing, the side that you would never see on the T.V. crime dramas, but it was essential to explore every tiny detail and make sense of the enormous amount of data they would be receiving.

Andy McKinley was sitting in front of a computer in the main briefing room, a phone stuck between his shoulder and his ear as he typed something into the machine. He acknowledged Russell with a movement of his eyebrows while muttering the occasional, "Yes," or "OK" into the handset.

When the call was over he said, "How did it go with the press office?"

"Thankfully, I'm not needed. The chief super will brief the journalists at five-thirty, concentrating on what happened today. If the press make a connection between today and what happened ten years ago, Kelly Ingram's got a plan to offer them some answers without making it clear that we think it's the same killer. Have you met Kelly Ingram?"

"Aye, a couple of times."

"What do you think of her?"

"She comes across as being a bit eccentric, a bit airy-fairy but I wouldn't want to cross her. I saw her tear strips off a young D.C. who was naive enough to answer a press question with something other than a 'no comment.' He caused a minor embarrassment but the way she exploded at him made it sound like he had proposed hanging pensioners who drive too slowly. It was all a bit over the top but I suppose she's got stress in her role, just as we have in ours," he said with understanding.

"Do you think she's good at what she does?"

"I don't know but the braid seem to think she is and that's all that matters."

"I suppose so. What progress - if any - are we making?"

"A progress of negatives, if you know what I mean. We've ruled out seven of the clowns so far. They're just kids trying to pick up some extra cash while they study at college or university. We've not found a hardened criminal yet, nobody that stands out as an obvious psycho." He cracked a weak smile.

"And here was me hoping that we'd have one in custody telling us that it was a 'fair cop' and asking to be put in the jail and never let out."

"Some hope. Somehow I doubt we'll find the killer among the official participants of the event."

"No. It's all part of his pantomime. What about the owner of the company?"

"He's down south at some trade show or something? We're trying to get hold of him."

"Any other connections to April the first?"

McKinley shook his head. "Nah. Another dead end I think."

"It's still worth a look, but I think you're probably right. The knife?" Russell tried not to let his desperation show.

"Nowt so far. We've searched the buildings and streets with direct access to the square and now widened it out to include the surrounding streets."

"How many officers?"

"Sixty on the search if you include the forensic techs."

"Good."

McKinley looked pensive as he said, "What do you think about this? Why would you leave a ten-year gap if you feel you've been so wronged that you're willing to kill innocent people in an attempt to get revenge?"

"It's like I said earlier Andy, there's something about it being a 'big' anniversary. I can't think of anything else."

"It's just bloody weird if you ask me."

"You won't get any argument from me on that score."

Russell found an empty desk and rang the mortuary. Dr Thomson confirmed that the post mortems would begin the following morning at ten o'clock. Russell thanked her and turned his attention to the computer where he read through his e-mails. This had turned into the worst 'day off' he had ever endured and he would be glad to see it come to an end. The afternoon drifted into early evening and the station began to empty. Russell waited until McLelland returned from the press conference.

"How did it go?"

"Not bad. No one had made any connection back to ten years ago but it probably won't be long once they find the leaked story. Even some of the old hands were shocked by what happened but they'll soon fit the pieces together and begin asking questions. Anything happen while I was away?"

"I'm afraid not, sir."

"I'll see you in the morning. Hopefully things will start to move in a more positive direction."

***

Russell finally got home at seven-thirty, feeling the strain of an investigation that had already opened old wounds.

"Is he back?" Karen asked when he walked into the kitchen of their two-bedroomed flat.

"Looks like it," he replied placing a kiss on her cheek.

"Are you hungry?"

"Not really, I'll just have a sandwich."

He walked through to their bedroom, stripped off and showered under a very hot flow of water. He allowed the powerful jets to massage his shoulders; pounding away some of the knots that were already beginning to appear. Although it was the first day of the case, he felt as if suddenly the weight of ten years was on him; the pain of seeing that little murdered girl had haunted him long after it had happened and now it was back. Guilt was now piled on guilt as more people had died because he and the team had failed to catch the Harlequin first time round.

He finished the shower, dressed in some casual clothes and walked back to the living room where Karen had laid out a couple of sandwiches and a cup of tea. She talked incessantly about the search for a dress and Tom tried to respond appropriately in the right places but his mind was elsewhere. His only distraction came when the news began on the television. The majority of the broadcast concentrated on the bombing of Iraq by Allied Forces. The Americans had coined the term 'Shock and Awe' for the huge bombs they were dropping.

"Shock and awe is just another way of saying terrorising," Russell observed.

"That man needs to be removed, Tom," Karen replied.

"Maybe, but a lot of innocent people are going to die because the real reason is, we need their oil."

"He's got terrible weapons and is willing to use them," she argued.

Russell kept his own counsel and continued to watch the bulletin. The three murders in Glasgow got a very brief mention; there wasn't even time for McLelland's press conference.

Talk about a good day to bury bad news Russell thought.

McLelland did appear on the local news, serious and articulate but looking strained. The reporter delivered her piece to camera from in front of the crime scene in a sensational way, claiming that the citizens of Glasgow were now living in fear. It was typical of the increasingly opinionated news style that was replacing well-reported facts. Russell sighed in disgust and wished his wife good night as he headed for bed.

CHAPTER 13

A nother day, another briefing. There were now nearly forty detectives assigned to the case and it looked like the vast majority of them were attending the morning meeting. Russell had once again joined McLelland in front of the incident board. It took some time for the room to fall into near silence.

"Good morning, everyone," McLelland said, stilling the last few murmurs.

"We're going to go through our tasks from yesterday. I'd like to start with the search for any similar crimes. Who was looking into that? If you could give your name and station before you report, I know some of you but it would help me if you could introduce yourself."

A female detective raised her hand. "D.S. Ellen Clarkson, Maryhill, sir."

"Ellen would you like to come forward."

She stood up and made her way to the front of the room where she opened a notebook. "Myself, D.C.s Shaw and Mulgrew looked into some one hundred and fifty three murders that occurred on 1st April over the past twenty years. Six of those were in the U.K. only one of which remains open but it was related to a robbery. The Interpol database produced the rest of the results, with the vast majority of them in the U.S. There was only one open case that might fit with what we've seen in Glasgow. The ritualistic murder of a fifty-two year-old man in Denmark. The victim was Klaus Eriksen and he did have a connection with Scotland; he had worked here for two years in the nineties. The Danish police said that his body was laid out in a clearing in a forest with pagan symbols carved into the surrounding trees, they have been unable to find the culprit." When she was finished she snapped the notebook closed.

"Thanks Ellen. Tom?"

Russell shook his head. "I don't think so, sir. If he had been here in 1983 then maybe, but it doesn't feel like our man."

"I think you're right. Are we agreed that we can put this aside?" McLelland asked the team.

Everyone nodded or mumbled their agreement.

"Right, next up any luck with the murder weapon, Andy?"

D.S. McKinley responded, "Yes, sir. A forensic technician found it around seven last night in an industrial bin in North Court, a lane just off St Vincent Street."

"Fingerprints?"

"Fingermarks," a youthful-looking man at the back of the room said.

"Sorry?"

"If they haven't been identified, they are fingermarks rather than prints, sir."

McLelland's face flushed but he kept his voice steady when he asked, "And you are?"

"D.C. Jackson, sir."

"Just finished your forensics course, detective constable?"

"A month ago, sir."

"Let's just presume that those of us with more experience than you know the difference between the definition of fingermarks and fingerprints and that we use the expression prints as a shorthand."

"But sir…"

McLelland raised his voice slightly as he warned, "That's enough, detective constable. At this moment we have more important things to worry about than semantics; like the fact we are chasing a killer who is responsible directly or indirectly for the deaths of twelve people."

Although he was now red faced with embarrassment, the younger man would not back down. "But sir, it's important to use the correct nomenclature to avoid confusion or miscommunication."

The younger man had succeeded in erasing the last of McLelland's patience. "Constable, get out of my fuckin' sight before you find yourself busted back to uniform." He pointed at the door. The fact McLelland had reacted so vehemently to the young man was a sign that he was definitely feeling the pressure of the Harlequin's reappearance.

There was a ripple of laughter from some of the older officers as the persistent young detective learned a harsh lesson and was forced to leave the room with his tail between his legs.

"Bloody hell," McLelland sighed. "Sorry, Andy you were saying?"

"The knife's clean, nothing that forensics could use. In the same waste bin we also found the clown costume the killer was wearing, it's on the way to the lab to be checked for DNA."

"Well, that's something, I suppose. Cheers Andy. Victim profiles. Let's start with Mr Jenkinson."

An overweight man with a thick moustache came to stand beside Russell and McLelland. "D.S. Ben MacDonald, Govan station," he introduced himself before continuing, "Martin Jenkinson wis fifty-four. He wis married to Sharon Jenkinson and has two grown up daughters who live down south. He wis originally fae Sussex and he moved tae Glesga for work twenty-two year ago. Nae criminal record and nae obvious connection to 1st April '83. That's all ah've goat at the moment, sir." His speech was delivered with gruff efficiency.

"Thanks, Ben. Has his family been interviewed yet?"

"No, sir."

"Can we have the report on the young man, Jordan wasn't it?"

Another female detective made her way to the front. "D.C. Amanda Robertson, Shettleston. Jordan Callender was twenty years of age. He was studying Web Design at the College Of Building and Printing. He received a caution last year for possession of a class 'C' controlled substance but no other record. He lived with his family in Dennistoun. Initial interviews with his folks have found no significance in the date April 1st 1983."

"Thanks Amanda. Last up Mr Ashad."

A young male detective stood up. "D.C. Ally Tyler, Stewart Street, sir. It's a bit of a mystery. I contacted the Turkish Embassy in London and on their initial investigations they couldn't trace any contacts for Mr Ashad. From what they discovered in their records the only Mehmet Ashad they could find who was born on the date that was shown on the passport, died of leukaemia when he was two. They think there may be a gap in their records and are going to investigate further. The only thing I can tell you is that he arrived in the U.K.

three months ago according to immigration, and that he has been staying in the Holiday Inn for a couple of weeks here in Glasgow." He returned to his seat.

"Thanks for that, Ally. Very mysterious but he's unlikely to have direct connection to the killer, so make sure you stay in touch with the embassy to ensure that the poor guy's family are informed."

"Will do, sir."

"We seem to have nothing that would connect any of these people with the significant date and the killer. There's obviously another level to this and it would seem to point to the promotions company. How are the interviews with the staff going?"

D.S. McKinley answered once again, "We'll finish them today but I don't think any of the performers have anything to tell us that will help. They were hired specifically for that job, they don't really know much about each other and if I'm being honest, the majority of them aren't the best witnesses, shock I suppose."

"Have you spoken to the owner yet?"

"He'll be back in Scotland tomorrow. He said the promotion was booked a few months ago and he'll have to check the records when he gets back."

"That's a priority for tomorrow. Let's get as many witness statements checked today. Someone might have seen something that will help us. He's taken a huge chance doing this in such a public place."

Russell agreed. "I think it seems like he was trying to make a bigger statement. We didn't allow him too much in the way of publicity last time and I think he feels that his grievances - whatever they may be - need to be aired in public this time round."

"So let's hope he's slipped up. We'll need the CCTV checked as well. D.S. McKinley, can I ask you to sort out the allocation of tasks once again?"

McKinley nodded.

"You going to the mortuary?" the chief superintendent asked Russell.

"Yes, sir. I'd like D.S. Clarkson to accompany me."

"Ellen, you're with D.I. Russell."

"Yes, sir."

"Get to work and bring me some results, please."

As the detectives began to funnel out of the room, McLelland turned to Russell. "I don't imagine there'll be anything we can learn from the P.M.s but keep me informed. I'll head back to Pitt Street and brief the A.C.C. and then we'll prepare a press statement."

"See you later."

***

Lucy Thompson and Dr Roy Dent were waiting for the two detectives when they arrived at the mortuary. As there was no way to corroborate Mehmet Ashad's identity, his body would be left intact until someone could be found to make a formal identification.

Dr Thompson took the lead on the investigation of the body of Martin Jenkinson. She had completed the initial external investigation when the door of the viewing room opened and Assistant Chief Constable Ian Dunsmore walked in. He cut an imposing figure at over six feet tall, his broad chest covered by his uniform, with a line of medal ribbons decorating it. A uniformed assistant who was carrying a notepad accompanied him.

"Sorry I'm late, folks," he said loudly.

"Sir," Russell acknowledged him while wondering what he was doing there.

As if reading Russell's thoughts he said, "This one's a bit too public for us not to be fully in the loop. I thought I would pop down and see what the docs have to say, Tom." His voice boomed in the limited space of the tiny room.

Russell knew that Dunsmore had been in the military and at times it appeared that he thought he was still on a parade ground as his volume never seemed to dip below thunderous.

"We've not long started, sir. Dr Thompson has just finished the external examination."

"A.C.C. Dunsmore and this is my assistant, Sergeant John Gordon." He said formally offering his hand to Helen Clarkson.

She shook it while replying, "D.S. Clarkson, sir." She then acknowledged the sergeant with a nod.

"Excellent. Carry on doctor," he leaned towards the microphone that connected the room to the autopsy suite. Russell was pretty sure Thompson would have been able to hear him through the glass without the help of the intercom. Thompson returned to announcing her findings as Dent noted the details. As she worked through the established procedure, she found Mr Jenkinson to have been in good health before that fatal moment of chance robbed him of his life. She confirmed her theory from the scene that the knife had cut through his liver and that it was the cause of his death.

Dent took the lead for the post mortem of Jordan Callender. Russell noted that the pathologist was almost effusive, at least by the standards of his normally humourless character. When he removed the young man's ribcage to look at the internal organs, there was admiration in his tone as he said,

"The heart has been punctured with a single stab between the fourth and fifth rib, piercing the left ventricle and killing the subject immediately. It would have taken a very precise blow to achieve this with a single action."

Russell asked, "Are we looking at someone with medical knowledge?"

"It's poss…" Thompson tried to answer but Dent interrupted her.

"It's more likely that it is someone trained by the military in hand-to-hand combat."

Thompson gave him a withering look. "Can we continue please?" she said abruptly. Professional differences weren't going to be aired in front of the police officers but it was obvious that Thompson would have words with Dent later.

There was no sign that Dent understood his colleague's feelings as he returned his focus to the cadaver.

Russell thought there was evidently tension between the two doctors and the whole short cameo was revealing. They continued their work but even through the glass, Russell could feel how icy their relationship was.

By one-thirty, one of the mortuary technicians was stitching together the pieces of the unfortunate student.

"How are we doing with the investigation?" Dunsmore asked when the post mortem was over.

Russell briefed him on what they had learned so far and it was obvious that the senior man was less than happy.

"It's a bad one, Tom. The press are bound to put two and two together about what happened ten years ago and then we'll have the politicians crawling all over us."

"I understand that, sir but we can't do anything other than to keep working the case and see what we find."

"OK but keep me informed."

"Chief Superintendent McLelland is running the case, sir."

"Of course, yes but you'll make sure that he's on top of it, won't you?"

Russell wasn't sure what the A.C.C. was saying, but he wondered if Dunsmore held McLelland accountable for the failure to catch the killer after the last series of murders. "Yes, sir."

On the drive back to the incident room, Ellen Clarkson asked Russell more about the original crimes. He told her all that he remembered, it was a case that was etched into his memory and he could recall much of that terrible time. From the finding of the original trio of bodies through to the suicide of D.I. Newman, they were images that crawled through his nightmares like predatory spiders, preying on his weakness and taunting him with his failure. The discovery of the three bodies in George Square had only added more pain to the psychological and emotional scars of doubt and regret that he had stored. For her part, Ellen Clarkson could see how much the case was possessing Russell and she hoped that she would never let the job get to her in that way. She thought she would quit if she ever let her career overtake her life and character in that way.

***

When the two detectives arrived back in the office it was obvious that something had happened; the atmosphere in the room had been dampened and Russell's first thought was that the killer had struck again.

"What's up?" he asked.

Andy McKinley replied, "You've to go in and see the chief super right away."

"Why? What's so urgent?"

"You'll see when you get in."

He did as requested and when he knocked on the door of the office, the chief superintendent shouted angrily, "Come in."

He opened the door to find two people sitting opposite a red-faced McLelland. On the left was a rangy, thin-faced man in his mid-forties and on the right a slightly younger woman with perfectly coiffured blonde hair. They were both dressed in navy blue suits and Russell knew instinctively that they weren't part of the Strathclyde team.

McLelland said curtly, "This is Detective Inspector Russell."

The man stood up and offered his hand. "Harry Coldfield and this is my colleague Jennifer Smyth," he said with a refined English accent.

Russell shook each of their hands in turn, all the time wondering who these people were and what they had done to get under McLelland's skin to the extent that he looked ready to burst.

Russell's answer came in the form of an announcement from McLelland. "D.C.I. Coldfield and D.I. Smyth will be taking over our case."

"What?" Russell exclaimed.

"They've come from London on the authority of the Home Secretary."

Russell knew what McLelland was saying. It was the discreet way of saying that they were from Special Branch and that meant that all decisions relating to the case were being taken out of the control of the Strathclyde force.

"What the hell do you want with our case?"

Coldfield gave a measured response. "It is a matter of national security."

"Bollocks."

"Your opinion is of no consequence. We will be taking over the case. A team will arrive from London in a few hours and we will need some help from your foot soldiers but we will be running this investigation."

"Sir?" Russell looked to McLelland.

"Sorry Tom, but there's nothing we can do about this."

"This is bullshit. There's nothing about this case that is relevant to what you do. This is some crazy bastard bent on revenge for God knows what reason, but it is just that." As he was speaking, the reason they were there suddenly dawned on him. "Mehmet Ahmad. This is what this is all about, isn't it?"

"We don't need to explain ourselves to you or anyone else. You will follow orders." Coldfield was unmoved by the anger being directed at him.

Russell began to think out loud. "The Turkish authorities could find no trace of him. Let me guess, maybe he was a Kurd, which means he wasn't really Turkish but Iraqi. Did you get him out to ensure that Saddam didn't get his hands on him or was it just because you knew that you were going to bomb the hell out of his country?"

Coldfield's façade crumbled and he growled a warning; "You keep your little fantasies to yourself. Don't dare repeat that outside of this room. I'll remind you that you are bound by the Official Secrets Act in the same way we are."

"Bingo. Well, you can think what you want but this is nothing to do with whatever group of spooks Mr Ahmad worked for, he was just an unlucky victim of timing and circumstance. If he had arrived two minutes later he would have been a witness, not a corpse lying on a mortuary slab. You know I'm right, sir." Once again he turned to McLelland for support.

"Apparently our experience of this case is irrelevant, Inspector Russell. We have our orders." McLelland's defeated tone indicated that he would not be able to back his D.I. and that Russell should let it be.

"Aw fuck off." He turned and stormed out of the office. When he reached the incident room he said, "I'm going for a walk."

***

An hour later he returned and was told once again to go to McLelland's office. This time McLelland was alone.

"Sorry, sir," Russell said as he took a seat, knowing that he had let down both his boss and himself.

"I know how you feel, but when the orders come from that high up there's nothing we can do. They don't want you involved with the case in any way and have been asked that you be reassigned."

McLelland was ready for another outburst but Russell had been expecting to be removed from the case. He said simply, "Fine."

"That means no involvement, Tom. I know how personal this case is to you but you can't get in the way of these people. They don't play by the same rules that we do."

"All this is going to do is divert resources to a wild goose chase, while the trail for the real killer goes cold. Do they really think that Saddam Hussein is going to send an assassin dressed as a fuckin' clown to kill a spy? I think he's got more to worry about right now, don't you?"

"Tom, I am on your side honest, but it's pointless arguing."

"Why won't they listen to us? It's obvious that this is related to a previous case, a case we have already worked."

"I suppose when the normal rules don't apply to them, they begin to think they can't be wrong. I think you're probably right about the Iraqi angle and if that's true they are more than a little paranoid that Hussein or his sympathisers will begin operations within Britain. They think that Mr Ahmad, or whatever he's called, will be just the first of many. If you worked within the intelligence services, you'd probably be just as fearful."

"It's nuts, they're wasting their time. Anyway I'm going home. Send me a text to tell me where I've been reassigned."

""I will. I'm sorry Tom."

Russell lifted his coat from the rack in the incident room and left without a word to any of his colleagues.

***

Karen wasn't home when Tom arrived back at their flat. Once again he stood under the shower trying to loosen yet more knots of tension that had built up since he had met Coldfield. Shower over; he dressed in jeans and a T-shirt before heading to the kitchen. He wasn't much of a cook but he could manage to prepare a decent omelette. He chopped onions and mushrooms; the rhythm of the knife on the board was a little more frantic and angry than it would normally have been. He was already frying the ingredients in the pan when he heard the door of the flat open.

"Hello," Karen hollered.

"Hello."

"You're home early," she said walking into the kitchen.

"I'm off the case."

"What?"

"The spooks from London arrived and decided it was a matter of national security."

"Eh?"

"Exactly. Anyway I told them they were talking rubbish and they weren't too happy, so I got the boot."

"That's crazy, don't they know you've been working this case since it started?"

"I don't think they believe that what happened ten years ago is the same case, they're too busy chasing shadows."

"Did you make any progress with the investigation today?"

As they sat down to dinner, Russell ran through what little he had discovered before the bombshell. When he mentioned Ellen Clarkson, Karen began to interrogate him. It was a regular part of the pattern of their relationship. Any female colleague seemed to be regarded as a threat and she would quiz him intently. After the day he had suffered he was in no mood for her irrational jealousy.

"Karen, she's a detective sergeant who happens to be a woman. I work with Andy McKinley who is also a detective sergeant but he happens to be a man. I've had a shitty day and the last thing I need is your fuckin' paranoia." He immediately regretted his anger but before he could apologise, Karen got up from the table and stamped away in the direction of their bedroom, leaving her omelette half eaten on the plate. Russell pushed his own plate away, his appetite suddenly gone. He knew that only part of his frustration with Karen came as a result of the day he had endured. He was becoming increasingly annoyed by her constant belief that he had a wandering eye. She had been the only woman he had looked at ever since they had started to go out together, but her own insecurity meant that she suspected him of chasing other women. For Russell, what had started as a minor irritant that he could laugh at was now a major and widening gap between them.

He threw what was left of the omelettes into the bin and curled up on the couch, the T.V. remote in his hand. He drifted off to sleep and woke at two o'clock in the morning, with a painful neck and sticky eyes. He put the television off and went to a bed that was cold, both literally and emotionally.

CHAPTER 14

When he looked at his phone the following morning there was a text from McLelland telling him to report to Pitt Street. He guessed he was going to be told what a naughty boy he had been upsetting those important people from London.

Before he arrived to discover his assignment, he rang Ellen Clarkson.

"Hi Ellen, it's Tom Russell."

"Oh hello, sir. Aren't you coming in?"

"No, I've been reassigned, I'm just about to find out where they've dumped me. Can you do me a favour?"

"Well…" She was hesitant.

"It's nothing that will get you into trouble. I just want to know what the 'Tinker, Tailor' brigade is up to. Nothing useful probably as they're on completely the wrong track."

"I suppose so."

"Magic. I'll give you a ring later."

"OK, sir."

There was no way that he was going to let them remove him from a case this important without a fight.

He walked into the reception area of the H.Q. building and was asked to go up to McLelland in his regular office.

"Are you a bad boy too?" he asked the chief when he reached his office.

"Not quite. Look, Tom I know you're pissed off but we have to play the hand we've been dealt. I'm asking you to bear with me. I want you to go to the archives…"

Russell interrupted him. "Bloody hell, are you putting me out to pasture?"

"No, but you have to appear to be as far from this case as possible. But the archives are quiet, you'll have access to old files, particularly the cold case files," he said the last bit with heavy emphasis. McLelland's hardline approach of the previous night had softened now that he had had time to think about it.

Russell took the hint. "Ah, you mean the cold case that has nothing to do with the current one."

"Exactly."

"Are you sure about this, sir? You'll be in bother if the braid find out."

"Why? I assigned you as far from the current case as I could. The new case is a suspected assassination apparently. What harm can you possibly do in the archives?"

Russell smiled with appreciation. McLelland was playing the political games with the skill of someone who had climbed the promotional ladder by avoiding the potential broken rungs. He had complete deniability if Russell got involved in investigating 'The Harlequin', while at the same time being in a position to claim the credit should the younger man find something. Russell knew that his investigative and management skills were good enough to allow him to follow

McLelland up that tricky ladder but that he would never be able to navigate the bureaucratic pitfalls with the degree of skill his mentor had shown over the years.

"I'll try not to let you down, sir."

"I'm sure you'll be fine. Did you see the newspapers?"

"No."

"They're putting together the connections, not surprisingly."

"It was inevitable."

"It just makes things more awkward if they start asking questions about how the investigation is going. Special Branch won't want anyone knowing they're running the show and we'll be the fall guys when no one is caught."

"The perils of rank, sir," Russell said with a sardonic smile.

McLelland grinned back. "Aye, very good. Get out there and investigate the real case."

"Aye, sir."

***

Russell went straight from the meeting with McLelland to the archives where he reported to Sergeant Ken Harris. The ageing sergeant was a former detective who was coasting his way through his final months before he could collect his pension. Russell had worked with him before when they were both based in Partick. As a detective, Harris had been a very methodical and dedicated plodder. A man who would track every angle of a case until he found a lead that he would then pursue until it panned out. If that failed he would go back to the start and find another route. He was a solid analyst and was always a capable member of the team. Time and a chronic back problem had caught up with him, but he hadn't been ready to be pensioned off due to ill health, he had wanted to be useful. Now he was tied to a desk, supervising a couple of civilian workers, in the depths of the archives where the light was fluorescent and the coffee dreadful.

"D.I. Russell, to whit do we owe this pleasure?" he asked with a broad smile.

"Ken, how are you? It's good to see you," Russell said with genuine warmth.

"Ah'm not too bad. Whit's an important person like yirsel' daein' doon the dunny?"

"I've been temporarily reassigned."

"Whit?"

"Special Branch are in town and I think I might have upset them a wee bit."

"Say nae mair." Harris tapped the side of his nose. "Spy stuff. Ye shouldnae upset they boys, ye know. Ye could end up disappearin' aff the face o' the Earth wi' nae questions asked." He laughed although he did seem sympathetic to Russell's situation.

"Basically, I'm here to tell you that I'm here all day. If anybody comes looking for me, I'm off to lunch or in the lavvy. If you catch my drift."

"And what will ye be up tae really?"

"I can't tell you, Ken. Just in case they torture you."

Harris chortled. "It's aw right ah cin take it."

"I'm going to do some real policing and work the case the way it should be getting worked."

"The George Square thing."

"That's the one."

"It's that bastard again, isn't it?"

"I think so and this time I want to make sure I nail him."

"Good luck, Tom. It's time that he wis caught and punished for whit he did. Particularly efter whit he did tae the wee lassie."

"Look, I need a wee bit of help before I can get started. Can you possibly get me some information from the HOLMES database? I need access to the names, addresses and phone numbers for some of the people involved with this latest incident. I can't log in myself or the spooks will get me booted out of the service."

"Sure, nae problem. Whit dae ye need?"

Harris logged into the computer and navigated his way to the case notes. Russell told him what he required and then jotted down the information as Harris supplied it. When he had everything he needed he said, "Thanks for that, Ken. Look after yourself."

"You too, Tom."

***

Russell had to know if there was a direct connection between any of the victims and the killer. He had already dismissed Ahmad as being the link. Even if there was a possibility that the mystery man from the Middle East was involved, there was little point trying to pursue it, as Special Branch would be focusing all their efforts in that direction. That left the other two victims as possible links and of those, Martin Jenkinson seemed to be the more likely.

Mr and Mrs Jenkinson lived in the Jordanhill area of the city. Their home was in the middle of a Victorian terrace fronted by small gardens. It looked safe and secure; far from the terrors of life in a big city but even here violence could reach out a grasping hand and throw lives into chaos.

When Russell rang the doorbell, he was hoping that a Family Liaison Officer wouldn't open it because he didn't want his private investigations to get back to the ears of the people who were now in charge of the case. He waited a few seconds before ringing the bell once more. He could see a figure approaching through the ornately crafted, stained-glass window of the front door. It swung open and an attractive young woman dressed in a sea-blue jumper and black jeans stood in the doorway. Her eyes were filled with sorrow and her complexion was hauntingly pale. Russell reckoned that she would be in her early twenties, but her grief was weighing heavily on her and had robbed her of some of her youth.

"Detective Inspector Russell, I wonder if I could have a few words."

"Come in. We thought you would be here sooner."

"It's been very busy, there were a lot of witnesses and they were the initial priority."

She seemed to accept an excuse that sounded weak to Russell's ears but it was the best he could come up with a short notice. As she stood to one side, Russell entered the house. The young woman directed him to a door on the left of the hall.

When he walked into the room he found a middle-aged woman and another woman who could only be her daughter, so striking was the similarity between them.

"Mum, this is a detective from the police."

"Tom Russell." he said before adding, "I'm sorry for your loss Mrs Jenkinson."

"Thank you, inspector. This is my oldest daughter, Caroline and my youngest, Josephine." She indicated the older sister as being the one who had opened the door to him. He shook the hands of the siblings and was invited to sit on a long sofa.

"I don't suppose you're here to tell us that you've caught the person that murdered my husband?" She seemed strangely calm and Russell wondered if she was receiving help from her doctor to cope with the adversity she was living through.

"I'm sorry, but no."

"What have you been doing that it's taken you this long to come and speak to my mother? I thought when I flew up that you would already have been here to speak to her," Josephine said sharply.

"Jo," her mother rebuked.

"That's fine Mrs Jenkinson, I understand your daughter's concerns. You should have been allocated a Family Liaison Officer. Has that not been arranged?"

"No."

"I'm sorry about that. I'll get it organised when we are finished here. To answer your question, this is a very complicated investigation. We have three separate victims, a huge number of potential witnesses and our resources are finite. As this appears to be a completely senseless attack we have had to concentrate those resources on gathering information of those who were at the scene. It's not normal procedure but this is not a normal crime."

Mrs Jenkinson replied, "I understand. Now how can we help you?"

"This may seem a little strange but I need to know a little about when you first came to Scotland. Can I ask you when you first arrived in Glasgow?"

"What's that got to do with who killed my father?" Josephine was on the attack again. Her mother's calm was not mirrored in her raging daughter.

"If you can bear with me, I will explain," Russell replied patiently.

After a short pause for thought, Mrs Jenkinson said, "Eh... we arrived in the January of eighty-three."

"We have reason to believe that the killer is seeking revenge for something that happened in April of that year, to be precise on April Fool's Day of that year. Can you think of anything that happened on that date that might be relevant to our inquiry? It may have seemed trivial at the time but it has significance for the killer."

Josephine stood up angrily. "Oh this is ridiculous. How can my mother hope to remember something like that? It sounds like you don't have a single idea why my father was killed and now you're stumbling about in the ancient past trying to find something."

"Jo, sit down and let mother think." It was Caroline's turn to try and rein in her sister's misdirected grief.

"What is wrong with you? Can't you see they're incompetent and that they will never find out who killed Daddy?" She left the room abruptly.

"I apologise for my sister, inspector. She always was a bit of a drama queen." Caroline's statement unmasked a little of the family's divisions.

"It's quite understandable after all that has happened," Russell conceded.

Mrs Jenkinson said, "I've been trying to think but I can't remember anything. What kind of thing were you thinking of?"

"I don't know. It could be an argument or a prank gone wrong."

She paused for a few seconds before saying, "No, I honestly can't think of anything like that. Martin wasn't one for practical jokes and he was a very peaceable man. He wouldn't get into a serious argument with anyone. He was a good man."

Her final sentence seemed to break the spell and for the first time she looked upset.

"I'm sure he was, Mrs Jenkinson. It was a long shot, anyway."

"Why did you want to know?" Caroline asked.

"Ten years ago there was a series of crimes that were directed at one person. The first of April 1983 was believed to be the date that had significance for the killer. I was wondering if there was any link between any of Tuesday's victims and that date."

"You think it's the same killer?" she asked in surprise.

"We have reason to believe so, but I can't give you any more details."

"Is there anything else, inspector?"

"Not at the moment," Russell said as he stood to leave.

Mrs Jenkinson felt the need to explain something before the detective left the house. "I was scared to come to Glasgow at first; the city has such a violent reputation but Martin persuaded me. I grew to love it and we made a good life here but it turns out my fears have been realised."

"I know, Mrs Jenkinson and I will do everything in my power to ensure that there is some justice for your husband, I promise."

"Thank you, inspector."

Caroline escorted him to the front door. "I hope you keep your promise," she said.

"I intend to. I'll get that liaison officer organised. They should be in touch this afternoon."

"Thank you."

Russell walked back to his car, disappointed that a simple task like assigning the F.L.O. had not been done and irritated at himself for making excuses for the failings of an investigation which was heading in completely the wrong direction. When he had settled into the driver's seat, he reached for his phone.

"Ellen, it's me. Can you talk?"

"Just one moment, sir." There was a pause and when she spoke again there was an echo. "I'm set."

"Where are you?"

"In the stairwell. What do you want?" she said impatiently.

"Can you make sure that the Jenkinsons get an F.L.O. allocated to them as soon as possible, please?"

"Shit, has that not been done already?"

"No, they haven't seen anyone. What's going on?"

She spoke quietly as she answered, "The spooks have got us investigating every person from the Middle East that's arrived in Britain in the past three months. They've already hauled in for questioning two poor Egyptian women and a journalist from Qatar. Stumbling about in the dark would be the best way to describe it."

"It's what they do. Why use a scalpel when you can use a chainsaw?"

"I take it you've been to see Mrs Jenkinson?"

"Yes and her daughters."

"Anything useful?"

"No, it was a remote chance but it was worth the attempt. The younger daughter seems to blame us for her father's death but that's understandable."

"Poor thing. Right I better get back. Where are you going next?"

"I'm going to track down the owner of the promotions company, if the attack wasn't directed at one of the victims, it must have been directed towards him."

"Good luck."

The call over, Russell drove off in search of lunch before he would continue his own investigation.

CHAPTER 15

The company was called Gltz Events, Promotions and Marketing. Russell thought the dropping of the noun from the name was a bit pretentious and pretty stupid but he guessed that it was perfectly acceptable in the kind of circles the company would do business in. The offices were in West George Street, in an eighties structure of glass and steel. The lift door opened out onto a plush reception area where the company logo dominated the wall behind a very attractive young woman who beamed a false smile at Russell as he approached.

Warrant card in hand he said, "D.I. Tom Russell, I'm here to see Mr Hastings."

Her smile faded a little. "I'm sorry, Mr Hastings isn't in the office at the moment."

"Can you tell me where he is? It's very important that I speak to him."

Russell could see her become flustered as she wondered what to tell him. "To be honest we're not sure where he is. He was due back today from his trip to London but he hasn't arrived and we can't reach him on the phone. I thought maybe he had missed the last flight from Heathrow but the hotel he was staying at said he had checked out and not returned."

"What airline was he flying with?"

"B.A."

"And you've tried his phone?"

"Yes, but it goes straight to voicemail. It's not like him, he likes to be in contact with the office at all times."

"Does he live with anyone?"

"No, he was divorced from Mrs Hastings four years ago. There's not been anyone since." The wistful way she said it made Russell think that she was hoping that Hastings might cast his eye in her direction.

The detective's thoughts were already turning to Deirdre Nichol's body. The Harlequin may be following the same pattern by attacking Hastings's company followed by killing the owner.

"Is there anyone who can tell me about the customer who requested the promotion in George Square?"

"One moment, please take a seat."

Russell walked to a comfortable black leather chair while the receptionist picked up the phone. When the call was over she said to him, "Mr Davies will be with you in a moment."

Five minutes later a harassed man in his early forties burst through a door and said with a distinct Welsh accent, "Detective Inspector Russell, I'm so sorry to keep you waiting. I'm Bryn Davies. Please come through, we can have a chat in Gregor's office."

He was tall at well over six feet and his mass of long brown hair streamed behind him as his huge stride carried him down a corridor between the sectioned work areas. Each area had three or four desks that were separated from their fellows by brightly-coloured paneled screens. As he followed him, Russell could here the buzz of multiple conversations, phones ringing and keyboards clicking. Eventually at the far end of the larger workplace, Davies showed him into a smaller office that was behind a glass partition. When the door was closed, the noise suddenly disappeared. His host moved behind a very modern desk and invited the detective to sit. Russell settled into another comfortable chair and examined the man. He was dressed in a smart but casual grey shirt, a gold cross visible on the top of his breastbone between the open folds of the collar. The wrinkles around his eyes betrayed the fact that he was a little older than his hair and clothes suggested. He was tanned and looked to be healthy, the very picture of success.

"Can I get you anything to drink? Gregor's got some nice malt whisky stashed away if you fancy something stronger than tea or coffee." Davies said.

"No thank you, sir. Not when I'm on duty."

"Of course, of course. I believe you're looking for some information."

"That's correct, I'm hoping you'll be able to tell me a little about who commissioned the promotion on Monday."

"I have the details here." He flicked his hair away from his face as he lifted a piece of paper. "The company is called 'Harlequin's Tears' and the promotion was a preview event for a new restaurant of the same name that is opening in July. The specification said that if it went well, we would be commissioned to organise three other similar stunts on the run up to the opening, as well as promoting the opening itself. I guess that won't be happening," he said with a sad smile.

"How were you paid?"

"Unusually, we were paid upfront by company cheque."

"Did you meet anyone from Harlequin's Tears?"

"No, it was all done over the phone and by e-mail."

"Is that normal?"

"No, but it's not unheard of. If people know us or have used us before they might just phone up and book us again. There's no need for the hard sell when people know what you can do."

"How did you recruit the young people who took part in the event on Tuesday?"

"They were mainly drama students and some circus performers. The proposal said that we had to make it an engaging performance, so we sourced people with the necessary talents. The restaurant paid considerably more than we might have expected from that size of business, so we had to make sure that they got their money's worth."

"Did the contract specify the number of performers?"

"There had to be a minimum of sixteen people."

"And it specified the costume?"

"The costumes were supplied and we received very specific instructions regarding the make-up."

"And it had to be in George Square?"

Davies nodded. "Yes and at exactly that time. There was a huge penalty if we were late."

Russell absorbed what he had been told. "Basically, you had to find the performers and make sure that they were in the right place at the right time. There was no real creative input from your team, is that correct?"

"Absolutely."

"It seems strange to me that someone would pay you that amount of money for a relatively small amount of work. Didn't you wonder about it?"

"To be honest, not really. When we're working with large companies, they will often have a full plan in place that we have to act upon. When the sales team told me what had been offered and requested, I presumed that it was maybe a new chain of restaurants. I didn't check the details I'm afraid, we're in the fortunate position that we are very busy."

"Thanks for your time, Mr Davies. If Mr Hastings gets in touch would you ask him to call me? Here's my card."

"I will. After what happened on Tuesday, we're all worried about him."

"I understand. Thanks again." Russell walked back through the office, thanked the receptionist and pressed the button to call the lift.

When he stepped out into West George Street, he immediately dialled McLelland's number.

"Tom?"

"Sir, Gregor Hastings is missing. He hasn't turned up at the office and the staff can't get a hold of him."

"He's definitely back from London?"

"No one knows for sure, he could be in the air I suppose but something tells me that's not the case."

"Get on to the airline and find out if he was on that flight. If he was, we've got a problem."

"Yes, sir. I'll let you know."

He walked back into the building and asked the security guard on duty at the desk if he had a phone book.

"Naw, Ah cin look up the number on the computer if ye want."

"Yes please. It's the British Airways desk at Glasgow Airport."

The man moved the mouse hesitantly and clacked slowly on the keyboard. Russell was frustrated at the delay but he had to acknowledge to himself that he would not have been able to use the computer any more efficiently.

"Got it," the guard said. He wrote the number on a yellow notepad and handed the page to Russell.

"Thanks."

Back on the street he started walking in the direction of Pitt Street as he dialled the airline.

"British Airways, Glasgow Airport. Simon speaking, how can I help?"

"My name is Detective Inspector Tom Russell. I was wondering if you can help me regarding a passenger who was due to fly to Glasgow last night from Heathrow?"

"I'm not sure if I should," the man said sounding perturbed.

"I understand your reluctance but this is very important. We need to know if this gentleman was on the flight as his life may be in danger."

The stress in Russell's voice was enough to convince Simon. "Oh... what is his name?"

"Gregor Hastings. He should have been on the last flight, I'm sorry I don't know the exact time."

There was a short period where the noise of a busy airport was all that Russell could hear before the airline employee said, "Mr Hastings both checked-in and boarded the flight which arrived in Glasgow at 11:40 last night."

"Thanks for your help, Simon."

"You're welcome, I hope the gentleman is OK."

"So do I. So do I."

By the time the call was over Russell was turning into Pitt Street only fifty yards from the entrance to the headquarters building.

McLelland knew before Russell spoke that their worst fears were beginning to be realised.

"We need to tell Special Branch to take a hike, we need bodies on this to find Hastings before it's too late," Russell said forcibly.

"I know. Give me a minute and I'll speak to the A.C.C."

McLelland rang Dunsmore's office. When he was put through he laid out what Russell had discovered and what he believed needed to happen.

"I thought D.I. Russell had been reassigned," Dunsmore observed.

"Sir, that was my decision. I didn't believe that the version of events being spun by Special Branch was likely, and I felt Tom was the best man to keep investigating the real crime."

"Let me make a few phone calls." Dunsmore hung up.

McLelland and Russell sat in contemplative mood as they waited on the word from the top. They both knew that the A.C.C. would have to speak to the chief constable and then maybe Whitehall to get the case reallocated. The decision may have to come from the Home Secretary. Russell hoped that whomever took the decision would do so quickly.

After twenty minutes the call finally came. "You've got agreement, Mark. The chief constable wishes to be kept informed, so let me know of any developments immediately."

"Yes, sir."

"We'll speak about you disobeying orders when this is all over."

"Yes, sir." McLelland hung up and said to the handset, "Arsehole."

"Let's go, Tom. We've got a case to run." He called Andy McKinley and told him to collect as many of the team together within the hour for a briefing. McKinley sounded delighted to hear that they were back in control of the case.

***

Coldfield was clearing papers from the desk at Stewart Street Station when McLelland and Russell arrived.

He didn't bother with a greeting, instead he warned, "You better be right about this, McLelland."

"Oh we're right and we've always been right."

Russell was even more blunt. "You've cost us valuable time on this investigation and your fannying about playing spy has possibly cost an innocent man his life. So get out of our way and fuck off back to London. Maybe you'll listen to the people on the ground before you barge in and lay down the law."

"We were acting in the interests of national security."

"No, you weren't. You were acting in the interests of national paranoia. Keep us scared and we'll stay in line. Well this is Glasgow and we don't scare easily."

"Tom," McLelland warned.

"We'll be keeping an eye on you, Russell," Coldfield warned.

"Look at me; I'm quaking in my boots."

Coldfield lifted the box of papers and walked quickly out of the office.

"That might not have been too wise, Tom."

"I don't give a shit. These halfwits are so full of their own importance, they didn't have the sense to listen to us and look what's happened. They wasted resources chasing ghosts while the real killer slips under their radar."

"I know but they can make life really difficult for you if they want."

"Aye, right."

"We need to get a search organised for Hastings. Andy should have the troops organised within the next half hour or so."

That half hour dragged and Russell occupied himself by calling Gltz followed by Hastings's home and mobile numbers. Hope of finding him safe and well diminished with every negative result.

Finally they were ready to go to the incident room. McKinley had managed to pull together about half the team of detectives and there was an almost celebratory atmosphere when Russell and McLelland were greeted with a round of applause.

'Let's get back to some real police work," McLelland said by way of introduction. He allowed Russell to tell them all that had happened earlier in the day and the concerns that the killer had been active once again. Assignments were given to check CCTV and interview Hastings's neighbours, family and colleagues.

"It's vital we find Mr Hastings as quickly as possible. Report anything you discover to D.S. McKinley, he will disseminate the information to the rest of the team. Understood?" McLelland asked.

"Yes, sir," was the unanimous reply.

Russell decided that he wanted to take a look at Hastings home and asked D.S. Clarkson to accompany him. As the meeting broke up, they headed to Clarkson's car.

***

Hastings lived in a penthouse flat in Clyde Street, which enjoyed a panoramic view of the river. Rain had begun to fall on the city; the skies were dark with slow-moving clouds that were crammed with the promise of a long period of heavy rain. The downpour made both detectives scurry to the door of the building where Russell had to press a few of the intercom buttons before getting a reply from a woman on the third floor. He introduced himself as he showed his warrant card to a closed-circuit camera that was positioned above the row of buttons. The entrance opened with a click; Russell held it open, waiting for two uniformed constables who had followed them from the station. They were there to provide the muscle should they need to break down the door of Hastings's flat.

All four climbed the stairs to the third floor where a woman was waiting outside her flat.

"Is everything all right?" she asked as she looked at the short battering ram that one of the constables was carrying.

"Yes, of course. Thanks for letting us in."

"Are you sure?" She looked doubtful.

"Absolutely."

It was obvious that she was desperate to learn more but Russell remain stoic and waited until she retreated back into her home.

The flat that Hastings owned was directly above where the curious woman lived. Russell knocked the door a couple of times; the second time was louder than the first and was accompanied by a shout. When there was still no reply, he rang Hastings home phone once again with exactly the same result.

"Open it up," Russell said to the constables.

The door withstood the first blow but surrendered in a brief shower of splinters with the second strike.

Russell and Clarkson pulled on some gloves and walked into the flat, leaving the constables to wait outside. There was a narrow stairway that led from the short hall to the second storey of the flat. The hall opened out into a kitchen and dining area that then led to a living area three steps below. The balcony was beyond the broad expanse of full-height windows. All of the ground floor of the flat was covered in highly polished genuine cherry wood flooring. To Russell's eye the furniture was modern, tasteful and expensive. He walked through to the living area and was relieved that there was no sign of either a body or a struggle.

"Very nice," Clarkson observed.

"Aye, he's clearly doing well for himself. We better check upstairs." He led the way to the second-floor landing that contained four doors. They tried each of them in turn, looking into two guest bedrooms and a toilet before finally entering the master bedroom. The room was decorated with refined masculinity, simple and minimalistic. The king-sized bed hadn't been slept in and there was a single navy blue suitcase lying on it; on the handle was the airport baggage tag that had been attached at Heathrow. Russell tried to open the case but it was locked.

"Looks like he didn't get time to unpack," Clarkson said.

"Let's have another look downstairs."

They both went to search the kitchen and living room. There was nothing to suggest that Hastings had even made himself a cup of tea on his arrival from the airport.

"Maybe the killer was waiting and watching for him to come back." Clarkson theorised.

"Aye and then called him. If he tempted him out of the flat, Hastings must have known who it was."

"We better get forensics to have a look, in case the killer came into the flat."

Russell called McLelland and told him what they had found.

When he was finished, McLelland said, "It's not looking good is it?"

"No, it's not."

"I'll get forensics over. Let's hope they can find something."

Russell returned to the station by taxi while Clarkson stayed to interview Hastings's neighbours. She completed her task at six-thirty after waiting for the majority of them to return home. No one had heard anything, some of them didn't even know who Hastings was.

Russell sat in the incident room until well after nine o'clock, hoping against hope that a piece of information would help them to find Hastings. The CCTV cameras on Clyde Street had captured him exiting a taxi at the flats at quarter past midnight and then leaving on foot ten minutes later. The cameras tracked him to the South Portland Street footbridge across the Clyde but failed to pick him up on the other side. The area would need to be canvassed for information in the morning.

McLelland walked into the office at ten o'clock and after he had been briefed said to Russell, "There's nothing else we can do tonight, Tom. Get yourself off home."

Russell complied reluctantly, "Good night, sir."

"Good night, Tom."

CHAPTER 16

Russell's phone rang at quarter to seven the next morning and he knew what he was going to hear before he even looked at the display to see who was calling. Ellen Clarkson's name on the screen only confirmed his fears.

"Sorry to disturb you sir, but a body's been found in Ruchill Park."

"You didn't disturb me, Ellen. I've been waiting on the call most of the night. Hastings?"

"Looks like it. The chief super's on his way to the scene, will I tell him you'll get him there?"

"Aye. I'll be there as soon as I can."

"It's at the flagpole, so you should come in off the Benview Street entrance."

"Cheers."

For Russell the drive to the park was filled with dread. Another death meant another layer of remorse and regret for him. Life as a detective was only satisfying when he was getting justice for the victim of a crime, but failing to catch the person responsible always brought a feeling of failure, and when the culprit used his freedom to continue killing it was even worse.

In his career, Russell had never come across anything quite like this. There was obviously a motive, revenge was indeed a strong one but the cold way that he had gone about it made this a very strange murderer. Revenge was normally about raging passion not clinical calculation.

He arrived at the park twenty-five minutes after Clarkson's call. He drove through the gates and up to where the blue and white tape fluttered in a strong breeze. The park sat on a hill that left it exposed to the elements and a squally shower was drenching everyone when Russell drew to a halt just outside the cordon. He suited up and walked in the direction of yet another body.

The flagpole was situated on a mound that offered a view across the whole city. A spiral path led up to it and at the top an inner cordon had been established. McLelland was waiting for Russell when he ducked under the tape.

"Good morning, Tom," the chief super greeted him with a grim look.

"What's the story?" Russell asked.

"The park ranger found him this morning during his first patrol of the day. It's another level of freakishness."

The situation of the body made it difficult to erect a tent around it and instead the technicians had surrounded the pole with screens. When the two detectives arrived a female technician stepped out of the screened off area to allow them to look at the body.

Gregor Hastings had been tied to the bottom of the flagpole; a rope had pulled his head back, revealing a line of crimson death that was traced across his throat. His eyelids appeared to have been stitched to his forehead, leaving his eyes open and staring off into the distance. He was dressed in one of the harlequin suits that had been used during the performance in George Square; it hung loosely on his angular frame and it appeared he was naked under it.

"Bloody hell," Russell muttered in disgust as he took in the terrible sight. He stepped closer and noticed something in the murdered man's mouth. "Can you take a picture of this, please?" he shouted to the technician. She did as she was asked. With the tips of his fingers Russell got a hold of the item and gently pulled it out through Hastings's teeth. It was the now familiar calling card of the Harlequin and when Russell turned it over written on the back was the same date, 1st April 1983.

"Same again," Russell said to McLelland who bobbed his head in agreement.

The technician handed him an evidence bag from her case. He placed the card in it and showed it to McLelland before giving it to the woman to record and reference.

McLelland was standing shaking his head, "What's this all about, Tom?"

"Fuck knows," Russell sighed.

"What about the eyes?"

"Where is he looking?" He stepped out of the protected area and tried to establish the direction that Hastings's head had been positioned to 'look' at. He moved his head in and out of the screen as he calculated the direction.

"The university, he's looking towards the university."

The Gothic architecture of the main university building loomed over the West End of the city like an educational behemoth. It was easily visible from the top of the mound.

Russell's mind began to tick over and think through all that had happened. "What if the Harlequin had hoped to drug university students when he got Petterson to place the hallucinogens in the cakes?"

"A vendetta against the university?" McLelland asked trying to follow his logic.

"It could be or maybe it was something that had a connection to the university back in 1983. Deirdre Nichol attended Glasgow Uni, didn't she?"

"Yes but I think she would have left by '83."

"I'll lay good odds that Hastings was there too. I'm sure there's a connection between them."

During their conversation Professor Lionel Marriot strode up the mound already dressed in his protective clothing, a mask dangled below his chin and he was carrying his forensic case.

"Good morn...ing, gentleman." He was panting due to the effort of climbing the short hill. Russell hadn't seen the pathologist for a couple of months and he was shocked to see how much weight the man had lost.

"Are you OK?" McLelland asked.

"On my last legs old boy. Too many cigarettes. Asthma and goodness knows what else killing the old lungs and me with it probably." His barking laugh was laced with a customary black humour.

"Should you be here?"

"No it should be Dr Dent but he's taking a personal day, whatever that's supposed to be."

"I meant should you be working at all?"

"I'm just doing my time until they find a replacement. Anyway what have you got for me?"

They moved towards the screened area and when the body was revealed, Marriot said, "It's enough to drive you up the pole."

McLelland and Russell ignored the comment. They were used to the professor's tendency to crack jokes at a crime scene, but after all that had happened in this case, neither detective could be bothered to offer even a polite smile.

"He wasn't killed here obviously and he has been redressed. It takes quite a lot of dedication and persistence to get clothes on to a cadaver." He leaned in closer to the corpse and pulled gently at the costume. "Velcro. That would have made it a bit easier I suppose."

'Death is due to blood loss and he wouldn't have lasted very long once the carotid had been sliced." He walked round the corpse, noting the position of Hastings's hands and commenting on the knots. When he came round to front of the body he stared at the stitching on the eyes. "Very skilled work."

Marriot began a more detailed examination as McLelland pondered, "How did he get the body up here?"

"The path's wide enough for a car, maybe he just drove up." Russell said.

"I suppose so, tricky though."

As they talked more of the forensic team arrived and then Ellen Clarkson joined McLelland and Hastings.

"Sir, the park ranger is ready to be interviewed if you would like to speak to him."

McLelland asked, "Anything significant?"

"Not really. The body wasn't here last night. He didn't see anyone around the park when he closed up and no one this morning when he opened up."

"Any idea how the killer would have got in? Aren't the park gates locked at night?" Russell wondered.

"Cut through the chains on the gates at Benview Street, apparently."

"It's easy done with decent bolt cutters, I'd imagine. What do you think about the placement of the body?" Russell was curious to know what Clarkson thought.

She replied, "It's obviously very public, seems to be an attempt to humiliate the victim and attract more press attention."

"What about the eyes?"

She shivered involuntarily. "Creepy. Looks like he's staring at the university."

"That's what we thought too," McLelland said. "We need to canvass the area, see if any of the residents in the flats overlooking the park saw or heard anything during the night. Can you organise that as quickly as possible, sergeant? I don't want to lose any more time."

"Yes, sir."

Inside the screens, the work of the forensic team was now well under way. The crime scene photographer was completing a video tour of the body and the surrounding area. He would then turn his attention to photographing in the same methodical way.

"There's not much else we can do here. We should head back to Stewart Street." McLelland said

"Aye, right enough, " Russell replied morosely.

***

The news had obviously reached the ears of the press pack as Russell and McLelland had to push through a throng of reporters and cameramen at the entrance to the station. Questions were shouted but the two detectives had nothing to say other than that a press conference would be held later that day.

The team of detectives who were waiting to be briefed in the incident room had also heard the news about Hastings death. Russell could sense their disquiet and there was also a degree of puzzlement as they tried to understand the killer they were tracking. There was a broad range of experience in the room but no one had come across a crime spree quite like this.

McLelland was darkly serious as he led them through the events of the past few hours. The description of the condition of Hastings's body brought gasps of shock and expressions of revulsion.

"I've arranged with Professor Marriot that the post mortem be conducted today as soon as is practicable. Andy, I want you to take Ellen Clarkson with you when she gets back. We know what the cause of death was but I want to know what else may have been done to Mr Hastings - if anything - before his untimely end."

"Yes, sir." D.S. McKinley nodded.

"We need to find the connection between Deirdre Nichol, Gregor Hastings and what happened on the first of April, 1983."

Russell was desperate to understand the motive, so he said, "Sir, I'd like to do that."

"You'll need some help. D.C. Shaw and D.C. Mulgrew, you work with D.I. Russell to find that link. Find it and we'll be a bit closer to understanding why these crimes are happening and hopefully who is committing them."

As the meeting came to a close, some of the detectives were allocated to help with the questioning of the people who lived around the park. The mood had improved a little as the briefing finished and work began in earnest once more.

McLelland told Russell, "I'll go to Pitt Street and get the press conference out of the way. They'll be in the mood for a lynching no doubt, but I'll do my best to avoid the gallows and buy us a wee bit more time."

"Good luck with that," Russell replied.

When the chief superintendent had gone, Russell sat down with the two youthful detectives that had been told to help him.

"I'm going to phone the university records office, I need the two of you to speak to friends and relations of the deceased. We need to establish connections and they may not be obvious. Deirdre Nichol and Gregor Hastings were the same age, so they probably were in the same year at uni but they may not have been in classes together. I want you to ask about their interests, any clubs they may have been in together or if they were a couple back then."

"Where should we start, sir?" D.C. Shaw asked.

"Start with family members and work out from there. There should be a comprehensive file on Deirdre Nichol but you're going to have use your initiative to pull together the information on Hastings. Be discreet and sensitive when you're asking questions, particularly with those close to Hastings. Check with family liaison and make sure that they have been in touch with his family before continuing. I don't want you to be the one to break the news of his death. Do you understand?"

They nodded their acceptance and Mulgrew said, "I'll take Mr Hastings's family. It might be better if it's a woman speaking to them."

"I don't mind which of you does it, as long as it's done properly and with tact."

They left him alone as they went in search of files and contact information. Russell lifted a telephone book on to the desk in front of him and found the section for the University of Glasgow. He scanned through a long list of numbers before finding the direct number for the records office. Some of his colleagues would have used the computer, but he was sure that the analogue method was quicker for him.

"Glasgow University records office, Tracy speaking."

"Hi Tracy, I'm hoping you might be able to help me. My name is Detective Inspector Tom Russell and I'm in need of some information about students that would have studied with you in the early eighties."

"Can I ask what this is concerning?" she asked guardedly.

"It's an ongoing murder investigation and we believe that there may be a connection through the university between the victims."

"Oh, I see."

"We think they may have been attending the university some time around 1980. Their names are Deirdrie Macintosh and Gregor Hastings."

"Of course, of course. It might take a while to dig back into the archives. Can I ring you back?"

"That would be great. Thank you."

He gave her his number before hanging up and then decided that he needed a cup of coffee to kick-start his tired brain. A visit to the small canteen also secured a roll and bacon to allow him his first meal of the day. Shaw and Mulgrew were sitting at their own desks when he returned, phones stuck to their ears and pens poised above their notepads. The clock on the incident room wall seemed to turn very slowly as he sat drinking the coffee and eating his breakfast. When it had ticked round to twelve o'clock the phone rang.

"D.I. Russell."

"Inspector, it's Tracy Paterson at the university."

"Hello Tracy, thanks for getting back to me."

"Deirdre Macintosh was a student from 1980 through to 1982 and earned a B.A. in Business Management. Mr Hastings was here during the same period, his degree was in Marketing."

Russell was pleased that some link had been established. "Were they in a class together?"

"Let me have a look. Eh… no there were no subjects that they shared."

"What about clubs or social organisations?

"I'm sorry we don't keep those records unless it's sport and there's nothing listed for either of them."

"That's fine. You've been a big help."

She sounded pleased as she said, "Have I? That's great I hope you catch who did this."

It wasn't as clear-cut as he had hoped but the first connection had been verified, the only difficulty was that they weren't at university in 1983. He hoped that Shaw and Mulgrew might be able to draw together the threads into something more cohesive and concrete.

He sat staring at the clock once again while picking up the occasional piece of conversation from the phone interviews that the two detective constables were conducting. By one o'clock the frustration had become too much for him and he went for a walk, trying to dodge the wind-driven showers that were still making an appearance every now and then,

McLelland was sitting in the office when he returned.

"Hi Tom, any news?"

Russell told him what he had learned from the university.

"So there is a possibility they knew each other back then?"

"Hopefully. How were the press hounds?"

"Biting. It's going to be almost impossible to stop this spinning off into flights of fancy. They've got a juicy murder to add to the pile of the other bodies that have mounted up. I would never have thought that I would be glad of a war to keep us out of the headlines."

"Deaths of innocent people in Iraq are a almost incidental to the fireworks show," Russell observed cynically.

"But those fireworks are the focus for the press at the moment. It won't be long before Iraq gets relegated to page two."

"True enough."

The chief super's mobile rang. "McLelland."

Russell sat in silence as the other man listened and replied.

"OK... Right, yes I understand... Thanks Ellen."

McLelland ended the call and turned to Russell once again. "That was Ellen Clarkson. The post mortem showed that Hastings had been tortured before he was killed."

"Poor bastard," Russell said softly.

"Sir, I think you better see this." A shout went up from the other end of the room. The sound of the television news filled the air as it was taken off mute."

A news reporter was in the middle of a breaking news story. " ...believed to be of murder victim Gregor Hastings have appeared on the internet. The forty-one year-old man was found this morning in Glasgow and these pictures appear to show him being tortured by the killer who calls himself the Harlequin. The website - which is called the Harlequin's Den - first appeared today at 11:45 BST and includes a number of distressing images."

'Put that thing off,' McLelland shouted, his face red with anger.

The television was muted once again and silence fell on the room.

"I want that fuckin' thing taken down this instant. Someone get hold of the I.T. squad and get that website down," he bellowed.

"Yes, sir," replied the officer who had pointed out the news story.

"Can this get any fuckin' worse?" he sank his head into his hands.

Russell was as distressed as his boss about the website. The Harlequin had moved on to a completely different level of seeking out publicity. He was accelerating his behaviour and Russell wondered if this time he might not stop at Hastings. If there were others within his sights he might not wait another ten years to finish his mission of revenge.

"I.T. are on it, sir. They're trying to trace the I.P. address and they've initiated a denial of service attack to prevent people accessing the site."

McLelland looked up. "Good, with any luck he's made his fatal mistake."

Half an hour later the technicians informed them that the I.P. address could not be traced and McLelland's hope evaporated. He left the incident room and retreated to his temporary office.

At two o'clock, D.C. Shaw stood up from his desk and approached Russell. "Inspector, I think I might have something."

"Go on then."

"Deirdre Macintosh was a member of something called the Jester's Balls. According to a friend that I traced through her ex-husband, she was a member at the same time as Gregor

Hastings. She thought that Hastings was possibly one of the founder members of the organisation.

"What did the organisation do?"

"She wasn't very forthcoming but she said it was something to do with practical jokes."

"What's this woman's name?"

"Christine O'Donnell."

"Where is she?"

"She lives in Moodiesburn."

"I think I'll go and have a word with Ms O'Donnell.

Russell told McLelland where he was going and then took Shaw with him to head to Moodiesburn.

***

Within thirty minutes the car was pulling into the drive of a semi-detached house that dated from the sixties. Christine O'Donnell opened the door to them with an anxious look on her face.

Russell offered the official greeting. "D.I. Russell and this is my colleague D.C. Shaw."

"Come in."

She was in her early forties with features that looked careworn and bore the wrinkled scars of the struggles of her existence without masking her fine bone structure. She was stout with thick arms and legs that were wrapped in loose leggings. Her hair was dyed a dark shade of purple but there was a line of grey showing at the roots.

She guided them into the living room, which was decorated in beige tones and was covered in pictures of her family; Russell noted two children but no sign of any photographs of a partner. He thought that the worn down air she projected might be the result of the life of a single parent.

"Ms O'Donnell, thank you for speaking to us."

"This is about Deirdre and Gregor?" she asked as her hands circled around one another in a gesture of anxiety.

"Yes, it is. You may be aware that Gregor Hastings was found dead this morning. We believe that his death may have a connection to Deirdre's and I believe you told D.C. Shaw what that connection might be."

"I can't be sure," she replied.

"I understand that, but if you can tell us all that you know, you will be helping us rule out a link to this club you spoke of, at the very least."

She took a deep gulp of air and said, "Gregor set up the Jester's Balls club when he joined the university. The idea was that the members would play practical jokes on each other and other students. We would sponsor one another to execute the jokes and raise money for good causes."

"A bit like 'Rag Week'," Russell suggested.

"Yes but it would continue all through the academic year."

"So how did this sponsorship work?"

"At the monthly meeting we had to pick three jokes that would be played the following month."

"You were a member of this club?"

"Yes, Deirdre persuaded me to join. I think she only joined because she fancied Hastings who was a friend of some guy she knew. Anyway, once the jokes had been agreed, each of the members had to pledge a certain amount of money to pay if it was completed successfully. You had to show evidence that it had been done, normally a photograph. The more daring the stunt, the more money you had to pledge. It started off with buckets of water above doors and super-gluing staplers to desks but as time went on it got more daring."

"In what way?"

"During third year, Gregor was dared to steal the wheels from a vintage car owned by one of the professors. It was a beautiful open-top sports car, an Austin-Healey I think it was. He took on the challenge but the car toppled off the jacks he was using. He damaged the chassis and the bodywork of the car. Professor Turner was livid and threatened to throw the culprit out of the university but he never found out that it was Gregor."

"This all happened while you were at university. What about after you finished your degree? In 1983 to be precise."

The woman's anxious behaviour increased and suddenly she stood up. 'Can I get you something to drink?"

"No, that's fine Ms O'Donnell. Please take a seat and tell us what happened."

She perched herself on the edge of her chair. "The committee in charge of the club decided that we should keep it going. We would hold meetings every April Fool's Day and celebrate with a fund-raising event of some kind. In 1983, April the first fell on a Friday, so we decided to have a weekend event that included a dinner-dance thing at a country hotel out near Falkirk. Deirdre came up with this horrible practical joke for us to play." She stopped talking, looking guilty.

"I think you know that this might be very important. If it was something illegal and you were involved, we don't care. The murder is our only concern."

"No, it wasn't illegal just immoral. She came up with this idea where her and two other women would pretend to be attracted to three guys we knew from uni. She asked me to do it but I refused, so it was Deirdre and two other members of the club. The idea was that they would take these guys to their rooms and the woman who persuaded the guy to undress first would be the winner. There were three people with cameras who were meant to record what happened to each of the men. The three guys they picked as targets were the shy type, the ones who struggled to talk to women."

"So what happened that night?"

"Deirdre had organised the invitations to the three guys. They were told that they were going to be invited to join the club. The dinner started at seven-thirty and the women made sure they were sitting next to their targets. They plied the guys with drink; there may even have been drugs involved, I'm not sure. They spent the evening dancing and flirting with the men and at about eleven, Deirdre led her man up to the bedroom. The other two followed at five-minute intervals and the remainder of the club were split into three different groups. Deirdre had told us to wait half-an-hour to go up to the rooms. By this time everyone was pretty drunk and everybody thought that it would be a good laugh. It was far from it."

"What happened when you got to the room?"

"The three rooms were on the same floor, all next to one another. When the groups were in position, we waited until eleven-thirty five and that's when the three girls opened the doors. We all rushed into the rooms, each group had a camera to record how far the women had gone in getting the guys naked. Gregor had the camera for our group and when we burst in, we found Deirdre's conquest completely naked on the bed. His penis was erect but it was tiny and there was a lot of cruel mocking. He sprung up from the bed and went to throw a punch but Gregor put his arm up to protect himself and Roy punched the camera instead. The poor sod broke bones in his hand and damaged nerves."

"Roy?"

"Roy Dent, he was still a student when it happened. He was in the fourth year of studying medicine. I heard that he had to take a year out and that he had to change his plan to be a surgeon."

Wade reacted. "Sir, isn't tha…"

"Yes, D.C. Wade it is. Sorry, Ms O'Donnell, you were saying?"

"Apparently the nerve damage meant that he has a slight tremor in his hand, particularly when he is under stress. He had planned to become a surgeon like his father and grandfather but instead he had to choose something else. Forensic pathology, I think."

"Do you know who else was involved in the incident?"

"There were a few others in the room, including me, but I think Roy blamed Deirdre and Gregor." As she spoke the implications of her story became obvious to her. "You don't think that the murders are related to that night do you?"

Russell lied. "We don't know, but it's something we'll have to investigate."

She became contemplative. "I think that night was when my life started to go downhill."

"In what way?"

"I wasn't proud of my part in what happened and I cut myself off from anyone who was involved. I feel that I might not be isolated if I hadn't been there."

"What about your husband?"

"Buggered off. Left me with nothing thanks to a pre-nuptial agreement that his father made me sign before we were married. I was naive enough to believe that we were genuinely in love. We were divorced six years later as a result of 'unreconcilable differences' and the agreement was allowed to stand. Six months later he had moved to London with his new girlfriend He sends money for the kids but that's it."

"I'm sorry, it must be difficult."

"I made my bed, at least that's what my mother tells me." She offered a weary smile.

"D.C. Wade will take a formal statement from you just now if that's OK, that'll save you a journey."

"Shame, I could have done with a day out, even if it was just a trip to the police station." Her eyes lit up with genuine humour, even if it was laced with pathos.

"I'll just have a word with my colleague in private if you don't mind." Russell indicated with his head the Wade should join him in the hall.

"Sir?"

"Get as much detail as you can. I think we may have broken this case but don't let her know just how important this is. Don't tell her what our suspicions are. I don't want her clamming up because she gets scared."

"You can rely on me, sir."

"I'll send someone to pick you up but I'm going to head back into town."

"That's fine, I think the poor woman will appreciate the company."

"I'm going after Dent before he kills again, wish me luck."

CHAPTER 17

R ussell walked to the car but before he could do anything he had to speak to McLelland.

When the chief superintendent answered, Russell said, "Sir, I need a word urgently."

"What's up?"

"I'd rather not say on the phone. Where are you?"

"I'm still in my office at Pitt Street."

"I'm in Moodiesburn, I'll see you in twenty minutes."

He started the car as he put the phone into his pocket. He debated with himself whether it was important enough to merit the lights and sirens before deciding he couldn't risk Dent getting away because he'd driven too slowly. He lit them up when he reached the main road and drove quickly but safely back into the city centre.

When he reached the headquarters building he swiped his pass without even acknowledging the officer at the front desk. He raced up the stairs two at a time to get to the second floor. McLelland was waiting for him when he arrived at his office.

"What the hell's up, Tom?'

"I think I know who the Harlequin is, and you're not going to like it."

"Who?"

"I think it's Dr Roy Dent."

"The pathologist?" McLelland said with a surprised laugh, but the smile soon evaporated from his face as he realised that Russell wasn't joking. "You're serious. Why?"

Russell sat down and began the long story of the Jester's Balls club. He took his time detailing every stage of the tale in the same way that O'Donnell had laid it out for him.

He finished up by saying, "Dent had access to the hallucinogens, he obviously has medical skills and he was privy to the information on the Blakes' deaths."

"I don't believe this. Have we got anything substantive on him?"

"No, all we've got is the woman's story. It's going to be tough trying to prove it; he knows forensic procedures as well as anyone. We might be able to trace the money he used to pay the promotions company but even that might not be enough."

"Fuck, this is a mess," McLelland shook his head, lay back in his chair and stared at the ceiling.

"What do you want me to do?"

The chief superintendent moved forward again. "We'll need a forensic accountant to check the Harlequin's Tears Company and who might be involved. Dent will probably have buried his connection with the company and it'll take an expert to unpick it."

Russell sighed. "I think in the interim, we should put surveillance on Dent."

McLelland wished they could arrest Dent and get him off the streets but without evidence they wouldn't be able to hold him very long. Dent would know how little they had, and he knew exactly how the system worked. He could only hope that Dent wouldn't make a move before they could find the proof they needed to prosecute the case.

"I can start the surveillance right now."

McLelland nodded. "Are you sure? He's bound to know your face."

"I'll need to be the secondary, we'll need at least one other person."

"We need to keep the number of people involved in this to a bare minimum. People we can trust. I know Dent might not be the most popular guy in the world and I doubt he's got many friends in the force, but if someone leaks this and he finds out, he'll be off and we'll never get our hands on him."

"What about Ellen Clarkson? She was helpful to me during my brief exile."

"You contact her directly, you'll need the backup immediately, I'll clear the paperwork later."

"Will do."

As Russell stood to leave, McLelland said, "You are sure about this, Tom? If we're wrong we'll be lucky to be pounding the beat when they're done with us."

"It's the only thing that makes any sense," Russell replied, confident that his instincts were right.

"Get to it and god help us all."

***

In order to watch him, Russell had to find out where Dent was. Marriot had said that Dent was taking the day off and he hoped his quarry was at home but he had to be sure.

Russell dialled the number for mortuary; he was gambling that he might get Dent's home address from them. It was probably in the police records somewhere but he wanted to short cut procedures a little.

"Hi, it's Detective Inspector Russell, I was wondering if Dr Dent was available."

"Hi Inspector Russell, it's Graham Rowson here."

"Hi Graham," Russell presumed from the man's tone that he must have met him some time in the past but had no memory of it. There were a number of forensic pathology technicians at the morgue and they tended to work quietly in the background anytime Russell visited. Rowson wasn't a name he recognised.

"No, I'm afraid he' got the day off. It's Doctor Thompson and Professor Marriot today. Do you want to speak to either of them?"

"No, it's Doctor Dent I need to talk to. I need him to clarify something in an old post mortem report. It doesn't tie with my notes and I want to be sure I've got my facts straight before I take this to court."

"Is it urgent because Dr Dent is due to go to a conference this weekend in Birmingham, so he won't be available until Monday?"

"Do you think I could maybe get his home address, it's just that the case is due to start tomorrow."

"I suppose so. He's not far from here, he's over in St. Andrew's Square in fact. I could pop over and get him if you like."

"No, it's fine. If you give me the number I'll go visit him. It'll get me out of the office."

He supplied the number and Russell thanked him.

Was Dent really going to a conference or was it some attempt at an alibi or even worse escape? Was his need for revenge satiated by killing Hastings or were there other targets that he was planning to go after in the next few days? Russell couldn't afford to let those thoughts creep in; he had a job to do.

He dialled Ellen Clarkson's number.

"D.S. Clarkson."

"Ellen, it's me. I need you to help me with some surveillance. You have to keep it to yourself, so make some excuse to the others. It's vital that you don't say where you're going."

"I understand," she said her voice sounded flat and disinterested.

"I'll meet you at St Andrew's Square as soon as you can possibly get there."

"Yes, that's fine."

Russell could sense that she was desperate to ask what was going on but she had managed to maintain the pretence that the phone call was of no consequence. Secrecy between detectives wasn't a normal part of working on a murder case and Russell hoped that she respected what he had told her.

***

He waited impatiently at one corner of St. Andrew's Square hoping that Dent wouldn't leave before Clarkson could arrive. The time ticked on and Russell's anxiety increased. Finally, after twenty minutes Ellen Clarkson pulled her Ford Focus up behind his car. She got out and Russell met her on the pavement.

"You made it. Any problems?"

"No, I just told them I was checking a witness statement."

"Good. I know this is going to sound crazy but I think Roy Dent is the Harlequin."

"The pathologist? You're kidding."

"No, it's a long story but he has a link to both Deirdre Nichol and Gregor Hastings. That link is strong enough to give him a motive."

Clarkson looked stunned as she said, "What's the plan?"

"We have to keep an eye on him while the chief super tries to find some evidence that will stand up in court. All we've got is a story from twenty years ago and a lot of circumstantial evidence. Have you had many dealings with him?"

"No, not really. I worked one scene that he was the attending pathologist at but I doubt he even noticed me."

"He knows me all too well but there's no one else we can use at the moment. We need to keep this between ourselves, we can't afford Dent getting wind of it."

"Hence the secret squirrel stuff."

"That's it. Right, let's make a start. You see if there's a parking space around the corner that will give you a view of his flat. I'll go round to Steel Street and pick you up as you go by. I'm not sure if he'll recognise my car but I don't want to take the chance that I'll spook him."

"OK, sir."

"Keep your radio on, it'll be quicker than using the phone."

They returned to their cars and drove to their respective vantage points. Clarkson drove halfway round the gentrified square, where she had a perfect view of the block where Dent lived. Russell found a space in Steel Street, on the edge of Glasgow Green.

It was close to three o'clock when they settled in to their respective places. At four-twenty a traffic warden approached Russell's car but a flash of his warrant card was enough to make the woman walk on and turn her interest to another vehicle further along the street. Shortly after she left, raindrops started to patter gently onto the windscreen.

Steel Street leads to the road known as Saltmarket. Due to its proximity to the High Court, the street is popular with lawyers. These aren't the sumptuous, elegant chambers of the Inns of Court that flourish in the shadow of the Old Bailey in London; they are slightly sleazy shop fronts where the drug addicts and thieves could find a solicitor to defend them in their latest brush with the law. Russell tried to avoid watching the parade of solicitors and criminals walking passed his car, there were too many who would know his face.

Time moved like a snail and Russell's concerns grew, maybe Dent had slipped away while he was waiting on Clarkson. At six o'clock the rush hour traffic was just beginning to subside as a black taxi pulled up outside Dent's block. Clarkson could barely see it through the rain that was now falling steadily and blurring her windscreen.

"Sir," Clarkson's voice disturbed the quiet interior of Russell's car.

"Ellen?"

"There's a black cab outside his flat."

"Let me know if it's for him."

Silence descended again as she watched the door of the building intently and Russell drummed gently on his steering wheel.

Dent emerged a couple of minutes later wheeling a suitcase.

"Here he comes," Clarkson announced.

"I'm set, Ellen," Russell said as he started the engine of his car.

The detective sergeant moved out as the taxi pulled away from the kerb. The taxi turned into Steel Street and then left on to the Saltmarket with Ellen about two cars back. Russell pulled out but the lights at the junction turned red before he could follow them through and he had to stop.

"Shit," he said as he pulled up at the junction. "Have you got him Ellen?"

"The taxi has turned on to Clyde Street," she replied.

"Keep them in your sights. I'll be with you as soon as I can "

The traffic lights ran through the full sequence before Russell was able to drive off in pursuit.

"Ellen, where are you?"

"Still on Clyde Street."

Russell turned right on to the street that followed the course of the river. He sped through the junction at Stockwell Street just as the lights were about to halt his progress. He drove past St. Andrew's Catholic Cathedral and on towards Jamaica Street.

"We're going under the bridge, sir," Clarkson announced.

"Understood."

A few seconds later she said, "We're turning into Oswald Street, I think he's going to Central Station."

Russell was stopped by another red light, this time on the junction with Jamaica Street and screamed a curse in frustration. What should he do? If Dent got on a train, he might never return, but if he tried to take him in they might lose their only chance. When the lights did change he accelerated quickly, drawing an angry blast of a horn as he cut in front of a bus, he drove under the railway bridge and turned towards Hope Street.

"Confirmed, sir. He's going into the station."

"Follow him in but don't get too close."

"Yes, sir."

He had another brief stop for traffic lights at the intersection of Oswald Street and Argyle Street before driving up the ramp that led into the old railway station. The tight spiral opened out on to the broad concourse and in to the short-stay car park. A taxi was moving towards the exit ramp and Russell caught a glimpse of Dent walking in the direction of the platforms through the rank of parked vehicles. He passed Ellen Clarkson's Focus just as she was getting out and he managed to find a space at the very end of the same row.

He rushed to join the detective sergeant. "I'm not sure how to play this, Ellen," he confessed.

"I don't think we can let him leave the city, sir," she replied.

"No, I suppose not. I'll follow him to the train, you wait at the end of the platform."

They walked swiftly to the departure board where they discovered that the Birmingham train was due to leave from platform 2 at twenty-five to seven. The long sleek form of the bright red and grey train was pulling to a halt at the buffers just as the two detectives arrived at the end of the platform.

"Ring the chief super, we might need backup. Wait here and make sure Dent doesn't make a run for it."

Russell began to walk up the long platform that was crowded with passengers disembarking from another train as well as the people waiting to board the Birmingham-bound coaches. While trying to spot his quarry he had to dodge the surging current of people and luggage trolleys heading for the exit. He finally saw Dent waiting to board the first-class coach at the far end of the train. The doors slid open with a sigh of air and he watched as Dent lifted his case onto the train.

His heart pounding, he climbed the steps on to the carriage two down from the coach Dent had chosen. He rushed through the buffet car, where he attracted a stare from one of the train crew before walking through an empty first-class compartment. When the door slid open and he stepped into the final coach, he could see a lone figure. Dent looked up from his bag and straight at the detective. Russell thought he could sense a little bit of disquiet in the pathologist's glance but it was replaced by a strained smile as the detective approached. The smile was the clue that Dent was both surprised and disturbed at the sight of Russell bearing down on him.; Dent smiled very rarely.

"Detective Inspector Russell, are you off on a trip?" he said as he sat down.

"No, doctor. We need to talk."

"I'm off to Birmingham for a conference. If it's about the post mortems from Tuesday you will have to speak to Dr Thompson, I'm afraid?"

"I don't think that anyone can answer these particular questions other than you."

"Take a seat, we've got fifteen minutes before the train is due to depart," Dent said reasonably.

"I'd rather we did this back at the police station, if you don't mind. I'm afraid you won't be going to any conference this weekend."

"It all sounds a bit ominous, inspector. Have I done something wrong?" Russell was impressed at how well Dent had regained his composure but he did notice the smallest of tremors in the physician's right hand.

"Please, doctor I don't want this to be difficult. I think you probably know why I need to talk to you. I've spoken to someone who was a member of the Jester's Balls' club. Someone who was there in 1983 and they've told me what happened at the hotel."

"Ah, yes." His poise disappeared and a momentary look of rage crossed his face.

"I'd like you to accompany me back to the station and we can talk about what happened to you. What transpired that night was truly awful and I'm sure you would like to tell your story."

"I'm sure you'd like that, inspector. Listening to my tale of humiliation and pain." His bitterness was no longer rippling below the surface; it was beginning to swell into something menacing.

"Not at all. I want to hear your version of events."

"I'm sure." Dent stood up and Russell was relieved to see that the doctor seemed resigned to his fate.

"I'll need to get my case." He pointed to the end of the carriage where the luggage was stored.

Russell led the way towards it and waited at the door while Dent lifted his bag from the rack and placed it on to the floor. The detective stepped on to the platform and turned to help the doctor with his case. Dent launched the luggage at him and it knocked an unsuspecting Russell to the ground. Leaping over the prostrate man, Dent turned and ran towards the end of the platform in the direction of the tracks.

Russell, feeling both angry and embarrassed, pushed the case aside and got to his feet. The pathologist had a thirty-yard start and Russell was horrified to see him running towards the expanse of track that led away from the station. With no other option he ran after the man he now believed to be a killer.

The station is the main terminal for a number of services to and from the city, including the mainline trains to London. Russell chased Dent out on to the busy matrix of interconnecting tracks. Slow moving trains rumbled to and from the station as Dent ran out on to the bridge across the Clyde. Russell tried to keep sight of his quarry while worrying about the deadly engines and wheels that would slice him to ribbons if they caught him during their journey over the rails. He followed Dent across three sets of parallel tracks and watched in horror as the killer raced in front of an oncoming multiple unit painted in the blue and purple livery of ScotRail The driver blew the horn and Russell turned away expecting the worse. When he looked back the train was rolling past. He stood within the safe haven of one of the pillars that held the signal gantry; his view of Dent was blocked. When the train had finally rolled by, he could see Dent running towards the edge of the bridge. With a quick glance to either side, he ran after the doctor, lifting his feet to clear the rails and being careful not to put them down where points might close on them. Every breath was painful as the fear and effort threatened to overcome him.

When the detective looked up once more he could see Dent climbing the ironwork at the edge of the bridge. He stood briefly and glanced back at his pursuer before jumping off and into the River Clyde some way below.

"No," Russell shouted in vain. He reached the point from where Dent had leapt, clambered up the iron structure and tried to see into the dark waters. The river was being rippled by the strong breeze that was blowing, as well as the constant rhythm of the rain. Russell wasn't sure whether some of those ripples were the result of Dent's plunge, but what he knew for sure was that there was no sign of his prey.

"D.S. Clarkson," he shouted into this radio.

"Sir, where are you?"

"Out on the bridge, Dent jumped into the river, I'm going after him. Ring McLelland and get the boat out and as many officers as possible along the banks."

"Into the river?" she asked.

"Yes, just do as you're told."

"Yes, sir."

As the conversation finished, Russell took off his jacket - which held both his radio and phone - climbed the iron lattice and jumped into the black depths thirty-five feet below. The chilling water shocked his body and he struggled not to take a breath that would have resulted in a lungful of river. He was momentarily disorientated, not sure which way was up. He relaxed enough to let his buoyancy take hold and he then kicked his legs to take him to the surface. He gasped in a welcome breath of air and tried to get his bearings. The combination of the railway bridge and the George IV road bridge robbed that part of the river of any illumination. He used his arms to propel him in a circle as he searched for any sign of Dent. The short waves in the river lapping against him added to his problems as he tried to pick out any sign of the doctor. He swam for a short time downriver but it was obvious that Dent was nowhere to be seen. As the cold began to overcome him, he swam to a jetty and hauled himself out. As a result of the entertainment he had provided, the people who lined the banks greeted him with cheers but he didn't feel like responding in a positive way.

He peered into the water, hoping that Dent's body would float to the surface but in his heart he knew another chance had gone. There were now several police cars, an ambulance and a fire crew on the quay above the river. The paramedics came and offered him a blanket and asked him if he wanted to go with them to the hospital to be checked out but he refused. A few minutes later he was joined by McLelland who had been directed to where he was by a combination of the emergency service personnel and the gawping Glaswegians who had watched the drama unfold.

"What the hell happened, Tom?'

Russell recited the story through chattering teeth as the cold continued to penetrate into his bones. As he told the whole sorry tale, he was both resigned to, and frustrated by his failure

"We'll keep searching, he can't have got far," McLelland said by way of encouragement.

A systematic search was organised along the riverbanks but there was no sign of the doctor, neither alive nor dead. The fading light meant that the diving team could not be deployed that night and they would have to wait until the following day to make a detailed underwater survey.

Ellen Clarkson arrived carrying his jacket; an officer from the British Transport Police had retrieved it from the bridge. The group stood huddled on the quay for an hour, hoping that some sign of Dent would appear somewhere along the great stretch of water but their wait was in vain.

Bitterly disappointed, the senior officers returned to Pitt Street. Russell was still wrapped in the blanket from the ambulance as they briefed an extremely annoyed A.C.C. Dunsmore.

"You should have waited for backup, Tom," Dunsmore admonished.

"I know sir but I didn't have much time to make the call," Russell said defensively.

"Let's hope that we find his body because I doubt we're going to catch him alive, do you?"

McLelland felt protective towards Russell and he was tempted to tell his superior where to go but instead he muttered, "We've circulated his picture to all forces across the country, sir, so there's still a chance."

"That's twice he's slipped away. We're in for a time of it from the press."

Russell was feeling cold, miserable and angry but he bit his tongue, the obsession with the press really rankled when there were victims families who were the ones that the senior officers should be focusing on. He simply said, "Yes, sir."

"I think you should take a little time off D.I. Russell, while Chief Superintendent McLelland and I clean up your mess."

"Yes, sir."

"Get out of my sight." He dismissed Russell with a wave of his hand.

Russell thought about throwing his warrant card across the desk and walking away from his job but being a detective meant too much to him. Instead he slammed the door and retreated down the corridor and into himself.

CHAPTER 18

The following days got even worse for Russell. The search for Dent proved to be fruitless, both in the water and on land. Some of the detective team were of the opinion that Dent must have drowned but as he had once been on the university swimming team, that seemed unlikely. It was impossible to say whether he had drifted downstream, swam upstream to a quieter area of the city or if he had climbed out of the river before the police could react but it amounted to the same thing, he had escaped justice once again.

The press were all too aware what had happened as there were plenty of passengers on the trains who had witnessed the chase and Dent and Russell jumping into the river. Police competence was questioned and analysed by the broadsheets, the tabloids gloried in the failings and called for heads to roll. Questions about Special Branch's role in diverting resources of the investigation for no good reason were never asked because no one was ever told.

One week after Dent had escaped, Russell was called to an enquiry to identify what went wrong. A panel of three senior officers from Lothian & Borders put his decisions under close scrutiny. McLelland and Clarkson were also put in the spotlight for their part in the failure to catch the Harlequin. Russell had warned Ellen Clarkson that she should tell the panel that she was following orders and although she argued the point with him, she finally gave in. It was two weeks before the report came back. McLelland was censured for failure to control an officer under his command. Ellen Clarkson was excused of all blame although she was warned to ensure that she worked within standard procedures. Russell was heavily criticised for poor decision-making in light of flimsy evidence and was told that he would be ineligible for promotion for three years. The report did admit that he was probably correct in his identification of the culprit but believed he had handled it badly. He was withdrawn from the pool of officers dedicated to murder investigation and reassigned to the squad that looked into illegally imported, and fake goods. It was a demotion in all but name but he didn't care, no punishment they could have suggested would have been as bad as knowing that he had failed to capture the killer.

* * *

Over the next ten years, Russell's thoughts would drift to the Harlequin every time the first of April came around, dreading what might happen but as time slipped away, a hope that it was finally over began to take root in his thoughts. He had no idea how wrong he would be.

PART THREE

April 1st 2013

CHAPTER 19

Karen Russell looked at her reflection in the full-length mirror, adjusted her hair one more time and then straightened her skirt. She was ready for her big day.

This day was important because she had an opportunity to sell a substantial property that would net her the largest commission she had ever received from a single sale. In the six years since she had become an estate agent, she had done fairly well selling the family homes and flats that made up much of Glasgow's housing market, but today was different. The property she was going to visit was a substantial old farmhouse that had been renovated and modernised, it was surrounded by a large tract of land and could sell for a seven-figure sum. When the client called the office he had asked specifically for Karen and she was desperate to ensure that she would be the one who would complete the deal. It was unusual to have to work on Easter Sunday, but the client insisted it was the only day he was available. From what she could gather he was an Italian property developer who had been in Scotland for a short time. His name was Ruggero Pagliacci and Karen hoped that he would have those classic Italian looks. In her fantasy she thought that maybe she could be more than his estate agent, but she knew it was only wishful thinking. He was probably balding, fat and in his sixties.

With one final glance in the mirror, she picked up her handbag and mobile phone, locked the door of her flat and headed to her car.

***

The house was out in the shadow of the Ochil Hills in Stirlingshire, a forty-minute drive from Glasgow city centre. Despite April being only a day away, small flakes of snow were falling in occasional flurries as she drove out to the house. All across the country, winter was still holding spring at bay as trees remained bare and the daffodil flowers were still tucked up in the warmth of their buds.

She had left herself plenty of time to make the journey, worried that work on the roads or the weather would delay her. She was desperate to be on time to make sure that her relationship with the client didn't get off to a bad start. A slight delay on the M80 due to workers filling in potholes was all that hampered her and she turned into the drive of the house five minutes ahead of schedule. The drive was lined with large pine trees and when she pulled up in front of the house, she could see that the description of the property she had been told to expect was on the modest side. This was no farmhouse, but a glorious villa in the Scottish Baronial style. She was already calculating a possible selling price and the commission she would earn from it.

At the door of the house there was a gloss black BMW 5 series, but there was no sign of the owner. She crunched her way across the gravel in front of the house and rang the doorbell. The old-fashioned bell rang faintly somewhere deep in the house. There was no reply, and she tried once more but there was still no sign of life in the great building. She stepped back on to the gravel and made her way around to the back of the house. There was a garage and a small block of stables at the rear and she shouted, "Hello, Signor Pagliacci. Is there anyone here?"

Once again there was nothing to suggest that there was anyone else on the property and a little flicker of fear made its way into her mind. She walked closer to the stables and called out once again. When there was still no sign that the client was going to appear she turned with the intention of waiting in her car, suddenly she heard the sound of another foot on the gravel. Before she could turn to see who it was she felt a hand grab her around the waist and another was clamped to her mouth. Her nose was engulfed in a smell that was both sweet and antiseptic, and caused her to feel light-headed. The Chloroform fumes soon overtook her and her legs folded. As she was about to lapse into unconsciousness she realised that Signor Pagliacci was not who he claimed to be; instead of her Italian fantasy, she was staring up into a cruel mask. The Harlequin's face grinned back at her and then the world turned black.

***

Hayley McLelland was puzzled when she received a mysterious e-mail from her father; it wasn't like him to be so spontaneous. It read:

> Hayley,
> Meet me at the graveyard at Cadder Church in Bishopbriggs at 7pm. I've got a surprise for you. No questions.
> Dad

She knew that since he had retired he had become passionate about tracing the family tree and she could only imagine that he had found something significant in the old churchyard. Why he couldn't wait until tomorrow when they were due to go for lunch she couldn't imagine. She knew there was no point in phoning him to see what it was all about; ever since she was small he had loved to delight her with something new and exciting, he would never tell her what this mystery was. Although she didn't share his enthusiasm for the ancestry project, if it kept him happy it would be worth the trip.

Due to the holiday, the traffic was relatively light as she made her way out to the suburbs. Only five miles from the city centre and she could see the Campsie Hills and surrounding countryside. She thought that living in a huge city where you could drive for hours without seeing a field must be awful.

The sun was beginning to set between the clouds that carried wintry showers across the landscape and there was a pink tinge to the light. She turned into Cadder Road, made her way over the Forth & Clyde Canal via a narrow bridge and found her way to the church. The Easter services were obviously over, as the only car she could see was a black BMW. She checked her watch it was five-past seven. It wasn't like her father to be late. Having never visited the church before she decided to wander around while she waited for him. The ancient gravestones were uneven and on many of them the engraved text had been worn away by rain, wind and time. She had been walking for about five minutes and there was still no sign of her father. As she reached the point of the graveyard furthest from the entrance she felt that there was someone watching her. She turned to see a man wearing a mask, a manic grin painted on it. She was about to scream when he punched her hard in the solar plexus. The wind rushed from her lungs and her scream died on her lips. His hand covered her mouth and she slipped into a deep sleep.

***

Joseph O'Donnell was ready for a party. He had spent the afternoon with his mother and his sister having Sunday lunch. His mother had insisted he be there as it was Easter Sunday, but he had no idea why that made any difference; his mother hadn't been in a church since she was divorced from his father and it seemed weird to celebrate when she no longer believed. He had been the dutiful son and stayed until the meal was over and hung around reluctantly for a short time to keep his mother happy.

He had received a text from Gerry, a mate he had met at uni. There was a big party tonight at a flat in the West End and Gerry promised that it was going to be a cracker. By the time Joe got back to his own digs in the halls of residence in Port Dundas it was already eight o'clock. After he had showered and dressed it had gone nine but that was still early to make an appearance at a party. There was a bottle of vodka in his bedroom and he poured himself a large one. It was always good to have a little something to get the party started. He felt the liquid burn its way to his stomach and he was ready to go. He pulled on a leather jacket, locked up his room and walked out into the chill air. He had only gone two steps when he felt someone come up behind him and a hand was placed across his nose and mouth. As his knees buckled, the unseen person caught him. The last thing he focused on was a clown beaming a creepy smile at him.

CHAPTER 20

Tom Russell's Easter weekend had not been one he was going to remember with any fondness. 'Good Friday' had been anything but, and it didn't get any better from there.

He had spent Friday morning at a briefing session all about the new Police Scotland organisation that was about to replace the eight regional forces on the first of April. Despite all the political posturing, it was simply an exercise in saving money and some of the details had caused both the public and serving officers some concern. At the briefing Russell and the rest of the detectives at Helen Street station were given more information about how they could now be assigned to any major incident across the whole of Scotland. No longer were they restricted to Glasgow and the surrounding area. They could be called to an incident in Aberdeen or Wick at a moment's notice. The worst thing was that for many places across the country they would have to travel to and from the scene every day. There was no money in the budget for a hotel room for the length of an inquiry. The braid had already dismissed the general principle that local knowledge would be required to adequately investigate any crime, but the specifics of how the new system was going to work had brought the detectives grievances into sharp focus. Russell was not one of those that voiced his concerns; he was too long in the tooth to expect common sense to prevail among those who ran the police force in Scotland. He had a good idea that the first time an Edinburgh 'polis' turned up to lead an investigation in Glasgow there would be a great deal of resentment, and the same was true for any Glaswegian detective going anywhere else. In truth, as the city with the most detectives, it was more likely that the 'Weegies' would be the ones to be sent elsewhere, with all the discontent that would create. He decided there was no point in worrying about it; the job would be the same just with added complications and extra mileage.

Friday afternoon brought him far more personal and immediate problems.

Andy McKinley was a detective that Russell had known for over ten years but when he turned up in Russell's office it wasn't for a social visit to catch up on old times. McKinley was now part of the Ethics and Standards department; the team who were responsible for dealing with public complaints and ensuring that the force was free of corruption and unethical behaviour. Despite the majority of cops hating those within the ranks who were 'bent', the officers of the E&S were regarded as traitors who ended careers and were, to a sizable number of officers, as much the enemy as any career criminal

"Andy?" Russell said when McKinley's considerable bulk filled his office doorway.

"Can I have a word?" he asked as he closed the door behind him.

Russell was already wary, there was no warmth in McKinley's demeanour. "Sure, what's up?"

"I shouldn't be doing this but I'm here because we go back a long way and I think you need to be told. You're about to be investigated."

Russell's stomach flipped. "I see. What about?"

"Your relationship with Malky McGavigan, and in particular the deaths of two Serbian nationals back in January. A team is coming from Dundee to begin the investigation on Tuesday. I hope you've got your story straight, Tom."

"There's no story to get straight. There is no relationship between me and McGavigan other than he's a villain and I'm a cop who would like to see him rot in jail."

"I don't think that's how other people see it. I've told you; it's up to you what you do with the information but I wasn't here. Understand?"

"Fine Andy."

McKinley turned to leave when Russell said, "And thanks."

The visitor walked away without another word.

Russell blew out a long breath and cursed his brother. "Eddie, you're a fucking useless bastard."

Eddie Russell's gambling had landed him in hot water with a Serbian gangster and he had turned to his brother to help him out. Malky McGavigan had taken care of it on Tom's behalf in a way that wasn't quite what Russell had intended, and now it looked like it was about to come back and haunt him.

Russell picked up his phone and tapped on Alex Menzies name.

"Sir?"

"You going out with Noel tonight?"

"No, he's on-call. Why?"

"Fancy a beer?"

"Sure, what's up?"

"Nothing, just fancied a beer, that's all."

Alex wasn't fooled, there was something wrong with her boss and the only way she was going to find out what was bothering him was to join him for that drink. A quiet night of telly and a glass of wine disappeared as she said, "OK."

"I'll get you in the Station Bar at seven, I'll leave the car in Stewart Street overnight."

If he was going to leave the car it was obvious it was going to be a long session for him. Alex would settle for an orange juice while she listened to whatever was eating at him.

***

The bar was quieter than on a normal Friday night and the two detectives managed to find a table. After they had bought their first round, Alex settled into the chair opposite Russell and waited.

He took a deep draught of his pint of Schiehallion ale and sighed. "Complaints are after me."

"What? Why?"

Russell began to tell her what Andy McKinley had told him. When he was finished Alex asked, "How much of it is true?"

"Most of it, even if it's more innocent than it might appear."

"I remember you let McGavigan off with the assault charge when he swung that punch at you in the car wash."

"All I was trying to do was prevent a blood bath between the McGavigans and the Wrights. I thought that Malky McGavigan in prison would have exacerbated an already volatile situation. That was all I was thinking but I could see how it could be twisted into something else."

"Was that why he did you the other 'favour'?

"No, not at all. I promised him we would find who killed his son and we did. When the Serbian gorillas arrived there was no way to deal with them without my brother getting dragged in to it."

"Did you tell McGavigan to kill them?"

He looked shocked. "Absolutely not. I thought that he would get his goons to scare them off. I suppose I should have known better."

"Sir. I'll do what I can to help. Tell me what you want me to say."

"Naw, that's not on, Alex. You tell them what you remember from that time and if I have to fall on my sword, then that's what I'll have to do but I'm not taking you down with me."

"If you're sure."

"I am. Thanks anyway."

They sat drinking for another two hours, Russell slipping slowly into a drunken, morose mood while Alex watched, concerned. She drove him home and advised him to get a good night's sleep.

He waved unsteadily as she drove away and when he arrived in his flat, walked to the kitchen to retrieve a glass and a bottle of 18 year-old Macallan Malt Whisky. He slumped into his sofa, poured a glass and tried to drown his sorrows.

***

He spent his Saturday morning nursing a raging thirst and a thumping head. As it needed to be done, he cleaned his flat, avoiding the use of the vacuum cleaner as his head would not have been able to stand the noise.

Around two o'clock he had recovered enough to start thinking coherently again. All of this was Eddie's fault and it was time he took some responsibility for his own mess. Tom had not heard from his errant brother since the Serbian incident in January. His mobile number was no longer in service and Tom presumed that Eddie had gone to ground to avoid any further problems with the Serbian thugs. Finding him may prove difficult but Tom had a good idea where to start.

***

The journey into the city centre on a crowded and warm train did not help him feel any better. By the time he disembarked at Queen Street station he was sweating and felt nauseous. He was pleased to feel the fresh, crisp air fill his lungs when he walked out on to the street.

His destination was a casino in Sauchiehall Street that he knew Eddie frequented when he was in Glasgow. Eddie's long-time friend, Chan Wu, was the owner of the Lucky Cat. Most of the bookmakers and casino owners in the city saw his brother as a pal, due in large part to his generous donations to their businesses, but Chan's was a different kind of friendship. He had been at school with him and was one of the few people to stick with Eddie through his various trials and tribulations. For reasons that were never explained to Tom, everyone referred to Chan as Clarty; a word that normally means dirty in the West of Scotland. Eddie did tell Tom that it had nothing to do with his cleanliness, but even Tom's best investigative techniques couldn't persuade his brother to reveal the secret of the less than complimentary nickname.

Clarty had a bit of a reputation within the police of the city as being someone who walked a very delicate wire between legitimate businessman and being a chancer. Nothing had ever been proven but rumours persisted of the casino's private gaming rooms being for more than one kind of game that patrons had to pay for. The kind of two-sided game where only one person ever got any money and was normally played horizontally. It was not legal and would generate considerable interest in Mr Chan's establishment from the vice squad should he ever be caught. Tom expected his brother to have friends exactly like the casino owner, never out and out villains, but the type of people who liked to live on the edge.

The Lucky Cat was on the second floor of an old, scruffy red sandstone building. Russell showed his credentials at the door and asked if Chan was available. The woman behind the desk was a pale waif with dyed black hair. She was thin to the point of emaciation, her skin paper white as if she had been blanched due to the low light of the casino; there was no need for pigment when the place was nearly as dark as a subterranean cave. She asked Russell to sit while she called through to Chan's office.

The gaming floor was busy with hopeful gamblers, praying to the fates that they would be kind to them for once. The vast majority were from the city's Chinese community that was centred in nearby Garnethill. There was also a tall, broad man playing Blackjack. He had Mediterranean features and a long, drooping moustache. He was casually tossing £500 chips on to the table as the cards turned. Russell shivered at the thought of throwing away that amount of money on the turn of a card.

The casino was decorated in a seventies retro style that was meant to be kitsch, but somehow seemed more like a journey back in time. Back to when 'Glesga' wore a blue boiler suit, sported a perm and smoked Woodbines. Now Glasgow wore a veneer of designer fabrics and ate humous, to hide from prying eyes the Primark jeans and fried pizza suppers that constituted the truth for large parts of the city.

After five minutes sitting watching the tables, Russell noticed Chan weaving his way between the games and the patrons, as he came towards him. Although younger than Russell, the casino owner looked a lot older. His greying black hair was slicked to his head by a gel that made it shine like that of a painted mannequin. He wore narrow spectacles on his flat, broad face. His suit was pale grey; his shirt and tie were both the same shade of maroon, the tie decorated with a gold tie pin that bore the number eight. Grotesque, gem-encrusted, gold rings weighed down his hands. He managed to overcome the great mass of gold long enough to shake the detective's hand.

"Inspector, this is a pleasant surprise." The strained smile betrayed that the visit may have been a surprise, but it was a long way from being pleasant.

"It's detective superintendent now Clarty, I've had a promotion."

"Congratulations. What can I do for a man like yourself on this fine day?" he asked with artificial good humour.

"I need your help. I want to find that useless brother of mine and I'm hoping you'll be the man to point me in the right direction.

"Come to the office and we'll talk."

Chan led the slalom back across the gaming floor and into a corridor that was even darker than the main part of the casino. They walked past a series of doors that Russell knew were the controversial private spaces where members played poker games.

Chan's office was decorated in a mixture of Chinese and Western influences, but he had chosen the worst of both traditions rather than the best. A four feet high, sitting, ceramic tiger was a particular low point.

"Can I get you a drink?"

He was tempted to have a 'hair of the dog' cure to tackle the remaining tendrils of his hangover but instead he said, "No, thanks."

"You're looking for Eddie?"

"I am indeed, there's a few things I need to discuss urgently with him. Have you seen him?"

"Not since he was up in Glasgow in January."

"Were you one of the people he tried to tap for money?"

"Yes."

"Did you give him any?"

"I owed him a small amount from a win he had a few months back, but that was all."

"The phone number I've got for him is out of service. I imagine that someone like you, a good mate I mean, would like to know where he is. Particularly when he owes you money."

"Tom, it's not like that with Eddie and me, he's a pal."

"Even the best pals can wear on you if they're constantly in hock to you. Do you have a number or not?"

Chan diverted the question and asked one of his own, "What's this all about?"

"When he was here in January, did he mention to you that he was on the run from a Serbian gangster by the name of Dragovic?"

"He might have mentioned it."

"Aye, well he hauled me into the jaws of his fuck up with him and now it's come back to bite me on the arse. I want him to do something he finds near impossible; take responsibility for what he's done."

"I'm sorry for your troubles but it sounds as if Eddie's going to be in real bother if he comes back. He's my pal, why would I do that to him?" As he spoke, he lifted his hands from his desk in a pleading gesture.

"I might be about to lose my job and maybe my freedom. That's not going to happen because of that wee shite."

Chan became defensive. "I'm still not hearing an argument as to why I should drop Eddie in it."

"He's already in it. If I don't get some cooperation then you might find yourself being dropped in it. A wee call to HMRC and I'm sure they would check your books a bit closer, particularly the VAT. The vice boys might decide on a raid just to be sure that there's no immoral earnings being taken in your private rooms. Of course if that were to happen, the licensing committee might get a bit nervous and who knows what will happen to your casino then." Russell drove home the threats in a slow, calm manner with a smile playing round his lips.

Chan's face fell into fury. "Eddie's right about you, you're a bastard."

"That's as may be, but I don't want to shut you down. However, I am so desperate to speak to my brother that I will do anything it takes."

Chan opened a desk drawer and retrieved a pen. He scribbled a mobile phone number on a scrap of paper and handed it to Russell.

"Cheers. Do I get a free spin on the roulette?"

"Fuck off."

Russell laughed all the way back out on to Sauchiehall Street. It felt like the first relief he had enjoyed since McKinley's visit. He walked back to Stewart Street to pick up his car and then drove home, via a chip shop where he bought a haggis supper.

The supper consumed, he decided that now was as good a time as any to call Eddie.

"Hello," Eddie sounded worried.

"Hello, it's me."

"Oh, hi, how's it gaun?" It was a forced note of happiness; Eddie was expecting the worse.

"Shite, as a matter of fact. All of it because of you."

"Aw, Tam, don't be like that."

Tom had resolved to himself that he would try and stay on an even keel no matter the provocation, but Eddie managed to get under his skin within less than a minute. "Don't fuckin 'Tam' me ya useless prick. 'Don't be like that!' I'm up to my ears in a mess you created and I'm facing jail time as a result. You need to crawl out from under whatever rock you're hiding beneath and come take some responsibility for this."

"I don't know whit ye mean."

"Your little Serbian escapade. I've got the 'Complaints' squad crawling all over my arse and if they think for a minute that I helped the two Serbs to meet their maker, I'll be heading for prison. That's not going to happen. I'll drop you in it so far you'll need a decompression chamber to avoid getting the bends."

"Tam, ye widnae dae that tae yir wee brother."

"I will. I'll make something up that'll make things even worse for you. If you come back, you might be able to spin some tale about self-defence, but if you don't, I'll tell them that you planned the whole thing. Don't for a minute doubt that I will."

There was a long pause and Russell was determined he was not going to be the one to end it. At that precise moment Eddie was nothing more than a perpetrator as far as he was concerned.

"Ah, need tae think aboot this."

"You've got 'til Tuesday. Then I spill my guts and you'll sound like fuckin' Al Capone. Understand?"

"Right, aye. Ah'll speak tae ye later." He ended the call. Russell sighed and tossed his phone on to the couch beside him. He had no idea if Eddie would do the right thing but the chances were, come Tuesday he would be on his own.

The rest of his evening was spent staring blankly at the television; the bland Saturday night offering was a good soporific if nothing else. By the end of the day his hangover had finally gone completely and he was ready to go to bed when his mobile rang.

"Russell," he growled.

"Sorry to disturb you, sir. It's D.S. Weaver."

"Hi, Frank what can I do for you?"

"I know you're not on-call tonight but D.I. Harrison has developed shingles."

"What's happened?"

"A fight outside a bar, one man dead."

"Fuck." Russell said quietly.

"It's a Cat B. sir I can get someone else."

"No, it's fine, where is it?"

Weaver gave him the details.

When he arrived at the scene it was obvious that it was a straightforward case. It was just another Saturday night, another punch thrown, another head hitting the pavement too hard and two lives over; one literally, the other figuratively. There were enough witnesses to fill three courts and in the end it was almost like a practise exercise in paperwork.

He arrived back to his flat at three the following morning; the worry over McGavigan and the Serbs had crept back into his mind during his trip home. When he got in, he polished off the remainder of the whisky and blanked out most of Sunday while the Harlequin was out collecting his victims.

CHAPTER 21

K aren Russell woke with a fuzzy head, a dry mouth and an aching body. Even with her eyes open it was still nearly black and it took a while for them to adjust to what little light was available

Disorientated and confused, she couldn't figure out where she was nor how she got there. As she shook the fog from her mind she remembered the face of the Harlequin and the panic began to rise from deep within her, a primal fear that had her heart thumping in her chest and sweat appearing on her brow.

"Hello, is there anyone there? Where am I? Let me out of here."

There was no reply. She pushed herself to her feet, still feeling shaky from the effects of the anaesthetic; she rocked before finding her balance. She could hardly see her hands in front of her as she stepped forward, arms straight, trying to feel for obstacles. She took two steps when she kicked something and a metallic sound rang out. She jumped in fright and then stood in the silence waiting for the trembling to stop. She edged forward once more for about six short paces before her hands came up against a barrier. She moved her fingers over it, feeling the cold metal that was arranged in a mesh. She realised that she was in a cage of some kind and suddenly the dread rolled over and threatened to suffocate her.

She croaked a weak plea, "Hello, is there anybody there?" Please."

She was startled once again when a voice to her left said, "Help me."

"Who's there?" Karen asked trying to not sound as scared as she felt.

"Where are we? What's happened?"

"I don't know. What's your name?"

"Hayley," the voice replied.

"Hayley, I'm Karen. It's going to be alright." She wasn't convincing herself, never mind the other woman, but she thought it was important to at least make an attempt to reassure her.

"What is this place?"

"I don't know, but you need to stay calm and we'll work it out."

"Help." Another voice, this time on Karen's right. It was a young man.

"Hello. I'm Karen."

"Help," he mumbled again.

A door opened and painfully bright light flooded into the space. It was so bright that all three captives blinked and shielded their eyes until a shadowy figure stood in the doorway.

"Welcome ladies and gentleman, contestants, to the Harlequin Carnival."

***

Monday was a bank holiday, but it was also the first day of the new Police Scotland organisation. As a result, there was no rest for the detectives. Russell woke to the sound of his radio at seven o'clock. His heart sank when the D.J. said, "It's April the first, 2013. What jokes have you got planned for this holiday Monday?"

It was April Fool's Day and the year ended in three. Russell hoped that there would be no reappearance of the Harlequin but a gnawing, grating feeling in the pit of his gut would not go away.

He showered and then dressed in a crisp white shirt, dark blue tie and dark grey suit. His polished shoes, gold cufflinks and tie clip completed his usual business dress.

For once the drive to Helen Street Station in Govan was brisk on the near-empty roads. He acknowledged some of his colleagues as he walked through the open plan area to his own office at the far end of the second floor of the building.

After hanging up his coat, he settled down at his desk, waiting for the computer to spin into life. His office included a private coffee machine that kept him supplied all day, much to the disgust of some of the other detectives. He brewed a cup and by the time it was ready, his computer was sitting at the login screen.

He needed to check some details of the manslaughter case from Saturday night before he could sign it off and pass it to the Procurator Fiscal's office. There was also the ever-present list of e-mails to plough through, a constantly high number that never seemed to diminish. That morning there were one hundred and forty-five unread mails in his inbox.

"Bloody hell, where does all this crap come from?" he muttered.

There were a number of mails regarding the new organisation, some of them duplicated as they were forwarded with comments and opinions from the Police Federation. He had three regarding previous cases, mainly queries from the Fiscal's office and one or two announcements about social events.

Close to the bottom of the list was a mail with the subject 'Happy April Fool's Day'. Everyone on the force was well versed in the need for vigilance with regards to computer security and in normal circumstances he would have dragged it straight into the recycle bin, but this was different. The mail had been sent from his own home e-mail address.

He clicked to open it. There was no message just a single Internet address; *www.pagliaccistears.com.* If he clicked on it and it resulted in a virus infection, he knew that he would be disciplined but as he was already facing the sack and maybe worse he thought, what the hell.

The Internet browser jumped on to the screen and the blue progress bar crawled, slowly revealing an animation. In the centre of the display was a Harlequin clown, laughing dementedly, beside it were the words, 'Come back at 10 a.m. for live fun'. The words disappeared and were replaced by a new phrase, 'Remember 1st April 1983'. The whole thing looped round to start again as the detective shivered.

Russell sank back into his seat and stared at the website. Two decades of nightmares came swimming into his head like voracious sharks, they were there to tear his life apart once more.

It can't be, it can't be was all he could think.

After five minutes he checked his watch, five to nine. He felt paralysed with the knowledge that something awful was about to happen. Finally he came to his senses and rushed to the door.

"Alex," he shouted out into the corridor.

"Sir," she replied from the large office she shared with the other detectives.

"Come here, quickly."

She did as he had requested and he directed her to the computer.

"Look," he said.

Alex looked at the screen, puzzled as to what was upsetting him.

"Sir?"

"He's back, that bastard's back."

"I'm sorry sir, you've lost me."

"The Harlequin, Roy Dent he's back."

Only then did Alex make the connection to ten years previously and the murders that had occurred in the city centre. She remembered there was some connection to the university as she was just finishing her degree when the murders in George Square happened and the details of the story were revealed.

"It must be a copycat, it can't be him. It's somebody playing a sick joke, surely?" she said doubtfully.

"No, it's him, I know it is. We need to get the I.T. bods on this right away. We need to know where that's coming from."

"Yes, sir. I'll give them a ring."

She had just left the office when Russell's mobile rang.

"Tom, it's Mark McLelland."

Russell knew what he was going to say. "You got an e-mail?"

"Yes, how did you know?"

"I got the same one."

"Do you think it's genuine?"

"I'm sure it is, sir."

"Just Mark these days, Tom. You don't think it's a copycat?"

"No, it just feels like the kind of escalation I expect of that bastard. Another play for publicity."

"What are you doing about it?"

"We'll get the e-crime boys to trace it and hopefully we'll be able to do something about it before he can play his sick games again."

"Why has he targeted us?"

"We got too close to getting our hands on him. We prevented him from completing his revenge, and now we've become his targets. Maybe he just wants to taunt us and let us know that he's still around. With this psycho it could be anything."

"Please keep me informed." As McLelland was speaking, the phone on Russell's desk rang.

"I'll need to get that, I'll be in touch, I promise."

After he put down the mobile, he picked up the handset. "Major Incidents Team, Detective Superintendent Russell speaking."

"Sir, it's Sergeant Kerry at Stewart Street. I've got a Christine O'Donnell on the line who would like to speak to you."

"Put her through."

"Yes, sir."

There was a brief silence before a click and Christine O'Donnell said, "Hello."

Russell guessed why she was calling but he said, "Ms O'Donnell, what can I do for you?"

"Inspector Russell, I've received an e-mail this morning," she said warily, as if she expected that the detective was going to dismiss her.

He didn't bother correcting her regarding his rank. He said simply, "Yes, as have I."

"The website?"

"Yes."

"Is it him?"

"We believe so, yes."

Her rising panic was clear when she said, "Oh God, what is he going to do this time?"

"I don't know but please don't worry, we've already got our computer specialists looking at the site and hopefully we'll be able to see where it's coming from."

"That's good. You'll put him away this time?"

"That's the plan. Don't worry we're on it." Russell offered a platitude but not one that he truly believed.

"I can't help but worry. What if he's after me?"

"I can have a uniformed officer come and keep an eye on you until it's over if you want."

"Please, that would make me feel a little better."

"Are you still in Moodiesburn?"

"Yes." She supplied her address to save him digging it out of the files.

"I'll get that organised."

"Thank you, I really appreciate this. Goodbye."

"Goodbye, Ms O'Donnell." He felt that he hadn't offered much help, but she was just one of a host of problems he had to deal with. At least he might be able to offer some reassurance in the form of a constable to keep an eye on her until this was over.

With a press of a button he disconnected the call. The nearest police station to where she lived was in Cumbernauld. Russell looked up the number in the force directory and rang it. A reluctant desk sergeant was finally persuaded to send a car to her address, checking that the cost would be taken from the budget of the M.I.T. rather than the local station.

"Fuckin' bean counters are everywhere," Russell shouted at the phone when the call was over.

His call to Lewis Baxter was not a comfortable one. Baxter was the newly appointed assistant chief constable responsible for operational matters in the West of Scotland. Baxter had come from the old Central Scotland force and this was his first day on the job in Glasgow. The product of an independent school, he had been fast-tracked through the ranks and was a career manager with a plummy accent, not the kind of cop that Russell had much time for.

After his initial description of what had happened and the background to the previous incidents he said, "There's little we can do at the moment, sir. We have no idea what he's got planned. I've got I.T. trying to trace where the site's being hosted."

"We need to prevent this leaking out, detective superintendent."

"Yes sir, but that's going to be almost impossible. Once this gets on to social media it will spread round the world in an instant."

"Do what you can, I'll be in touch." The call ended abruptly.

Russell shook his head and then moved through to the main office where Alex was sitting conversing with someone on the phone.

"Any luck?" he asked quietly.

She shook her head.

Russell stood poised at Alex's desk, hoping desperately that she would tell him they had traced where the website was being broadcast from.

Finally Alex said, "OK, thanks, Roger. Keep trying."

She turned to her boss. "Sorry sir, the signal's being bounced around the world. There's no way they can trace it. Roger said that he'd contact the Met. to see if they've got anything more advanced that might help but it doesn't look good I'm afraid."

"Shit."

"It gets worse. Roger said the website's already been publicised on social media; Dent must have posted it. There may be thousands watching that site at ten o'clock."

"I thought that would happen and it's exactly what he wants, publicity. I better contact the press office and warn them. Let me know if the Met. come up with anything."

Back in his own office he dialled the press office number.

"Helen Paterson," the press officer said.

"Helen, it's Tom Russell. I'm afraid we've got a major problem developing."

When he finished telling her what was happening she asked, "What are we looking at here? How bad is it going to be?"

"As bad as it gets."

"There's little we can do to stop this. That's the problem with the Internet; it's around the world in a blink. I'll get on to the providers and ask them to stop it but it's a case of bolting the stable door. The press will need to be briefed but they're probably all over it already. Great way to start our new organisation, Tom."

"I know."

"I'll keep an eye on that site but I'm not optimistic that I'll be able to spin anything from this. I'll let the media think that the inquiry is being run from here, that should mean you won't have them camped out at Helen Street."

"Thanks, I appreciate that. I'm sorry Helen, I know today was going to be busy anyway, but I thought it would be better if you were ahead of the game."

"I know but please, Tom, no more little presents like this."

Russell had done all that he could; all that was left was to wait until ten o'clock.

CHAPTER 22

Inside the cages, a masked man wielding a gun ordered the three captives to strip, threw a Harlequin suit to each of them and told them to put it on. The room was lit with a dim lamp and they could at least see each other. The young man had introduced himself as Joe O'Donnell and Karen thought he looked so youthful that he was like a boy. When the command came from their captor, Karen could see Joe become embarrassed as the two women stripped to their underwear, staring at the wall rather than their semi-naked forms. When it was his turn, Karen indicated to Hayley that they should do him the same courtesy.

Although she was absolutely terrified, Karen tried to remain unflustered. Hayley was so completely fearful that she had hardly said a word. She veered between total silence and then weeping copiously and noisily. Joe just seemed shell-shocked not sure what was happening or why. Karen knew all too well the story of the Harlequin, but she couldn't work out why she had been targeted. She wasn't sure that Tom would care very much what happened to her after their acrimonious divorce had left him with very little. The Harlequin obviously thought that he was exacting some sort of revenge on Karen's former husband, but she doubted that was the case. She did know Tom well enough to know that he would do all that he could to save all of them regardless of his feelings towards her.

When all three were dressed in their new apparel - each in a different colour - the masked man reappeared.

"Come with me, it's time to play."

***

In the briefing room of Helen Street Station, a laptop had been attached to a projector and a team of detectives were now assembled sitting staring at the screen. The computer clock showed it was five minutes to ten and the room was eerily quiet as a sense of foreboding gripped the group. Russell had already brought everyone up to speed, and during his talk his disquiet transferred to the team; his concerns became theirs. What could the sick bastard have come up with now?

Alex had asked Roger Green if there was any way that the I.T. team could at least prevent the site from being seen but despite their efforts, the address was re-routed before they could block it and as a result remained available.

Russell was standing at the back of the room, watching the digits on the computer clock move ever closer to 10:00, and he could feel every nerve and muscle in his body become tenser with every passing second. At the precise moment the clock flipped over to ten o'clock the looping message disappeared and a live video feed replaced it. The camera was focused on a dimly lit board, it was blue with gold stars and looked like something a magician or a circus performer might use.

Suddenly from off-camera a head appeared, the mask of the Harlequin with its insane, fixed grin filled the screen.

"Welcome everyone to the Harlequin's April Fool's Day Carnival. It is the reality game show to end reality game shows. Today we have three contestants who are playing for the ultimate prize, to see who lives and who dies. Let me introduce them to you. First of all our only gentleman contestant, Joseph O'Donnell." The Harlequin's voice was distorted but there was no mistaking his undisguised glee at what he was doing.

The camera cut to a petrified young man and Russell realised who it was immediately. Christine O'Donnell's son was so like her as to be unmistakeable and it was obvious that Dent's revenge-inspired spree was not over yet. The scene was accompanied by the sound effect of an audience cheering and clapping enthusiastically.

The clown face reappeared and he said, "Allow me to introduce you to our second contestant, Hayley McLelland."

Russell stared in disbelief as the fearful daughter of his former boss appeared on the screen. Make-up-laden tears streaked her face and her eyes were wide in terrified anticipation of what was to come.

"And finally," the Harlequin continued, "last by no means least, I give you Karen Russell."

As one, the detectives in the room spun round and looked at their detective superintendent. Russell's weight seemed too much for his legs to bear and he felt his knees buckle. His phone was ringing in his pocket but he ignored it; he couldn't deal with other people's troubles at that moment, the Harlequin had made his latest game a personal attack on those who had pursued him.

"Sir, are you alright?" Alex stood to offer him help.

"I'll… I'll be fine," he managed to reply.

The 'game show' was continuing and the host was back on screen. "Our first game is All Stars." He paused to allow more fake whooping and applause to be heard.

"The rules are simple, each of our contestants will propel three Ninja Throwing Stars at one of their opponents. They must hit the area of the board or be punished with a little pain of their own. The winner is the one who hits the board most often."

Joe O'Donnell was ordered to walk the length of the narrow lane and stand against the board. He was obviously unwilling, but the crack of a riding crop across his chest soon changed his mind. When he reached the board, which appeared to be about ten metres from the camera, he turned and stood shaking uncontrollably.

Hayley McLelland was first to throw. The Harlequin demonstrated the technique required and launched one of the sharp weapons towards the young man. The star embedded itself into the board about twenty centimetres from O'Donnel's right ear. The audience of detectives gasped and one exclaimed, "Bastard."

Hayley McLelland looked into the face of her tormentor but the blank mask offered her nothing. He handed her one of the weapons, her hand trembled as she took it from him.

"Miss McLelland please throw your first star." There was no clue in the voice of the Harlequin that he thought this was anything but a family television programme; it was filled with sincere joy.

"I… I… can't," the woman said.

Suddenly the show's 'host' switched from joyful to raging. "You can and you will." There was another crack and the crop scored her back.

Her scream was filled with shock, suffering and despair.

Russell's phone rang once again, but once more he ignored it.

The Harlequin snapped back into character. "Nerves getting the better of Miss McLelland there but I'm sure she's ready to go now."

Hayley managed to lift the star and throw it in the direction of the board. It missed the target and as soon as it did the whip cracked on her back again. Her costume was torn and blood began to seep from the wound and stain the cloth.

"Oh dear, a miss. Better luck next time."

She was now sobbing forcefully but she was compelled to take a second star. She let it fly from her hand and this time it embedded itself in the board close to Joe's left knee.

"Congratulations, Hayley, you've scored a point. Last try."

He handed her another weapon.

This time it hurtled through the air and landed on O'Donnell's left hip. He screamed in agony, the blade having penetrated close to the bone. The watching detectives winced and cursed at the sight of blood leaking from the young man, forming a red score on the diamond pattern of his suit. Russell could sense the anger growing but somehow no one could look away, the gory spectacle held each of them in a trance.

"Oh bad luck there Hayley, but you have scored one point."

Joe O'Donnell pulled the star from the top of his leg and the flow of blood increased. He hobbled away from the board, trying to maintain some dignity but there was a fire in his eyes. The Harlequin pushed Hayley towards the board and Karen Russell took her place at the other end. Russell was surprised to see his ex-wife seemed to be very still and unruffled. When she was handed the star, she walked into the throwing area and propelled it towards Hayley McLelland. She had aimed high and wide making sure that there was no way it would hit the younger woman. It hammered into the board about five centimetres from the top and ten from the left side.

"Congratulations, Karen. One point," the host said but it was obvious how annoyed he was at her, she had not even tried to throw close to the human target.

Her second star was equally well thrown, missing Hayley and landing securely in the board.

When she was passed the third, she made to throw once more but instead spun and threw it in the direction of her captor. There was a supportive cheer from the detectives but there was no sound to indicate that it had found its target. The Harlequin stepped forward into the frame and brought down the riding crop repeatedly on Karen as she cowered at his feet. After ten lashes he stopped.

Tom Russell could take no more and he rushed out of the briefing room.

Alex thought about going after him but she didn't know what she could say. She had to watch and hope to pick up some kind of clue as to where the grisly charade was being performed. Any little piece of information might be vital in putting an end to the horror.

On screen the Harlequin was saying through gritted teeth, "I'm sorry Karen that means you've lost all your points. Now it's Mr O'Donnell's turn."

The host dragged Karen to the board while Joe O'Donnell became the focus of the camera.

The pain in his hip was obviously causing him difficulty as he struggled to take a throwing stance but with considerable effort he finally steadied himself. Karen was equally shaky on her feet and for a time it looked like she would be unable to take her place. When the Harlequin indicated that he was going to use the crop again, she pulled herself into an upright position. Leaning back against the board, she closed her eyes.

Joe O'Donnell had played at being a ninja on a games console but this was not what he had imagined. All that ran through his mind was the thought that he may kill this stranger. Despite his efforts to avoid her, his first star grazed Karen's left forearm and buried itself in the board. The pain from the star made little impression on her, as the throbbing in her back was all she could feel. Joe kept apologising as he threw the second, which missed the board and brought another swipe with the riding crop from the sadistic host. When he let the third go, he was horrified to see it bury itself in Karen's right thigh, bringing a further scream and a stream of apologies from the young man.

"This round is a draw between Joe and Hayley with one point each. Well done, Mr O'Donnell and Ms McLelland you may survive our show, as for you Ms Russell you have some work to do to save yourself. Join us at four o'clock this afternoon for our second challenge on The Harlequin's April Fool's Day Carnival."

Every detective in the room seemed to breathe out simultaneously and then there was a rush of expletives, curses and vows that they had to find the Harlequin before he could broadcast his second sick show.

Alex shouted, "Quiet." The buzzing anger subsided.

"Right, we need to work this like any other case. Go and have a coffee, we'll brief back here at eleven," she ordered. Despite many of them being of the same rank as her, everyone seemed to be happy that someone had taken control and the meeting broke up.

Alex set off to speak to Russell. She found him in his office, his head buried in his hands. When he looked up she was shocked to see that he was crying. He turned away from her.

"Sir?"

There was no reply. She walked over to his chair and gently laid a hand on him. He brushed it away, disgusted that she had caught him at such a vulnerable moment.

"Sir, we need to start working the case and find where he's holding them before he can kill them. You need to take control." She was firm, realising that he needed to be shaken out of his current mood.

"This is my fault. I had that bastard and I let him go."

"It's not your fault," she replied angrily.

"I can't do this Alex, this is too much."

Alex never thought for a minute that her boss would be self-pitying. She wasn't going to let him wallow in his own guilt, while three lives were at stake. Her anger boiled over into the type of language she used rarely. "For fuck's sake, get a grip of yourself. No one knows this prick better than you and that means you're the best hope those three people have. Aye, maybe it is your fault that they're in danger, but that means you've got a moral obligation to help them get out of it. You can do whatever you want after we've caught the bastard but until then you need to pull yourself together, get off your arse and lead this team."

Russell turned and looked at her angrily. "You're sailing close to the wind there Detective Inspector. Show some respect."

"Get off your arse, sir," she replied with a sarcastic emphasis.

She broke the spell he was under and she could see that something had struck home.

He pulled a hanky from his pocket and wiped away the tears. "I did love her you know, even if it did end badly," he said calmly.

"I know, I've been there. If it was Andrew in that situation I would feel exactly the same, but you can't let it get in the way of doing all that you can to save her and the other two people."

He looked directly into her eyes as if taking a measure of her. "You're right. I just feel so guilty to have her in that position because of me."

"I understand but it's a destructive emotion. Be thankful you've still got a chance to help her. You're the best cop I've ever met and as I said earlier, no one knows this creep better than you. I've told the team to be back at eleven for a briefing, I'd rather you were the one giving it."

"I will be. I just need to call some people first."

"OK, I'll see you at eleven."

As she exited the office, she noticed that the door had been damaged, probably by Russell's fist.

He watched her as she left. Her fierce intelligence made her a great detective but as he got to know her better, he realised that she was also a strong leader. He hoped that the job didn't drag her down before she reached her full potential.

Lifting his mobile from his desk, he tapped on the missed calls icon. Mark McLelland's number was the first on the list and he initiated the dialling process.

"Tom." Russell could tell that his former boss had also succumbed to the same emotional torment as he had himself.

"I'm so sorry, Mark."

"What have you got?"

"Nothing as yet, we're about to start a briefing. We'll need to piece together how he got the three of them there. Any ideas about Hayley?"

"No, she was supposed to come round today, we were going to go for a pub lunch."

Russell's professionalism pushed aside his personal worries. "Did she say if she had anything planned for yesterday or maybe early this morning?"

"No, I don't think so. Are you puzzled as to how he managed to take them?"

"Definitely. To snatch three people and hold them captive isn't easy."

"Maybe he's got an accomplice.

"It's possible I suppose, but even if he has it won't help if we don't know who that might be."

"Is there anything I can do?"

"No, Mark. I don't think that would be a good idea. You're out of the loop now."

"I know this case, Tom."

"I understand and I know that you feel you need to do something, but please just trust me. In this situation Hayley and Joe are just as important to me as Karen, I promise."

There was silence and Russell wondered if asking McLelland to trust him with regard to the Harlequin was asking too much after what had happened ten years ago.

McLelland relented and realised that he would be better not getting involved. "Keep me informed, please."

"I will, I promise. I need to go, I have to speak to Christine O'Donnell."

"Cheers, Tom. Please, bring her back to me," McLelland's voice cracked.

"I'll do my best. Bye." Russell was relieved to end the call but the next one wasn't going to be any easier.

He tapped on the number of the other missed call.

When she answered, Christine O'Donnell was close to hysteria. "Oh God, Mr Russell he's got him. Did you see what he did to him?" Her words rattled rapidly down the line.

"I know, I know. We're doing all we can to find him."

"He's going to kill him, isn't he? It's all because of me being involved in that stupid prank. It's all my fault, oh my poor baby." She broke down and all that Russell could hear was her sobbing.

"Christine, it's not your fault. This is down to one man and only him. We're going to stop him but we need some help from you."

"What... what can I... do?" she said between gulps of air.

"Do you know where Joe was last night?"

"He was here yesterday for his lunch and then he was going back to his digs to get changed for a party."

"Where was the party?"

"In the West End I think. I'm not sure."

"OK, that's good we can ask his friends. I'll get a detective over to you and we'll take it from there. Try not to worry." He knew that the last sentence would be impossible for her, just as it was for him.

She realised that she might not be the only one who had a personal reason to be anxious about what the Harlequin had planned. "Do you know the older woman?"

"Karen's my ex-wife and Hayley McLelland is the daughter of a former colleague who worked the case with me previously."

"Oh God." She started crying once again. Russell told her that he would be in touch and was relieved when he ended the call.

Before he could do anything else the phone on his desk rang.

After Russell had confirmed his identity, the A.C.C. said, "I'm coming over. I'll be leaving in ten minutes."

"Yes, sir. We've organised a briefing for eleven."

"Wait until I've arrived before you begin." Once again the call was completed without any warning.

Russell had a feeling that life under their new A.C.C. was not going to be easy.

CHAPTER 23

The three captives were escorted back to the cages; this time they were placed all together in the same tiny cell. A plastic bag was thrown in beside them filled with bandages and plasters.

"Dress the wounds," the clown-masked man ordered before leaving them in the dingy light.

Karen's injuries were worse than the other two but when she asked Hayley to help there was no response from the younger woman. She was in a state of numb shock and instead it was Joe who stepped forward.

"I'll do it."

"Thank you," Karen said faintly. She pulled apart the Velcro of her costume and eased it off her shoulders. She made no attempt to preserve her modesty. She stood in her underwear in front of the teenager; his help was all that mattered. He still looked a little embarrassed but he bathed the wounds with an alcohol wipe that he found in the bag before using the padded dressings to cover the injuries. When he was done, he helped Karen to dress, adjusting the costume carefully to minimise her discomfort.

Then it was his turn and Karen treated the cut at the top of his leg. He winced as the alcohol stung on the two-inch wound and was glad when the procedure was over. Karen turned her attention to Hayley who had a welt with broken skin where the crop had come down on her back but it was relatively minor compared to what the others had suffered.

When the first aid was finished, they sat down at three sides of their cell, their feet almost touching in the centre. Karen struggled to get comfortable, the Harlequin hadn't supplied any painkillers in the impromptu first-aid kit and she could feel acutely the marks on her back.

"What's going to happen to us?" Joe asked.

"I don't know Joe, but we have to stay strong for each other."

"He's going to kill us," Hayley McLelland shouted.

"You don't know that," Karen replied firmly.

"I do, he's a psycho. He's killed loads of people, my father told me all about him."

"Who is your father?" Karen asked.

"Mark McLelland, he worked this case when he was still a policeman."

"My ex-husband is Tom Russell, he used to work with your father."

"See, it's revenge, he's going to kill us." The younger woman was now crying hysterically. Karen wondered if she should slap her but decided against it.

"Is that true?" Joe asked. He was too young to know much about the previous crimes, although he did remember that the police had visited his mother ten years ago.

Despite her pounding head, throbbing back and racing heart, Karen was determined to be the one to offer some sense of calm and reassurance. "First of all, this might be a copycat.

Secondly, even if it is the original Harlequin, maybe he's trying to draw out my ex-husband, your father and your mother. He knows how they will react and he wants revenge on them, not us." Although she managed to say it with real conviction, she knew her words were hollow.

"You think so?" Joe asked.

"Yes but we have to help ourselves. We need a plan."

Hayley dismissed the idea with a derisory laugh.

Karen remained positive and said, "There are three of us and only one of him. We need to be ready to take advantage of it if he lets his guard down."

"Aye, we could jump him," Joe said with enthusiasm.

"You can't just rush into it, Joe. We'll need to have a plan."

At that moment the room was flooded with light again as the door opened.

"We'll talk later," Karen whispered.

The door of the cage was unlocked and a tray was propelled onto the floor between them. A weak-looking porridge slopped over the sides of three metal bowls, the kind that were used to feed pets.

"Eat," the man commanded as he locked the door. When he was gone they were back in their twilight world. There was no cutlery on the tray but the three of them were so hungry they shovelled the watery food into their mouths with their hands. They were all famished and would need what little strength the porridge offered.

***

As requested, the Major Incident Team officers were back in the briefing room at eleven, but it was another fifteen minutes before the meeting could start.

With Baxter at his side, Russell was about to begin when the entrance of the Procurator Fiscal, Jacqui Kerr, delayed him further.

"I thought the Fiscal should know what's happening too," Baxter said.

"Take a seat," Russell said to the woman. The last thing he needed was Ms Kerr and her superior attitude, but he had to be polite.

One of the detectives rose from his chair but she said, "I'll stand here if you don't mind." She took up a position close to the door, leaning on the wall. Her face was set in its customary expression of disdain as she turned her attention to Russell.

The detective superintendent ran through the events of the day, mainly for the sake of Baxter and Kerr.

"This Karen Russell, is she related to you?" Baxter asked.

"In a manner of speaking, sir. She's my ex-wife."

"Ah. Do you think you should be leading this inquiry?"

When Alex saw Russell bristle she was about to speak, but he beat her to it. "With all due respect sir, I am the senior officer left on the job who has dealt with this case from the start. I know more about this man than anyone else on the force, there is no way that I will stand aside willingly," he said with barely controlled fury.

"I think that decision is mine to make, detective superintendent," Baxter responded.

Alex decided to mediate. "Sir, I feel that it would be better that the detective superintendent lead the team. His insights into this man would be invaluable to the investigation. I think continuity will help to short cut some of the procedures as we won't need to dig into files for information."

There was a positive mutter in the room, as the general consensus seemed to be with Russell being the S.I.O.

"Very well," Baxter said.

"We can't afford any further failures on this like last time, Detective Superintendent. We don't need your emotions getting in the way," Kerr added.

"I'll bear that in mind," Russell said sarcastically. "Can we get back to the case?"

Baxter nodded while Kerr ignored him.

"At the moment we don't have a lot to go on. We need to establish how he managed to grab all three of them. I need a team to look into the movements yesterday of each of the captives." He laid out what was required and teams were assigned to each of the three people involved.

"Next, we need I.T. to be on the ball. If possible, I want one or two of them to move here to facilitate easier communication."

"I'll speak to Roger Green and ask him to send a couple of folk over," Alex said.

"Good, get on that. Is there anything on that video that might help us? For example, can we isolate some sounds that might give us a clue to where they may be held?"

"It's worth a try. They've got an audio specialist in the team, I'll ask Roger about that as well."

"Next, if this is Dent rather than someone taking on the mantle, where the hell has he been for the last ten years? Obviously he'll be older now but he might have had plastic surgery to change his looks, and he will have changed his name. D.S. Craigan, I want you to form a small team with a D.C. and a couple of uniforms to try and trace what happened to him after he went into the river. Check bank accounts, family property, private cosmetic clinics, basically anything that will piece together where he's been and how he got back."

"Yes, sir," she replied.

"I'm going to have a word with somebody who might know who could have forged documents for Dent and what name he is going by now. Anybody got any other suggestions?"

The room stayed silent and a few shook their heads.

"Sir?" Russell asked the A.C.C.

"Make sure that your time is allocated properly on this investigation. I don't want any holes in the budget."

Fuck me, Russell thought, three people kidnapped and all he's worried about is his spreadsheets.

He didn't vocalise his opinion, instead he said to the team, "I want anything, and no matter how trivial it might be it's to be reported to a central communications team here in the incident room. Frank, can you please organise the comms hub. Make sure all phone numbers have been collated."

"Aye, sir. No problem." D.S. Weaver said.

"Get to it. Let's bring those people home, safe and sound."

The room was filled with a hubbub of chairs being pushed back, footsteps and voices. It dissipated into near silence as the team members went about their tasks. A small queue formed at Frank Weaver's desk as everyone checked with him that he had their mobile numbers. With mobile contracts changing due to the reorganisation, some of the detectives had been given new phones and the contact list was far from one hundred per cent accurate.

Russell made his way back to his own office to collect his coat. As he was about to leave, Alex appeared at the door.

"Do you want me to come with you?" she asked.

"Alex, you don't need to babysit me. I'm not going to do

anything stupid. I'm going to Nitshill to meet an old adversary of mine and then I'll come straight back. You get the I.T. stuff organised and when I get back we'll decide what to do next."

"If you're sure?"

"I'm sure."

A uniformed sergeant appeared behind Alex.

"Donnie, what's up?"

"Sir, I thought you should know that the press are outside. They know that your ex-wife is involved."

"Shit, so much for keeping them out of the way. It's OK, I'll deal with it."

"I'll make an appearance on the street and distract them while you get to the car," Alex offered.

"Not a bad idea, give me a sec."

He moved to the computer, logged in and found what he was looking for. The printer on his desk whirred and a picture of Roy Dent was deposited in the tray, which Russell folded and then put it in his pocket.

"I'm set."

While her boss went to the car park via the door at the back of the building, Alex strode purposefully to the gatehouse where the press were gathered; she called to them to walk round to the pavement on Helen Street. Once they were in place, T.V. cameras were hoisted onto shoulders, microphones, digital recorders and mobile phones were thrust in her direction while a variety of questions were asked about how Detective Superintendent Russell was dealing with this crisis. She let them shout for a bit longer than she would have normally, allowing Russell time to get into his car.

Over their heads, she could see his Insignia pulling away from the gates as she told the press to direct all queries to the press office in Pitt Street. There was a groan of annoyance and disgust from the journalists as they realised that she had denied them the chance to grill Russell. As far as Alex was concerned, being based at the most secure police station in Scotland definitely had its advantages.

CHAPTER 24

During the drive to Nitshill Road, Russell fought the urge to think too much about the situation Karen was in. He had to work this exactly as he would any other case if he was going to be able to help her; overly emotional distractions would only harm his chances of saving her.

His destination was a row of shops where Michael Kenny had a little watch repair business. The tiny space was cramped between a bookmakers and a sandwich shop. In the short line of buildings there were another two bookies, a pharmacy, a newsagent, and at the very end a pub that looked about as welcoming as a starved Rottweiler.

Michael's relationship with the law was based on the idea that it was more a set of guidelines, rather than hard and fast rules. He believed that as long as no one was hurt and he didn't get caught, anything was permissible. He had a reputation as a forger of incredible skill and had served five years for his troubles, but he was a slippery character. The watch repair business was a front, but he did have the skills required; the smaller the item the better he was at manipulating it. He could have made a real career for himself with a proper jewellers but he liked the game; skirting around the police with the same skill and dexterity that he used to fix watches and forge documents. The problem Russell had was that he couldn't help like the wee man with the milk bottle glasses, squeaky voice and insolent smile.

That grin was in full glow when Russell walked into the shop.

"Mr Russell, long time no see," Kenny said. He put down a watch and the cloth he was using to clean it, removed a pair of loupe lens glasses and put on his own spectacles.

"Michael, how are you?"

"Ah'm good, thanks. Yirsel'?"

"Not so good. I need some help."

"Noo, Mr Russell, Ah hope ye don't think that Ah'm involved in any nonsense," he said seriously, although Russell could still see the glint in his eye.

"Michael, I'm not here to cause you any trouble and I need you to be honest with me. This is about murder and kidnap, so anything you've been up to is irrelevant in the grand scheme of things."

Kenny realised how important this was, Russell's face showed the kind of strain that the little man had never seen before on any cop's face.

"Aye, nae problem. Whit de ye need?"

Russell told him a shortened version of the long story of the Harlequin. When he told the forger about the latest stage in the two decades of madness, Kenny's demeanour changed.

"Ah'm sorry fur yir troubles, Mr Russell. Whit cin Ah dae that will help ye?"

Russell took out the photograph of Dent and pushed it over the thin counter.

"This is Dr Roy Dent, we believe he is the Harlequin. He disappeared ten years ago, completely off the grid. He could only have done that with the help of somebody like yourself. I need to know if you recognise him or if you know who might have helped him."

Kenny took the photograph and peered intently at it.

"Ah don't remember the face. Ten year ago..." he was making a genuine effort to remember.

"That was about when the Iraq war started, if that's any help."

"Oh wait... aye, there wis somethin'. Ah remember noo. There wis a big rush joab roon that time. Some guy wis offerin' a fortune for a full set o' papers, passport, drivin' licence, the works."

"Sounds like it could be him. Do you know who did the work?"

"It wisnae me. This guy wis wantin' a rush joab and that's no' me, Mr Russell. Ah know ye don't approve but when Ah dae work, Ah dae it right. Ah heard that it wis Gerry Halkirk that did it. Second rater in ma opinion but it wid've passed muster. Just."

"This Halkirk, where is he based?"

"He wis oot Motherwell way but ye'll no' be able tae talk tae him, the cancer took him a couple year back."

"Shit. Is there anybody who might remember what name was used?"

"Naw, it's no somethin' ye tell other folk. We didnae keep records either, afore ye ask."

"Michael, if you could do some digging, just in case somebody knows what Halkirk did for him or maybe Dent's had to get other documents, anything you could find might help."

"Ah'll dae whit Ah cin, Mr Russell, Ye know Ah don't like any o' that violence pish."

"Thanks Michael." They parted with a handshake.

***

Karen Russell lay on her side trying to ignore the excruciating pain that seemed to engulf her. Hayley and Joe had succumbed to exhaustion despite their own agony; the tiredness in every bone and sinew had won. Karen's fear of what the Harlequin would do while she was unconcious was another reason that she refused to succumb to the need to sleep.

As she watched the two younger people rest, her thoughts turned to her own legacy. She and Tom had never been able to conceive, baffling the doctors as every test told them that it should have been possible. Karen had gone through a period of blaming Tom, believing the pressure of his work, his irregular hours and erratic eating had all contributed to their lack of children. However, after they were divorced, Karen began to re-evaluate. She realised now how unreasonable her behaviour had been; she could see a rival in every woman that he ever came into contact with. Her lack of trust had worn him down and when he told her he wanted a divorce, her first thought was that he must have somebody else. At the time she was so angry that the only thing she wanted to do was to punish him and with her lawyer's help, combined with Tom's reluctance to put up much of a fight, that was what she had done. It had taken some time but with no sign of another woman in his life and the mellowing of her own opinion, she had slowly come to realise just how poorly she had treated him both during and after their marriage. If she had been more understanding, more ready to trust him, they would still have been together today - they may have even been parents. She wondered what he was thinking about their relationship now. Did he just see her in the same light as the two other victims, that it was just another case to solve? Did he care if she survived, as long as he caught the Harlequin? She hoped that he did but she wouldn't have blamed him if he didn't. All she could do was try to survive and help the two young people to do the same. Maybe that would be a fitting legacy.

***

It was half-past one by the time Russell arrived back at the station. He had driven past the waiting press pack, whose members were in the middle of the biggest story of their careers and no one would talk to them. The fact Russell had sped past without so much as a pause had just added to their annoyance. Some of the T.V. crews had taken to interviewing other journalists in an effort to have something to offer their producers at the news channels. Those interviews were interspersed with discussions with psychologists and criminal 'experts' pontificating in the studio.

In the incident room, Alex was sitting with Roger Green and they were both peering at a laptop. Beside them were two other people that Russell didn't recognise; one of them was wearing a pair of headphones.

Alex introduced them, "Sir, this is Roger, the head of the Forensic I.T. team, this is his colleague Hugo Elgar and the audio technician is Stephanie Jensen."

All three acknowledged the detective; Elgar stood and shook his hand while the other two nodded. Russell was shocked at how young Elgar looked. He had heard about the hacker turned cyber cop but he hadn't expected him to look about twelve years of age. He wore his hair long and his clothes were shabby chic, at best. The rumour was that Elgar had cracked the police human resource database and created a record for himself. He then informed the security team what he had done and asked for a job. His unusual approach proved successful and he was given the job of tightening the security of the database he had just hacked. Having completed that task, he was moved into the forensic I.T. team.

The young woman looked a little more soberly dressed than her colleague. Despite her scarlet red hair - her muted pink blouse and simple blue jeans made her a closer approximation of Russell's idea of what a member of the force should look like.

"How are you getting on?" Russell asked Green.

"We're trying to map how he's organised the site but it seems to be using multiple hosts across the world. It's a very sophisticated piece of software that is behind this."

"Does this Harlequin guy have an I.T. background?" Elgar asked.

"No, he's a medical doctor, he was a pathologist in fact."

"He must have help from somewhere. This is the kind of stuff that only the best hackers on the planet would have, it's not something you can phone up your service provider to set up for you."

Russell was momentarily stunned; he had always felt the possibility was remote that the Harlequin would have help but now it was beginning to be a reality.

Alex said, "It makes sense, sir. Didn't you say that he had posted pictures of one of his victims ten years ago?"

"Yes but it was nowhere near this level of sophistication."

"Could the help come from another victim of the original prank?"

"Possibly. I'll speak to Christine O'Donnell, she might know. What about the audio?"

"Stephanie," Green said as he tapped her arm.

"Yes?" she removed her headphones and looked up. Russell could now see her delicately beautiful features and bright emerald eyes.

"Detective Russell was asking how the audio is going." Green said.

"Slowly I'm afraid. It's difficult to get it to the quality I need to do a proper analysis but I'm working on it. If we could get some more it might help."

"Yes, but that might mean we're watching someone die while we collect it." Russell said acerbically.

The technician looked abashed as she said, "I know, I'm sorry."

"No, I'm sorry. I know what you mean. Keep going folks and thanks for your help."

He retreated to the peace and quiet of his own office where he brewed a coffee. He regretted his little burst of pique at the computer bods; they had their problems in the same way he had his. There was no one thing that was going to tell him where the three captives were being held, it was going to take good police work in multiple disciplines to pull it together.

Christine O'Donnell's voice was filled with optimism when he rang her. "Have you got any news?"

"Not yet, I'm sorry. I'm looking for some help."

The hope gone, her tone was one of defeat as she said, "What do you want?"

"The other two men who were the victims of the prank thirty years ago, were any of them involved in computers?"

"No, one went on to be a lawyer, the other was some kind of engineer. Why?"

"We think Dent has an accomplice, someone with real skill in I.T."

"Oh. Are you any closer to finding them?"

"I've been out interviewing someone. I'm just about to be briefed about what progress has been made on how Joe and the others were abducted. I promise, I'll let you know when we get him back."

"If you get him back," she said bitterly and hung up.

Russell sighed as he sunk his head into his hands. He knew exactly how she was feeling but he knew he couldn't let her emotions or his own dictate what he did or let them stop him doing his job, even though it felt as if that was exactly what was happening.

CHAPTER 25

How had Karen and the rest ended up in the clutches of the Harlequin? That was Russell's next priority. He called through to the main office and asked Frank Weaver to brief him with the details of what the teams had discovered so far. He gave the detective sergeant five minutes to collate the information.

Russell took those five minutes to still his thoughts and prepare him for the next part of the day. He had to draw his energy and resilience from deep within him but by the time Weaver arrived, he was ready to go again.

"Come in, Frank. What have you got for me?"

Weaver sat in the chair opposite the detective superintendent, thinking how haggard the other man looked. He could only imagine what Russell was going through. He consulted a bundle of papers that he had collected from the investigative teams.

"Who would you like me to start with, sir?"

"Hayley McLelland."

He flicked through the papers before saying, "Miss McLelland received an e-mail yesterday allegedly from her father asking her to go to a church graveyard. I've spoken to former Chief Superintendent McLelland, who assures me that he didn't send the mail and the I.T. guys have backed him up on that score; they say the e-mail was sent from a different computer. Mr McLelland said that he has been researching his family tree and that he could only presume that his daughter thought that he wanted to see her in connection with that subject."

"So Dent or this fuckin' accomplice hacks Mark's account, sends the mail and grabs her. I take it this church is quite isolated?"

"Tucked away in a lane, sir."

"What about Joe O'Donnell?"

"He received a text from a friend about a party in the West End, that the friend didn't send. There was no party. As far as we can tell he left his student accommodation around nine but we can't pick him up on any CCTV and there's no record of a taxi picking him up, so we think he was taken soon after leaving the building."

"And Karen?"

"Her company said they received a call last week from the representative of an Italian businessman who wanted to sell a property in Stirlingshire. Apparently, he asked specifically for Ms Russell. The appointment was for early yesterday afternoon, as the alleged businessman was only going to be in Scotland until Monday morning. We got the Stirling boys to take a run out there and they found her car, and one other set of tyre tracks. The forensics team is on its way but it doesn't look as if there was much of a struggle. The officers at the scene think that bastard took her by surprise."

"I don't suppose she was expecting to be kidnapped."

"No, sir."

"What else if anything have we learned?"

He riffled the papers once more. "I think D.S. Craigan and the team might have made some progress with where Dent has been for the past ten years. His family has a place on the Isle of Man; they were loaded by all accounts. It would certainly have given him a bolt hole to hide in, somewhere far away from curious eyes."

"Interesting, it would certainly explain how he's stayed off our radar. I don't imagine the Isle of Man will be short of cosmetic surgeons. Has D.S. Craigan had any luck finding anyone who might have worked on him?"

"Not as yet, sir."

"He seems to know a lot about his targets. He must have been watching them for some time, particularly McLelland."

"Will I ask Mr McLelland if he noticed anything? Someone following him maybe."

"Possibly, but I think it's more likely that it's something to do with his computer."

"I really don't understand this guy. He's killed the two people that were most responsible for the prank, why does he keep going?"

"Ego. He believed we would never piece it together. He thought he was more intelligent than us and now he wants to exact his revenge on Mark and I, as well as the one other person he blames for what happened to his career. There's no point in trying to apply logic to a guy like this, there is none except inside his head."

Russell looked at his watch, which told him there was only two hours before the games would start again.

***

Hayley McLelland was sitting shivering, not from the cold but from fear, an all-encompassing terror that had both absorbed and overpowered her. She could see no way that she was going to get out of this situation alive. When she was a teenager, she had seen what effect the Harlequin case had had on her father. At the time of the murders and for about six months beyond them he had withdrawn from the family, attempting to isolate them from his irritation and distress. Hayley was in her twenties before he opened up about what he had lived through and why he felt it necessary to protect his daughter and her mother from the horrors he had seen. He had worked some truly terrible cases but the Harlequin had affected him more than any other, and that memory of his fear and frustration was what was now playing through Hayley's mind.

Karen seemed to believe that the police would find them, and that the three of them would survive this ordeal to get back to some kind of normal life, but Hayley thought that her optimism was misplaced. With only a day to investigate, why would they be able to catch him today when they couldn't catch him for twenty years?

She had no idea what time it was but she felt sure that four o'clock was approaching and that when that time arrived she would be vulnerable once more to the whims of the psychopath. The thought that she could be dead very soon brought on another shaking fit and her tears began to flow freely once more.

***

At ten minutes to four some of the detectives were congregating in the briefing room, trepidation and anxiety was written on every expression. The ex-husband in Russell felt sick and for a while he thought he wouldn't be able to face this, but his self-control won out and he joined the team in the room.

He had spoken to both A.C.C. Baxter and Helen Paterson in the past hour. Baxter's only concern seemed to be the political fallout and the image of the newly-formed force, rather than the lives of the three people involved. Russell's temperament was pushed very close to the edge of a career-ending rant but somehow he restrained himself from saying what he was thinking. Baxter was in a new job, desperate to make a positive impression and the worst possible scenario had landed on his plate on the very first day. Russell held on to that thought as the only way he could cope with his overbearing superior.

Helen Paterson had called available colleagues into the press office, curtailing their Bank Holiday plans. She had won a fight with the television channels over the broadcasting of the Harlequin's show. When she pointed out to them that they may be subjecting their viewers to both torture and murder at four o'clock on an Easter Monday, they came round to her point of view. Russell had thanked her on behalf of his team as well as the two parents who were dreading the next chapter in the horror story they were living through.

Alex joined him at the back of the room. "Roger and his team are still working on tracing the site, sir. Stephanie said she's hoping to get a better audio feed this time."

"Fine," he replied although it was obvious he was distracted.

The projector was switched on and once again the Harlequin's 'logo' filled the screen. As the clocked ticked over to four o'clock, the picture changed and there was the disturbing grin of the now familiar mask.

"Good afternoon everyone. Welcome to our second session. The next round of our Harlequin Carnival is called 'From

Russia with a bang" and I'm sure it's going to be explosive watching."

Russell's sense of foreboding became even more acute as the killer unveiled his latest twisted game.

"Here are our contestants." The camera panned to the right to reveal each of the three captives tied to a chair. They were arranged in a triangle, each of them facing one of the others about ten metres apart. The whole area was brightly lit and their faces were rendered flat and white.

"Ladies and Gentlemen, you may be familiar with the simple rules of our game. In my hand I have a revolver with a real bullet in just one chamber of the cylinder, all the other bullets are blank. I will spin the cylinder and our contestants will take it in turn to fire at one of their opponents. There is a one in six chance that they will shoot them, thus edging them closer to being the only survivor and winning the prize of release."

"Shit," Russell heard Frank Weaver say from the front of the room.

Alex was watching her boss intently but he seemed on the surface to be relatively calm or maybe he was just resigned to what was about to happen.

"Now one or two of our contestants may think it's a good idea to turn the gun in my direction. I must warn them that I have a pistol with twenty-two live bullets in the magazine. Their chances of survival would be far lower than mine, so we'll have no cheating from any of you." He finished the warning with a cheery tone, as if they were playing a child's board game.

"Now it is polite to allow a lady to go first, and as she is also at the bottom of our leader board, I'll turn to Karen as our first contestant."

He walked to where Karen was seated and spun the cylinder of the revolver, the sound echoed in the space and down through the camera. He handed the gun to Karen who had a fierce expression on her face. The Harlequin stepped behind her and Russell could see that Karen's right arm was the only part of her not strapped to the chair. Dent had positioned himself in such a way that there was no way that she would be able to point the gun in his direction. Karen was facing Hayley McLelland who was now weeping and wailing. Russell watched as his ex-wife raised the revolver, her hand was shaking as she pointed towards the younger woman. There was a long pause where everyone in the briefing room seemed to hold their breath. Karen put the gun in her lap.

"No, no, no," The Harlequin screamed. He walked to the chair pulled her hair to move her head backwards.

"There will be no cheating." He pressed the pistol against her temple. "Do you understand what the consequences will be for you if you don't pull that trigger?" he shouted into her ear.

"Yes," she replied quietly.

Russell felt both shock and an incredible sense of pride in the courage that his ex-wife was showing. He would never have guessed that she had such a resilient spirit.

On the screen the Harlequin was saying, "Good. Now play nice." He removed the pistol, leaving a visible red mark on her head.

When he had retreated Karen lifted the gun once again. As her hand continued to tremble, she took aim.

"No, Karen. Please Karen don't." The beseeching voice of Hayley McLelland filled the room.

There was a loud bang but there was no projectile. The hammer came down on a blank cartridge and there was an audible sigh from the group of detectives.

"April Fool!" the Harlequin squealed like some demonic schoolboy.

"Now, Ms McLelland." He took the gun from Karen Russell whose strength seemed to have evaporated as tears of relief trickled down her face.

Hayley was now a complete wreck and the Harlequin said, "Remember the pistol, Hayley. All you've got to do is point the gun at Joe there and pull the trigger."

After he had given the cylinder another spin, she lifted her hand to take it from him. The weight of the revolver seemed to surprise her and her arm dropped quickly.

Once again their tormentor had moved to a position of safety behind the contestant holding the gun. Hayley lifted the weapon in the direction of Joe O'Donnell who was gulping in a huge lungful of air. She closed her eyes and pulled the trigger.

This time the lack of projectile was greeted with cheers from the detectives. Russell didn't join in their celebrations, he was wondering how long the three victims would have to play this game; was Dent waiting for the live round to be fired before this would end?

As he was considering what might happen, a female constable walked to his position at the back of the room.

"Sir, sorry to disturb you but there are two detectives from Dundee wanting to see you now. They said they are from Standards & Ethics."

"You have got to be fuckin' kiddin' me. They're not due until tomorrow. Tell them I'm busy."

The woman looked nervous as she said, "They were insistent, sir."

"Do you want me to speak to them?" Alex asked.

"No, it probably won't do any good. I'll go and face the music. Anyway, I can't watch this any longer."

He followed the constable out of the room as Joe O'Donnell was being prepared to take his shot at Karen. Russell paused to look at the screen, wondering if this were the last time he would see his ex-wife alive.

CHAPTER 26

There were two of them, a detective inspector and a detective sergeant. They were waiting for him in one of the secure interview rooms; this was not going to be an informal chat.

The D.I. was called Ian Dickson; a stern-faced Dundonian that Russell knew by reputation. He was infamous for a regard for the rulebook that was almost pathological. He had a shiny bald head; what hair he did have was cropped close to the skin. His grey eyes seemed cold and remote as he stared at Russell. He was dressed in an immaculate charcoal grey suit with white shirt and blue tie. On his fingers was a signet ring with a single black stone that seemed almost frivolous on this rigid and serious man. His D.S. was introduced to Russell as Lee Foster. He was smaller than his colleague with a slight, almost feminine stature. His black hair was cut short on top but shaved in at the sides, the cut favoured by many military personnel. His face wasn't as stern as Dickson's but nor did he look like he would be the life of a party. His suit was cut from a cheaper cloth than his boss but in a more modern way. Russell wondered bitterly where they sent these guys to turn them into traitors, was there a special facility where their humanity and sense of loyalty to other officers was removed?

"Sit, please," Dickson commanded. He had warned the uniformed constable that they were not to be disturbed for any reason. There had been no handshakes between the men and as he placed himself on the edge of the chair across from them, Russell saw that they were going to make it a difficult examination for him.

Dickson made a show of opening a file in front of him to show Russell how important it was, and then turned on the tape recorder.

"It's four-twenty p.m. on Monday, April 1st 2013. This is Detective Inspector Ian Dickson. I am in the interview room at Helen Street Station, Glasgow, with D.S. Lee Foster. We are here to conduct an interview with Detective Superintendent Thomas Russell in connection with the murder of two Serbian nationals in January of this year. This interview is informal but Mr Russell has the right to a representative of the Police Federation to be present. Mr Russell if you wished this interview suspended until such times as a Federation representative can be present, we will do so."

Russell was tempted to say yes but that might cause him further grief and would mean he would have to face what was happening to Karen. He decided it was better not to know right at that moment whether she was dead, and if he was going to suffer at the hands of the 'Complaints' it wouldn't make much difference if his Federation rep was there or not.

"No, I'm willing to answer your questions," he said quietly.

Dickson continued his performance by looking through the file with great care; everything he was doing was a way of indicating that he was in charge. "In January of this year you were involved in an investigation into the death of one Gregor Wright, is that correct?"

"You know it is, it's written down in front of you." Russell's patience, which was already stretched to breaking point, was not going to survive if they were going to be long-winded and fussy about everything.

"Just answer the questions. Now during this inquiry you had contact with Malcolm McGavigan, a figure known to have connections with organised crime in Glasgow, is that correct?"

"If you mean did I talk to a known gang lord in the course of trying to catch a killer, then yes of course I fuckin' did."

"I would ask you to keep your anger in check."

"You are fuckin' kidding aren't you? I'm in the middle of an investigation to try and find a madman who has been killing for twenty years. My ex-wife may well be lying dead, fuck knows where and you're here pissing me about. How exactly am I supposed to keep my emotions in check in the middle of all that?"

"You listen to me. I'm not pissing you about. You are facing serious charges here, charges of conspiring with a known gangster to have two men killed. This isn't just the possibility of you losing your job; this could result in a long spell in jail. People like you are the ones who give us all a bad name."

"You know fuck all about me. Tell me, where do they take you for your lobotomy before you join 'Complaints' or do they just suck your brains out through your ears with a fuckin' straw?"

"Just answer the questions, smart arse."

During the exchange Foster was sitting back in his chair, with a supercilious grin on his face. It was all Russell could do not to get up and swing a punch at him.

"What do you want to know?"

"During the investigation into Wright's death, McGavigan's son was also killed."

"I'm not hearing a question."

"McGavigan assaulted you at the scene of his son's murder, is that correct?"

"Yes."

"You didn't arrest him, in fact you disappeared with him for about an hour and no charges were pressed. Why?"

"He might be a dangerous bastard, but he was still a father who had just lost his son. I could forgive him his reaction on that basis, and I had more to worry about than him taking a swing at me. I had to convince him that I would deal with his son's death and I needed him to keep his gun-happy minions from starting an all out war on the streets of my city. I don't know what happens in Dundee, but in Glesga we don't want citizens getting caught in the middle of a fire fight between two sets of fuckwits."

"How would keeping McGavigan out of jail help that?"

"McGavigan's a smart operator, he runs his outfit with an iron hand. If he tells them not to do something they don't do it. With him out of the way the chain of command might not have been so effectively enforced and some of them might get ideas above their station. Ideas like trying to use Alan McGavigan's death as an excuse to make a grab for more territory to deal their suffering in."

"Surely, the opportunity to put a known gang leader in prison should have taken priority?"

"How would I have put him in prison? He would have been charged with assault and his lawyer would probably have got him out on bail and then probation. In the short time he was in remand, I might have had another three or four murders to deal with, and some of those might have been innocent people. Maybe you've not been on the front line of real policing for a while, but when you're dealing with guys like McGavigan it's not always black and white. Sometimes you have to compromise to stop things getting worse."

"The law is the law. Your relationship with this man does not reflect well of you or the force."

Russell laughed. "Jesus, it's like talking to Robocop. What fuckin' relationship?"

"Cosy chats with villains where there are no witnesses does not instil confidence."

Russell sighed. "There were witnesses, we were sitting in a greasy spoon café, drinking a cup of tea."

"That's even worse but we'll move on. Your brother..." Dickson looked at the file again. "Eddie, isn't it?"

"Yes."

"He has a bit of a gambling problem apparently."

"So have any number of people, including some polis."

"A problem that seems to have him moving in some unsavoury circles."

"Again, like any number of people, including some polis. What's your point?"

"We have an understanding from one of our colleagues in the Met, that you contacted him to talk about a known Serbian gangster called Dragovic, is that correct?"

Russell managed to hide his surprise at the possibility that Jonny Holt had talked to them; he thought Jonny was one of the good guys. "Aye, so."

"What investigation was that part of? We don't seem to have any records that indicate Dragovic had any dealings this far north."

"You know or you wouldn't even be asking. I was interested in Dragovic because Eddie had gotten in deep with him. I wanted to know just how bad it was."

"According to Dragovic's record and the intelligence on him, it was very bad for your brother."

"It was. Dragovic is a particularly nasty piece of work."

Foster suddenly spoke up. "During the period that you were investigating the Wright murder and your brother's difficulties with the Serb, you had to attend A&E. Is that right?"

"Aye, I was mugged outside my flat."

"But that's not what really happened, is it Superintendent Russell?" Foster used Russell's rank like a club, battering him with sarcasm.

Russell's hot blood simmered with indignation at the implied slight. "You would do well to remember that superintendent bit, Sergeant." He added his own heavy emphasis to the final word.

"Answer the sergeant's question."

"That's what happened, I was mugged."

"We think that Dragovic sent two men in pursuit of your brother. We think those two men beat you up and tried to get you to tell them where Eddie was, and that those same two men ended up very dead in the boot of a car."

"I was mugged."

"We think that you arranged for McGavigan to take care of Eddie's problem for him. Basically, we believe that you are guilty of conspiracy to commit murder."

"I was mugged."

"It would be a lot easier on you if you just told the truth," Foster said.

"Aw fuck off, wee man. I've been playing this game a lot longer than you and you're really shite at it. I was mugged. I have no idea what happened to those men. They were bad bastards that were bound to end up in a boot of a car or at the bottom of a river somewhere."

"Why did McGavigan phone you when the case was finished?" Dickson asked.

It dawned on Russell just how vulnerable he was. The fact that they had already looked at his phone records meant the net was closing fast.

He remained calm as he replied, "He phoned me to thank me for finding his son's killer."

"That was nice of him. Do you have a lot of gangsters that are grateful to you?"

"Do you have a family or do your species just clone themselves? He was a father of a victim, calling to say thanks. Like any number of parents and loved ones have done down through the years. Spin it whatever way you want but that's what happened."

With Russell's intransigence the discussion was going nowhere. Dickson decided to end it and said, "Interview terminated at 4:35 p.m." Then he pushed the stop button on the recorder.

"I know what you did Russell and I'm going to nail you to a cross and put your body out as a warning to other dirty coppers."

"Aye, whatever. Can I go now and find out if a psychopath has murdered my ex-wife?"

There was a momentary flash of sympathy on Dickson's face before he nodded. Russell stood and walked out; his bravado disappeared and was replaced by overwhelming trepidation.

***

He raced from the room, back through the poorly lit corridor and up the stairs to the incident office. He knew as soon as he entered that there was bad news. The screen was blank, the detectives were sitting in complete silence and Alex's body seemed to be cloaked in grief; her shoulders hunched, her pale face only serving to emphasise the redness of her eyes. On seeing her boss, she composed herself and stepped forward.

'What? What happened?" he asked urgently.

"Karen's been shot. We think the bullet went into her thigh but we've no idea how bad it is as the video feed was cut almost immediately."

"Oh hell. Tell me what you saw."

"The bullet seemed to penetrate her leg and then go in the chair as there were splinters of wood, but he definitely hit her."

There was a period of silence as he tried to formulate a response. He didn't know what to say or do; it was like he had forgotten everything he had ever learned about working a case.

"Sir, what do you want us to do?"

"I... I don't know. What do you think?"

"We need to find where they might be. D.S. Craigan and her team are still looking at the financials. If Dent owns the property they are in it might help point us in the right direction."

"Aye, that's good. Let me know how they get on. I need to go to my office for a while." He hurried from the room, leaving his colleagues to their own thoughts and Alex in charge of moving the investigation forward.

She understood what Russell was saying. He needed time to straighten out his thoughts and function as a copper again. For twenty years the Harlequin case had been an irritant, an itch he couldn't quite scratch, but now it had become a dagger to his very soul, a painful wound that was infected with the pus of guilt. He needed time to dress that wound to allow him to continue the fight.

As he walked away, Alex shook off her own torpor and set off to rally the team.

***

Joe O'Donnell was still visibly shaken by what he had done. His plan had been to make sure that if there was a bullet in the chamber it would miss Karen, but controlling the weapon had been more difficult than they ever made it look on television. As he pulled the trigger, the muzzle had jumped up and instead of the shot going below the chair, the bullet had gone through Karen's left thigh and out into the seat. She had screamed, marginally before Joe did. Enraged and frustrated he threw the now safe but hot gun at the camera, braking the lens and toppling the tripod.

The Harlequin's delight at the bullet's trajectory was rapidly replaced by a feeling of rage at what Joe had done to the camera. He used the pistol he was carrying to hit the teenager and send him and his chair crashing to the floor. "Now they won't know what happened, you halfwit."

Joe's head rung with pain and the room spun around him like he was on a ride at a fairground. He was left in the same position while their captor took Hayley and then Karen back to the cages. Joe was dragged from the chair and staggered his way back to their prison while the Harlequin poked him in the back with the muzzle of the pistol.

When he had been thrown back in with the women, he began a catalogue of apologies.

"Never mind apologising, Joe. I need you to dress the wound," Karen managed to say through her pain.

He helped her out of the clown costume which was now soaked in her blood. She winced and cried out as he removed the tattered cloth from her legs. The bullet had travelled through her thigh, the entry wound was a small hole but the exit was a ragged mess. The bullet had broken up on its journey through her flesh, ripping it apart. He turned Karen so she was lying on her stomach so he could see both wounds more clearly. The blow from the Harlequin's pistol had left his vision blurry which combined with the poor lighting, was making the process even more difficult.

"Hayley, get over here and help," he shouted to the other woman.

"I can't, I can't."

"You can and you will. I need you to help me or Karen's going to bleed to death."

"No, no." Hayley's tears turned to hysteria.

Annoyed by her constant weak snivelling, he finally lost control. He walked purposefully over to her despite still being unstable on his feet. He dragged her up from the foetal ball she had curled up in and held her by the shoulders. He leaned in close and shouted at her, "Get a grip. I need your help or that woman is going to die because I put a bullet in her. I can't live with that, can you?"

Hayley lifted her face and looked into Joe's eyes. *Why didn't he understand that it was all a waste of time?*

He shook her. "Stop feeling sorry for yourself. That's what he wants. He wants us scared and unable to help one another. It's how he gets his kicks."

Somehow his words seemed to penetrate her frenzied distress.

"What do I have to do?"

He led her over to Karen and said, "I need you to see if there are any fragments of the bullet still in the exit wound. Hopefully, it's passed right through but we need to be sure."

Hayley overcame a bout of nausea to look more closely at Karen's leg. The flesh was raw and livid, blood still oozing from the wound.

"Here," Joe said as he handed her an alcohol wipe before he continued, "Karen, this is going to hurt but we have to clean the wound. Are you ready?"

"Yes," she replied weakly.

She found strength enough to scream as Hayley cleaned the affected area. When she was done, the younger woman looked into the wound track but she couldn't see anything that might be part of the bullet.

"I don't think there's anything there."

"Good." Joe reached into the bag of supplies and found two dressings, which he placed on each of the wound sites. With Hayley's help, he used a bandage to secure them in place while Karen moaned gently when the pressure began to tell and the agony increased.

"I'm sorry, Karen but it'll be better when this is done."

The bandaging complete, Hayley helped turn Karen round. She could see that the blood loss and the shock had drained completely the colour from the older woman's complexion and her eyes looked unfocused. Hayley wondered if their efforts had only delayed the inevitable.

CHAPTER 26

By five o'clock the incident room was alive with activity. There were detectives and uniformed officers working in every available space, some were peering at computer screens, and others were sifting through files while the rest took notes with phones clamped to their ears.

Alex was sitting with the I.T. team who were still wrestling with the tricky problem of tracing the source of the website. Stephanie Jackson had retreated to one of the empty offices to allow her to analyse the sound in an atmosphere that was more conducive to picking out details from an audio track.

They had had no luck in breaking the security surrounding the site and the screen now showed an animation telling people to come back at ten o'clock for the finale of the Harlequin's April Fool Carnival.

The social networks were ablaze with comments from all around the world and the tag #harlequincarnival was trending on all the major sites. It was a media disaster for the force but there was nothing anyone could do until they ended the kidnap or the Harlequin closed down his sick programme.

Alex was monitoring some of the posts and tweets, hoping that the Harlequin's arrogance would lead to a response that might help the team, but if he was involved at all it was as an observer not a participant. As she continued to read the streams of comments, Stephanie walked in bearing her laptop and an eager expression.

'I think I might have something."

She placed the computer on the desk in front of Alex and said, "I've isolated the voice track and the major sounds as well as I can, and removed them so we can hear the ambient noise."

She pressed the play button on the audio software but there was too much chatter in the room for Alex to hear what it was the technician was so excited about.

"Can everyone please shut up for a couple of minutes?" she shouted into the room. Slowly the talking died away. "Play it again," she said to Stephanie.

Into the silence there came a faint sound that was barely audible above the background hiss. Stephanie leaned over and adjusted some of the settings on the software. She played the noise again and it became a bit more obvious.

"Is that a jet?" Alex asked.

"Yes and four others can be heard in the time that it was broadcasting."

"So they're on a flight path somewhere. It doesn't help too much," Alex said.

"I know but this might narrow it down a little more." The technician clicked and typed before another sound was heard.

"Gulls?"

"Yes."

"So on a flight path near a body of water. I suppose if we can trace a property he owns with those characteristics it could be important," Alex said but there was little enthusiasm in her voice.

Stephanie looked deflated that what she had discovered wasn't enough to excite the detective.

When Alex realised that she had not been very grateful she said, "Thank you, Stephanie. It's at least a little more information."

She told the other officers to get back to work and the noise in the room went back to its previous level but Alex could feel that everyone was flagging. The emotional turmoil of all that had happened was taking its toll. She got hold of a uniformed constable and told him to organise a pizza run.

By quarter to six the food had been delivered to the desks, where they helped to revive the passion and energy of the team

Russell had spent some time in his office talking on the phone to Mark McLelland and Christine O'Donnell. He had hoped to offer them some comfort but after what had happened to Karen, it was the two parents who provided the support and succour for him. Mark McLelland had suggested again that he would come to the station but Russell had gently rebuffed him. McLelland had a lot to offer but this wasn't the time for him to come out of retirement.

Alex was wrestling with a slice of pepperoni pizza when the detective superintendent arrived back into the incident room. She had left him to his own devices in the period since he had retreated from the briefing.

"Grab a slice," she suggested, pointing to the open boxes at the end of the row of desks.

"No, I'm not very hungry but thanks. Where are we?'

Alex reported Stephanie's findings.

"That's good work, Stephanie. Thanks," he told her.

Ann-Marie Craigan walked from the group of desks that was the home of her small team.

"Sir, I think I might have something."

"I could do with some good news D.S. Craigan."

"I think I might know who his accomplice might be. Nicky Pettersen."

"What?" Russell and Alex said simultaneously.

"Pettersen."

"What makes you say that?" Russell asked doubtfully.

"I thought I would take a look at him as he was the only connection to Dent we had identified in relation to the crimes. He served three years for his part in the original conspiracy back in 1993. When he came out, he went to college to do an HNC in Computing that he then used to get into university and get a degree in Computer Science. In 2000, he set up an electronic security company with the help of an unknown investor. He sold that outfit in 2008 for £32 million and he is now apparently an investor in other businesses and property. I checked at Companies House, he is listed as a partner of a company called the Motley Bell Group. The only other listed partner is an offshore company called Ruggero Pagliacci Holdings, the same name as the mysterious Italian businessman that was supposed to be selling that property."

Russell brightened and said, "It's him, it has to be. Right, I want a full check on any property owned by Pettersen or any company that he's involved with. Look for warehouses, or maybe abandoned factories, anywhere where they could set up their freak show. Use as many people as you need, I want this to be the focus of the investigation."

Alex added, "Concentrate on anywhere close to water that might be on the flight path for Glasgow or Prestwick airports."

"Yes sir, ma'am. It might take a while."

"Do what you can but use every resource you need. We need to find them before ten o'clock."

Craigan hurried away and began calling others to her desk.

For the first time since he had realised the identity of the victims, Russell had hope.

***

Joe O'Donnell sat in silent vigil over Karen Russell. She had lost consciousness about twenty minutes after he had finished treating her wounds. Her face was still deathly white and her breathing seemed a little laboured, but he hoped that a period of rest might help her recover, if only a little.

He had no idea what the Harlequin had in store for them in his next charade but his belief was evaporating in much the same way as it had disappeared from Hayley. Throughout his teenage years he had played the role of hero in any number of games, blasting aliens, criminals and Nazis in the comfort of his own home. The type of violence he engaged in was pure fantasy, and he could never have imagined the awful reality. When he pulled the trigger and the deafening sound of the bullet being expelled filled his ears, he felt both physical and mental shock. The heat of the gun barrel had only hastened his decision to get rid of it, as it felt like death. The sight of the blood pouring from Karen's leg had affected him like nothing that had come before; even the cuts inflicted by the stars they had used earlier had paled into insignificance. Here was a very personal violent act in the raw, and he had committed it. He had tried to shift the blame to the Harlequin but his thoughts kept coming back to the fact that he could have aimed the gun further away or that he could have refused to pull the trigger. However, if he was honest with himself, he had been more worried about his own life; his own survival was more important to him than doing what was right, and that was what was playing on his conscience most of all.

As he sat watching a woman who had shown him kindness, and an incredible amount of personal courage, he hoped she would survive. If she didn't, then he didn't think that he could live with the guilt of knowing that he had killed her; his own life would become worthless.

***

By half-past eight a network of companies owned in full or in part by Nicky Pettersen had been revealed. The ex-prisoner's net worth was now reckoned to be around £80 million and the range of businesses he was involved in was extensive. He owned restaurants; a haulage firm and had created another software company specialising in apps for smartphones and tablets. His property portfolio was equally complicated and intricate.

As the depth of complexity became apparent, Russell had called Baxter to enlist the help of corporate specialists within the fraud squad. Two forensic accountants with the required expertise had been called in and were now sifting through the data with a keen eye.

Russell's nervous energy had him flitting between the various groups, hoping that his very presence would somehow help to produce the breakthrough. Time seemed to be racing and the clock hands moved on to nine o'clock and then half past in the blink of an eye. Everywhere you looked in the room people were yawning, stretching and rubbing tired eyes. The length of the day was only part of the reason for the fatigue; everyone felt Russell's pain like they were part of a hive mind.

Alex had joined the tedious trawl through the records and it was she who made the important discovery at ten to ten.

"Sir, I think I've found it."

The news of what she said went around the room in an instant and a hush descended.

"One of the property companies owned by Pettersen deals in factory space. It owns a former food processing plant close to the waterfront near Port Glasgow. It's not far from the airport."

"Sounds as good a place as any to start. Come on let's get going. D.S. Craigan, notify the Armed Response Unit and get them to follow us down."

"Yes, sir."

Alex put a brake on Russell's desperation to get going. "Sir, we'll need to wait on the A.R.U. We know that there are at least two guns on the premises, there may be more. We can't do anything until we have tactical support."

Russell looked like he was about to argue but the cool head and procedural sense of his D.I. had won out over the need to help Karen as soon as possible. He wouldn't be able to help her if he was lying with a bullet in him.

Ann-Marie Craigan called the A.RU. and gave them the details of the property. As they were based in Baird Street, they had a longer journey ahead of them and it would be ten minutes before they would be passing Helen Street. The plan was they would let the detectives know when they were getting close.

"Alex, you're with me. Frank grab some bodies and a car."

The two of them raced out to the car park and piled into Russell's car. Alex had barely pulled her seat belt across her chest, when the detective superintendent spun the wheels of the Insignia, pulled out into Helen Street, and waited with engine running for the response unit to approach. Frank Weaver followed with a couple of detective constables in a marked Ford Mondeo about two minutes later. While they waited, they ignored the pleas of the press corps as they tried to engage the detectives and shouted questions from the pavement.

The time dragged once more but at ten o'clock the sound of sirens filled the air and Russell and Weaver's cars headed for the M8. They added to the cacophony of sound with their own sirens and lit up the night with flashing lights. They were about twenty-five minutes from Port Glasgow, All Russell could do was hope that they would get there quickly enough to save three lives.

CHAPTER 28

The Harlequin came for the captives at five minutes to ten. Karen Russell had woken up about ten minutes earlier. She was hobbled by the pain in her legs, and had to be helped to walk by the other two. They were pushed back to the area the earlier 'games' had taken place and then on deeper into the building. At the far end, the lights and cameras had been moved to a space in front of a heavy, metal door. As they approached they could hear a humming noise filling the air like a swarm of insects was approaching. Having survived all that their captor had thrown at them so far, that sound filled them with new dread.

They were manoeuvred into position in front of the camera and at ten o'clock exactly, the Harlequin began his introduction. "Welcome, ladies, gentlemen, boys and girls to the final part of today's Harlequin April Fool's Carnival. Our third game is called, appropriately enough 'Three degrees'." The room was filled suddenly by the sound of the song 'When Will I See You Again' sung by the seventies girl-group, The Three Degrees. The Harlequin danced like it was his favourite tune and the three captors shuddered. The music stopped as swiftly as it had begun.

The masked clown stopped dancing and said, "Just a little April Fool's Day humour there. The game is simple; you are going to go inside this industrial freezer. The winner will be the one who doesn't freeze to death. All three will be placed in the room with the temperature at zero degrees." He walked across to a control panel beside the door and indicated an L.E.D. display. "After five minutes I will lower the temperature by three degrees, hence the name of the game. I will continue to reduce the temperature by three degrees every five minutes until such times as two of you have frozen to death. It's going to be very exciting. As they say, 'revenge is a dish best served cold.'" He laughed wildly before saying, "As Karen is the only one to have not won a round, she will be going in for five minutes on her own."

"No, you can't do that," Joe protested.

'Quiet!" The Harlequin struck the younger man with the back of his hand.

"It's OK Joe," Karen said quietly.

"No, I'm going in with you," he said defiantly.

The Harlequin replied, "Fine, it's your funeral, but just to make it a little more interesting we've got an extra surprise for you." He disappeared out of shot and appeared with a large bucket with water splashing in it. He threw the contents of the buckets over the three people, so they were instantly soaked, the thin costumes revealing the lines of their underwear. Collectively they struggled to draw a breath as the shock of the cold water affected them.

"Ms Russell and Mr O'Donnell you're up first." He removed his gun from his waistband and waved it to direct them to the door. Hayley stood in shuddering silence as Joe helped Karen towards the door. The Harlequin opened it and a blast of even colder air hit them. They walked to the middle of the room and the door clanged shut behind them.

***

Two minutes after they had created a small convoy with the mini-bus carrying the armed team, Alex's phone rang.

"Ma'am, it's D.S. Craigan. I thought you should know that he's putting them in a freezer. He says that he's going to keep turning the temperature down until two of them die." Craigan's Belfast brogue cracked with emotion.

Alex relayed the message solemnly to her boss. He didn't even acknowledge what she had said; instead he reacted by pressing the accelerator a little more firmly and took their speed above ninety miles an hour.

***

In the Helen Street briefing room the team were once more sitting in silent horror as they watched the final chapter unfold in the Harlequin's long revenge. Five minutes after he had put Karen and Joe in the freezer he forced Hayley to join them. When the door slammed shut on her, 'When will I see you again' began to play on loop. There was a camera mounted inside the frozen room and it showed the three of them huddle together, Hayley helped Joe to hold Karen up and all three moved around in a circle; none of them wanted to sit or lie down, afraid that it would only accelerate the freezing process. Ice was already beginning to form on the hair of the first two 'competitors' and the signs were that they wouldn't be able to last very long before hypothermia took its toll. The watching police officers were as powerless as the others around the world who had tuned in to see the finale; they could only hope and pray that their colleagues would arrive soon.

**

Ten minutes into the race, the little group of police vehicles had left Glasgow airport behind and were passing the junction that led to the Erskine Bridge. They were travelling as fast as was safely practicable, the traffic had been thankfully light and was now down to only an occasional car or lorry, but the police drivers knew they had a responsibility to those people as well as the Harlequin's victims. D.S. Craigan keeping them informed of developments by sending Alex texts. She had responded by telling the Irish woman to arrange ambulances from the Royal Alexandria Hospital in Paisley to get to the site.

**

Inside the freezer the temperature was now at minus twelve degrees. Karen no longer had the strength to stand up and the other two were beginning to feel the strain. They all sat in the middle of the room, trying to get some warmth from each other's bodies but it was only having a minimal effect. They kept moving to stop them freezing into a solid mass, taking turns to be in the middle to share what little heat was left. The encouraging words they had initially said to one another were now lost in their silent condensing breaths. Every one could be their last.

**

Russell was leading the convoy when they reached the end of the motorway and joined the A8, heading towards Greenock. Port Glasgow was a few miles down the road and their destination was getting closer. As they were no longer on the motorway, he eased back a little on the speed but he was still fifteen miles over the speed limit as cars moved across to give him a free path on the outside lane.

After another five minutes he killed the sirens and lights as they reached a roundabout. Alex guided him to their destination and all three vehicles pulled up in a line at the edge of the car park of the plant.

Detective Inspector Ruaridh McLeish, the leader of the A.R.U. team was a stocky Highlander with an abrupt, military demeanour befitting a man in his position. He called everyone to him at the back of the bus. He already had a diagram of the building on an electronic tablet. As he ran through the plan, Russell's feet itched to take him inside but he knew that in this arena, McLeish's word was the only one that mattered, so he listened and bided his time.

***

Karen Russell had fallen into unconsciousness as the temperature dipped to minus fifteen. Joe O'Donnell clung weakly to her, his limbs now stiff, his hands frozen into painful claws. He had begun to hallucinate and at one point he was convinced his mother was standing over him, when he reached out to touch her she disappeared and his thoughts drifted to their Easter dinner. Was it really only yesterday? He wished he hadn't behaved like a spoilt brat, he should have stayed with her for the rest of the day. At the time he presumed there would be many more Sunday dinners, now he wasn't so sure. Life was ebbing away and soon it wouldn't matter.

Hayley was also losing the battle. She had gone past cold and suddenly felt as if she were on fire. She had an urge to back away from the others and strip off her costume but something in her memory about it being a symptom of hypothermia stopped her, and she stayed where she was. She kept up an internal mantra telling herself that the heat was an illusion. Time was running out and it wouldn't be long before all of their struggles would end.

CHAPTER 29

There were three entrances to the old factory; the main entrance at the front; a bay for vans and lorries at one side and an emergency exit on the other. Two officers were sent to cover each side, while the six remaining armed men and women were ready to go in through the front led by McLeish.

Russell and the team would follow the initial attack when the armed officers had secured the scene. The delay only served to increase his sense of helplessness. He felt like he was the only one who could save Karen, that he owed her that much.

The radio on McLeish's vest crackled twice as the two teams guarding the alternative exits confirmed that they were in position. McLeish signalled to the others to move towards the main door and like the well-drilled team they were, they moved into their assigned places. One of the officers tested the door and found that it was locked. A short battering ram was brought forward. There was a pause as McLeish ensured that everyone was set and then using his fingers, he counted down from three.

The two officers crashed the double doors open; the lock offered little resistance. The battering ram was dropped and the team began to swarm into the space.

The air was filled with shouts of "Armed police" as they moved through a series of offices. "Clear," echoed through the building as the team visited a series of empty rooms and then the shouts changed suddenly to, "Armed police, get on the ground."

***

The temperature in the freezer was now at minus eighteen and Hayley had lapsed into an unnatural sleep and Joe was close to joining her. He thought he was hallucinating again when he heard faint shouts through the door, but they persisted and Joe moved stiffly to rouse himself.

In the large factory area, the Harlequin was slowly realising what was happening. He too thought he must be hallucinating as there was no way that anyone could have found his lair, but reality hit home when he saw the two armed men enter the old processing floor.

"Armed police, put the weapon down," one of them screamed at him.

He looked at them and then at the gun that he was still holding as he if he had forgotten it was there. The two officers were moving towards him with assault rifles pointed directly at him, laser sights lighting his chest. He was told to drop his pistol once more and the message finally travelled from his brain to his hand.

"Kick it away," he was ordered and as if in a daze he complied. He couldn't believe that this was how it was ending; it wasn't supposed to be like this. He had been told he would complete his revenge and would go back to the Isle Of Man to die.

"That ends tonight's broadcast," he said to the camera while the officer was telling him to get on to the ground and put his hands on his head.

***

No shots had been fired and Russell was convinced that it must be safe. Despite Alex's best efforts to stop him, he ran from the safety of the cars in through the doors. He charged past a few rooms - including one filled with three cages - until he saw one of the A.R.U. officers standing pointing a rifle into one of the open doors. Russell looked in to see Nicky Pettersen lying on the floor, while another member of the team secured his hands behind his back. The room looked like a cross between a television production suite and a data centre, with large monitors and a bank of machines all with flickering lights. It was an elaborate control room for the broadcasts and its complexity explained why the I.T. team were unable to find it.

Pettersen grinned. "Hello Detective Russell, I'm sorry but I think you might be too late."

Russell had a sudden urge to kick the prisoner's smug face like it was a football, but instead turned to the officer on the door.

"Where are they?" he asked her.

"Along the corridor and down to the right."

Alex had caught up with him and they both raced along to where he had been directed. He burst through a door and into a cavernous space. At the other end of the room he could see the lights and the entry to the freezer. McLeish and one of his team had opened it and the two detectives darted across the intervening space to help.

Joe O'Donnell had managed to crawl to the entrance and the two uniformed officers lifted him gingerly to clear the route into the frozen room.

Russell felt the blast of frigid air as he reached the entrance.

"We'll get Karen," he told McLeish and his partner. The two officers lifted Hayley as carefully as they could and took her out of the cold storage area. Then it was the turn of Alex and Russell to pick up Karen but it was difficult. She was so cold that their bare hands found it hard to get a grip of her. Her costume was frozen solid; there were signs of frostbite all over her exposed skin. Finally, they manoeuvred her out into the relative warmth of the old factory floor.

Russell reached for her neck to check her pulse. The depth of the cold he felt was like nothing living, and there was no sign that her heart still pumped her blood.

"No, you're not doing this to me." He began compressions on her heart, changing hands frequently as the cold was too intense for him to bear it for very long.

Alex had taken off her coat and wrapped Joe O'Donnell in it while two members of the A.R.U. were busy trying to stir Hayley McLelland's heart back to life. When Frank Weaver arrived she asked him to look after Joe while she went to help an increasingly distraught Russell.

"No, this isn't going to happen. I'm not having your death on my conscience. Come on, Karen. Please fight. Please." He was pounding her chest with more ferocious attempts.

"Sir, let me." Alex said gently as she rested her hand on his arm.

As she began to try reviving the woman, Alex could here the sound of ambulance sirens. Come on, hurry up, she thought as she pumped out the rhythm.

Russell was resting on his haunches as the paramedics arrived. There were eight of them and they rushed towards the victims. A quick triage was done as they wrapped their patients in foil blankets. Two medics were sent for portable defibrillation machines while the others took over the resuscitation attempts. Joe O'Donnell's effort to get to the door had led to him falling into unconsciousness, but his heart was still pumping albeit very slowly and with little strength.

"We've got a pulse," the paramedic said from beside the prone form of Hayley McLelland.

"Come on, Karen, Please show that stubborn streak one more time." Russell said as he watched the medical personnel continue to attempt to save her life.

The defibrillator arrived along with a doctor at Karen's side. Calls were made about voltage, the paddles applied and warnings to stand clear were shouted a number of times, but nothing the medic tried could stir a pulse. At ten forty-five the doctor said, "I'm sorry she's gone."

"No, you've got to keep trying," Russell shouted as he made an aggressive moved towards the doctor.

"No, Tom. No." Alex held him tightly.

"I'm sorry, but there's nothing more we can do," the doctor said. "I have to help with the other patients."

As his colleague held him in an all-enveloping embrace, Tom Russell wept like he had never wept before.

CHAPTER 30

A short time later the two other victims of the Harlequin were on their way to the Royal Alexandra Hospital where they would be reunited with their families. The doctor believed that despite what they had been through, they would make it.

Karen Russell's body lay still wrapped in the foil blanket awaiting the private ambulance that would take her to Glasgow Mortuary, a mile away from the station at Helen Street. Tom Russell sat on the floor beside her, holding her hand. The other police officers had left him to his private grief while they escorted the two criminals back to the station for interviews. Before they left, Alex told Weaver that she would lead the interviews but that she wanted to wait for Russell.

As he sat staring at the cold, blue hand that once had worn a ring he had placed on it, Russell was filled with regret and guilt. Regret that he couldn't make their marriage work, although it was Karen's jealousy that had finally driven them apart. He tried to think how he might have stopped her from seeing every woman as a potential rival, but he had been unable to understand it at the time and he was no closer to understanding it now that she was gone. The guilt was the feeling that had the tightest grip on him. If he had put Dent away ten years ago, this would not have happened. He had failed her and all of the victims who had suffered at the hands of the Harlequin.

Russell stayed lost in his thoughts until Dr Rajesh Gupta placed a hand on his shoulder. The forensic pathologist had his job to do before Karen could be moved to the mortuary.

"I'm so sorry, Tom," he said, his usual happy demeanour replaced with grim sympathy.

Alex had followed Gupta back into the room and she said to her boss, "We need to go, sir."

"Aye." He bent forward and kissed the lips of his former wife and said tenderly, "I'm sorry."

***

When they arrived back at the station, Alex had offered to drive Russell home but he refused; he wanted to be involved in the interviews. Alex was firm in her insistence that it wasn't possible, she even threatened to inform the A.C.C. if he persisted with the argument. No one could risk a successful prosecution because Russell couldn't control himself. He agreed to the compromise of being able to watch proceedings from the video room. Before the interviews could get underway, the assistant chief constable and the Procurator Fiscal arrived and indicated that they wanted to watch. Alex was in no position to say no. By the time Dent was led into the interview room there were six people watching the video feed; Russell, Baxter, Jacqui Kerr and three other detectives including Andy McKinley who was there to see the end of a case that had occupied a chunk of his career.

When the custody officer brought in Dent, Russell was shocked to see his condition. The former pathologist was wafer thin, his skin and eyes jaundiced, his hair just wispy strands on a near bald head.

Alex was joined by Ann-Marie Craigan and she began the interview by stating the date, time and who was present in the room. She asked Dent to confirm for the tape that he had refused his right to have a solicitor present.

"That's correct," he said.

Alex was about to ask her first question when Dent asked, "Are they all dead? Did I complete my revenge?"

"No." She wasn't about to give him the satisfaction of knowing what had happened to Karen Russell, he would know soon enough.

"Pity," was his reply.

She continued with the interview, going through each of the various crimes that were associated with the Harlequin. Dent sat calmly and admitted his role in everything, neither showing regret nor pleasure in what had happened. As Russell watched on, he wondered if Dent was under the influence of some kind of drug, he seemed so vacant and remote from what was going on. The same thought had obviously occurred to Alex as she asked, "Mr Dent, you don't seem too perturbed by what has happened and the consequences for you. Can I ask you why that is?"

For the first time there was a twinkle in his eye as he replied, "The simple reason is that I won't live to see the trial, never mind serve a prison term. I have nearly completed my revenge and now I can die. I'm sure the survivors will remember me long after I've gone." His smile of satisfaction caused Russell to curse him, drawing a withering look from the prissy Fiscal.

In the interview room, Alex said, "I see. What exactly is wrong with you?"

"Liver cancer. Stage three bordering on four I would imagine."

"You can be sure that we will make sure you get the best treatment available, to help you live in prison as long as possible."

"Oh there's nothing you can do, detective. My journey is over."

"We'll see." She turned away from him in disgust and said into the microphone, "Interview terminated at one twenty-three."

Dent was taken back to the holding cells, still wearing a smug grin.

The investigative teams had been sent home, many of them had been reluctant to go, wanting to show solidarity with Russell but the A.C.C. had pulled rank and made it an order. As a result the incident room was nearly empty when Alex and Craigan joined the group who had been watching on video in the now quiet space.

"Do you think he is telling the truth?" Baxter asked.

"Judging by how he looks, definitely," Alex replied.

"What about Pettersen?" Russell asked.

"We're waiting on his lawyer."

Tea and coffee was made and distributed to the exhausted detectives and visitors. The mood was not celebratory, as it normally would have been at the end of a momentous case. Instead a quiet sense of mourning settled on them. Even Jacqui Kerr offered her condolences to Russell.

As they continued to wait for Pettersen's lawyer, Mark McLelland arrived looking tired but relieved.

"Hi Mr McLelland, how are they?" Alex asked.

"The doctors reckon they will both survive, although it looks like both of them will lose some toes and Hayley's likely to lose a couple of fingers on her right hand due to frostbite."

"I'm sorry to hear that," Alex said.

"I just wanted to come and say thanks for all that you have done and to pass on my condolences to you Tom."

Russell could barely acknowledge his former colleague. "Thanks."

"Do you want a cuppa?" Ann-Marie Craigan asked McLelland.

"No, I'm heading back to the hospital. I just wanted to let you know how they were, and to pass on thanks from all of us."

He shook each of their hands before setting off to the hospital once more.

It was four o'clock in the morning before everyone resumed their places and Nicky Pettersen was brought into the interview suite. His lawyer was already in position and Pettersen settled in the seat beside him like he was at home in his favourite armchair.

Alex completed the formalities for the benefit of the recording.

"Mr Pettersen, would you like to explain your role in the events of the past couple of days?"

"What events would that be?"

In the observation room Russell was remembering a frightened young man, telling tales of a masked man who had offered him £250 to poison some cakes. It was a long way from the expensively attired, relaxed, forty something that sat across from Alex.

She answered the millionaire's question with a list of his crimes. "The kidnap, torture of three individuals, attempted murder of two of them and the murder of one more."

"I don't know what you're talking about."

"Strange, considering we caught you where the captives were held, in a building you own."

"I was merely helping a friend."

"In the same way you helped him twenty years ago."

"He wasn't a friend then."

"Mr Dent has confessed to all the crimes, so the worst you face will be conspiracy charges. You help us out and you might not spend the rest of your life in prison." Despite the anger and grief she was carrying inside, Alex was as detached and professional as she would be with any suspect in any case.

Pettersen laughed loudly. "He did, did he?"

Sensing a change in his client's attitude, the lawyer leaned towards him and whispered in his ear.

Pettersen brushed him away. "He's saying he did it all?"

Alex was puzzled by the sudden change, but she wasn't going to do anything that might stop him talking so she said, "Yes."

"Well that's not quite the real story. He didn't do it all, he didn't have the balls."

"What parts did he not have the balls for?"

"When I went to jail, he got in contact to say that he wanted to help me when I came out. He supported me through university and we became friends."

"That doesn't explain your role in all of this. What happened ten years ago?"

"We were in touch regularly and he started to talk about how the twentieth anniversary was coming up and how he wanted to get revenge on Hastings."

Alex sought clarification. "He wanted you to be involved again?"

"Yes, he said he didn't know how to go about it. He said he wanted to embarrass Hastings through the company he owned. I told him that we should revive the Harlequin as it was my idea originally."

"Your idea?"

'Yes, I thought a clown was the perfect April Fool's Day disguise. I made up the part about Dent visiting me dressed as the Harlequin, I thought that it was a bit of a laugh, leading you lot off on a wild goose chase. The calling cards were his idea, so I can't take credit for it all, but the Harlequin was definitely me." He smiled at the memory.

He had touched a raw nerve and Alex said abruptly, "Get on with the story."

"Life had gotten a bit stale, I needed some excitement. I came up with the George Square stunt. We had very little publicity for the Harlequin first time round, you lot kept it quiet. I decided to change that."

"Your murdered the three people?"

"Oh, yes and it was easy. Dent showed me where to put the knife so it looked like the scene at the Blakes; he had done their post mortems. We wanted to send a message."

"Who to?"

"Hastings, the world, whoever, and we did a good job I think."

"But that still wasn't enough?"

"No, Hastings had to die. Did you hear what that prick did to Dent and those other two guys?"

"Did you kill him?"

"Yes, after Dent had tortured him - he has quite a talent for it. As he was a doctor, he knows how to inflict pain. We made a good team." The grin returned as his trip down memory lane delighted him once more.

"What about posing his body the way you did? Didn't you think that it might have led back to the university?"

"It didn't make any difference. Revenge was all that mattered."

"What about the events of yesterday?"

"Dent told me he was dying, I thought he should finish the job before he popped his clogs. A bucket list kind of thing. He wasn't up for it at first, said he was too tired but I came up with the game show as the perfect way to go out in style."

Alex couldn't quite believe what she was hearing. "Why did you abduct the people you did?"

"In some ways O'Donnell was the worst of the lot during that prank, going along with it like a sheep. She could have stopped them but didn't, just drowned in self-pity afterwards as if there was nothing she could have done. I thought she should suffer and going after her son seemed like the perfect choice. McLelland and Russell got too close, forced Dent into exile, so they had to be targeted. McLelland's daughter was easy and Russell's such a loner that an ex-wife was all we could come up with. What is it with him anyway?"

Alex ignored the question. "Why exactly did you do all of this?"

"It was fun, that's all. I got a buzz from it."

"We'll need you to sign an official confession."

The lawyer managed to shake himself out of the shock of listening to Pettersen and said, "I'm sure that can wait until my client has had a night's sleep."

"I'm sure it can. Get him out of my sight," she ordered D.S. Craigan.

In the incident room, there was a brief meeting to go over what had been said, before Baxter ordered everyone to go home.

Alex offered to accompany her boss to his flat but he was in no mood and felt no need for company. He drove home, feeling more alone than he had ever felt in his life.

#

When Russell walked into his living room, dawn was breaking on the second of April. He was emotionally drained and physically exhausted by all that had happened. He noticed that the light was flashing on his home phone to tell him he had a message.

He thought about leaving it, expecting it to be some eager journalist but instead he pressed play.

"Tom, it's Eddie. Ah'm sorry aboot Karen, that wis tough. Jist tae let ye know Ah'm in Glesga and Ah'm gonnae hand masel' in the morra. You shouldnae huv tae be punished fur ma mistakes."

Russell deleted the message and went to bed, not convinced that Eddie would save him a visit from the Dundee detectives the following day. If he was being honest with himself, he didn't care any more.

EPILOGUE

Surprisingly, Eddie was as good as his word and confessed to the murder of the two Serbs but claimed self-defence. Russell made sure that the best possible lawyer represented him. Eddie said that he had gone to try to make a deal over the debt. He admitted taking a gun to the meeting and that he killed them when they had threatened him. He claimed to know nothing about the guns that were found in the boot of the car. The Fiscal accepted his plea, not wanting to stretch the case out and partially because she wanted to spare Tom Russell any more grief. The judge sentenced Eddie to ten years in prison. Eddie accepted that his lifestyle had led him to his fate, and when Tom visited he told his brother not to worry, that he would be safer in Barlinnie than he was outside. He convinced Tom that it would be a turning point and that he would be a better man when he got out. Tom's guilt at his brother's fate was tempered by all that he had gone through on his behalf, and the fact that he had more than enough guilt associated with Karen's death to last a lifetime.

Dent died three days before his trial was due to start and never faced justice, while Pettersen was jailed for life. At no point did he express any remorse for what happened, it had all been a laugh for him and his only regret was that he had been caught.

Karen Russell was buried on a bright sunny day in late April. Russell was used to attending the funeral of murder victims - it was something he did to keep himself rooted in why he did the job in the first place - but this was different. He stood closer to the graveside than he would for any other victim, Karen's mother at his side. Their relationship had never been a good one, even during Karen's captivity, she hadn't bothered to call him. There was some doubt that she would allow him to be involved in the service but she relented in memory of her daughter, although it was still very strained between the two of them. The lowering of Karen's coffin into the grave was a weight that he found difficult to bear, not physically but emotionally. He went straight home and took no calls from anyone for a while.

Unable to push aside his grief and guilt, he decided to take sick leave rather than face the daily grind of bodies, pain and heartbreak. At one point Alex thought that he wouldn't be back and there was talk of her being moved out of the Major Incident Team to head up a group in the Specialised Crime division but she resisted. She wanted to work with Russell again, a man she admired greatly. She was delighted when he decided to return to work six months after the Harlequin had been captured.

On that first day, she offered him a brief hug of welcome, there was no mention of what had happened, Russell held his emotions in check and then they got back to doing what they did best.

ABOUT THE AUTHOR

Sinclair Macleod was born and raised in Glasgow. He worked in the railway industry for 23 years, the majority of which were in IT.

A lifelong love of mystery novels, including the classic American detectives of Hammett, Chandler and Ross Macdonald, inspired him to write his first novel, 'The Reluctant Detective' featuring Craig Campbell. There are two further Reluctant Detective novels, 'The Good Girl and 'The Killer Performer as well as the short story, The Island Murder.

There are two other Russell and Menzies novels, 'Soulseeker' and 'Inheritance'.

Sinclair lives in Bishopbriggs, just outside his native city with his wife, Kim and daughter, Kirsten.